MW00488618

I AM...

T.H. MOORE

Published by:
In Third Person Publishing
P.O. Box 3591
Reston, VA 20190-9998
www.thmoore.com

Cover artwork and interior book layout by David Provolo

First Edition December 2019

Library of Congress Cataloging-in-Publication Data
is available upon request.

ISBN: 978-0-9779519-2-5

Jus·tice
/ˈjəstəs/
Noun

1. the establishment or determination of rights according to the rules of law or equity.
2. the quality of being just, impartial, or fair.
3. conformity to truth, fact, or reason.

"a concern for justice, peace, and genuine respect for people"

synonyms: fairness, justness, fair play, fair-mindedness, impartiality, lack of bias, objectivity, neutrality, lack of prejudice, open-mindedness, nonpartisanship; honor, decency, integrity, honesty, righteousness, ethics, morality, virtue, principle, trustworthiness, incorruptibility

—Merriam-Webster Dictionary

ACKNOWLEDGMENTS

As always, I'd be remiss not to thank my mother for all the sacrifices you made to provide me a quality education. Your steadfast work ethic and discipline laid a foundation that I'll forever be grateful for. Without you, I'm nothing. Tia Jackson, thank you for reading the original draft of my debut novel, *The End Justifies the Means*. I may have never decided to publish any of my writing had it not been for that defining moment.

Danitra Bell, thank you for encouraging me to continue writing. You convinced me my storytelling could be so much more than a personal hobby. Thank you to my editors, Megan McKeever, Susan Edwards, and Paul Zablocki, for running my story through your gauntlet of red tracked changes. Your wisdom and guidance are extremely appreciated.

A huge thank you to my team of beta readers, Sandra Terry, Bridget West-Armstrong, Debbie Ostrowski, Kemy Clermont, Natalie Jubinsky, Tracy Rivers, Tysheina Washington, and Yasmin Carlos. Your diverse backgrounds and points of views provided the honest feedback my story needed.

Thank you, Shonda Rhimes, for your award winning show *Scandal*. Especially season 4, episode 14, "The Lawn Chair,". It's a powerful and thought-provoking work of art. Thank you, Clifford Joseph Harris Jr., for penning "Warzone" and being one of few activists in my generation who inspire me.

Thank you, Jane Elliot, for your work in fighting racism. Thank you to my favorite social media troll and brother, W. Everett. You challenge my political views daily, even when we don't agree. I've learned valuable lessons about open, honest, respectful, and sometimes unsettling dialogue is necessary to truly bring forth change.

Finally, I'd like to thank all my friends, family, and loved ones not specifically named above. You all have supported me throughout this dream of being a writer and for that you'll always have a placed reserved in my heart.

"For it is not light that is needed, but fire; it is not
the gentle shower, but thunder. We need the storm,
the whirlwind, and the earthquake. The feeling of the nation
must be quickened; the conscience of the nation must be roused;
the propriety of the nation must be startled; the hypocrisy
of the nation must be exposed; and its crimes against God
and man must be proclaimed and denounced."

—Frederick Douglas

CHAPTER 1

"You know when you get home after work tonight, I'm going to put that thang on you, babe." Xavier playfully threatened his wife, Sandy, during their routine chat on her way to work.

"That thang, huh? Is that what you're calling it now?" Sandy replied, weaving in and out of traffic, doing her best Danica Patrick impression.

"Yes! That thaaang," he exaggerated. "It's my birthday, and you know I like to get a little freaky on my birthday."

"Oh, I know. Even Sean knows."

"What! You told Sean?"

"Of course not, babe!" she assured him. "I would never. But it only took him a few minutes to notice I couldn't sit down properly the morning after your thirtieth-birthday tryst. He definitely didn't buy the hemorrhoid story you and I came up with."

"I did get a little carried away, huh? I'm sorry, San," he said.

"Uh-huh, I'm 'San' whenever you're trying to be cute, so I'll forgive you," Sandy said, triggering a sly snicker from Xavier, followed by an unbridled burp.

"Eww! Nasty!"

"Sorry, it's the beer," he admitted.

"Are you already in your man cave?"

"You know it. It's almost game time, and we finally have a running back and defense worth bragging about. We're making the playoffs this year and after that the Super Bowl, baby!"

"I sure hope so," Sandy said, pursing her lips and shaking her head. "Just make sure I don't come home to another broken flat-screen if they disappoint you again."

"That was *one* time, San."

"Mmmhmm. And the last time, right?"

"I love youuu," Xavier sang.

"Mmhm, I love you too," she responded, smiling at the shirtless picture she'd saved to his contact profile so she could see it whenever he called. She could feel his bright smile emanating through the phone.

"Okay, love, I just parked at the hospital. I have rounds soon as I walk in the door, so I'll text you later in the day when things calm down. Enjoy the game. Me and you," she concluded.

"Me and you," he responded with their customary gesture of endearment, followed by a kiss he threw through the phone. Sandy returned the kiss and turned off the ignition. She exited the car, opened the rear door, grabbed her white coat from the plastic hanger dangling behind the driver seat headrest, and threw it over her forearm. It took her less than a minute to power walk the length of the employee parking lot and through the emergency room doors.

"Why are you at work, honey? Isn't today Xavier's birthday?" Sandy's well-groomed and chubby work husband questioned from the triage desk.

"Good morning to you too, Sean! He's at home watching football, so he'll be just fine until I get home tonight."

"Chile, all I know is if I had a big ol' dark, muscular policeman at home and it was his birthday, I'd be on my back instead of at work."

Sandy playfully cut her eyes at Sean.

"I did that all day yesterday," she admitted, snapping her fingers and cocking her neck to the side. The two friends burst into laughter.

"I know that's right." Sean raised both hands in the air and lowered his head as if praying.

"Okay, girl. I'll see you at lunch," Sandy said, blowing a kiss before heading into the heart of the emergency room. She greeted everyone with friendly waves and smiles before making her usual pit stop in the break room. There she found two nurses and the ER's chief physician, Dr. Murphy, already congregated around the TV, watching the start of the 49ers game versus Cowboys.

"Good afternoon, everyone," Sandy said as she approached the trio, maneuvering around them to grab the largest paper cup available for her coffee.

"Good afternoon, Doctor," the group said almost in unison. Sandy eyed the three large coffee thermoses, each with its own unique label.

Which one of you will be my best friend today? Sandy contemplated with a pointed finger oscillating in front of the French Vanilla, Jamakin Me Crazy, and Decaffeinated coffee options.

"I made the French Vanilla right before you walked in, Dr. Darboe, in case you're looking for which is the freshest," a Vietnamese nurse offered.

"Perfect," Sandy said, "French Vanilla it is." She winked at the bubbly young nurse before filling her cup. The heated beverage warmed her fingertips while its aroma flooded her nostrils, igniting a slight chill at the top of her spine.

"I bet you this thug doesn't stand for the national anthem again," Dr. Murphy blurted out as the break room TV screen showed cameras scanning the length of each team's sideline. The camera operators were searching for which players, this week, would take a knee during "The Star-Spangled Banner" to protest police brutality. It had been months since San Francisco's quarterback, Colin Kaepernick, had first refused to stand for the national anthem and instead took a knee, sparking an overdue countrywide debate about racism in America.

"I don't understand why so many people are upset. The way some are reacting, you'd think he'd set the flag on fire on the Fourth of July and doused the flames by urinating on it," the other nurse, a fair-skinned Dominican man with glasses, added.

"He's disrespecting our military," Chief Murphy said. "This is America! We stand during our national anthem. If you have a problem with America, feel free to leave!"

"With all due respect, Dr. Murphy, it's not the law or a requirement to stand during the national anthem. Standing is typically done out of tradition, but another American tradition is peaceful protests in the face of oppression. This isn't North Korea, for God's sake," the Dominican nurse said.

"Exactly!" the Vietnamese nurse agreed. "I grew up watching football with my father and brothers. I remember when the players all stayed in their locker rooms and weren't even on the field during the playing of the anthem. It wasn't until ten or eleven years ago the federal government started paying money to the NFL to really focus on promoting the anthem at their games to increase military recruitment. *That's* when the NFL mandated players come onto the field during the national anthem."

I can see where this is headed. Time to slip out of here, Sandy thought to herself, making her way toward the door now that she'd finished adding cream and sugar to her coffee.

"Not so fast, Dr. Darboe," Chief Murphy said. "You're not going to leave me here to debate these radical millennials alone, are you?" Sandy delayed her retreat at the beckoning of her boss, then turned to face the group again.

"This is a sensitive subject, and I'd rather not talk about politics or religion, especially at work. Sorry," she said.

"See! What did I tell you?" The chief pointed to the screen, ignoring Sandy's response, where cameras showed Kaepernick taking a knee in protest alongside two other 49er teammates. "Now there's two more thugs kneeling alongside him. He's lucky I'm not the owner. I'd have security drag him from *my* field and remove him from *my* stadium."

The Dominican nurse tilted his head and threw his chief a questioning gaze.

"You would fire one of your best employees over not standing for the anthem?"

"Without hesitation!" Chief Murphy asserted.

"Interesting," the nurse replied as Sandy watched the young man contemplate his next words. "Well, I'm from a military family, and none of my family who've served see any issue with what Kaepernick is doing. They've admitted that they prefer he stand. However, they also understand why he's not standing. My family members, both military and civilian, know this protest never was about the military. Our lying president would like you to believe that, but we know better than to believe a con man and the lies he spouts randomly day to day."

"Dr. Darboe, isn't your husband a police officer? Care to weigh in here?" the chief asked. Sandy's eyes flickered among the trio. She sipped her coffee, continuing to stall before responding.

"To be honest, I'd rather not say," Sandy said, prompting a look of disapproval from her chief. "However, I believe firing someone for peacefully protesting, even the national anthem, is extreme and goes against everything the flag stands for. Let me play devil's advocate." Sandy took another sip. "Our annual team trip to the Rangers' opening-day game—if someone in our group chooses not to stand for the national anthem, are you going to fire them?" The melody of the anthem playing in the background set an eerie mood while Chief Murphy pondered his response.

"Of course not," he answered sternly. "They can always join us in our section *after* the anthem is done being played. You all have a good day today," Chief Murphy concluded before exiting the break room.

"Out of the way!" a frantic voice familiar to Sandy yelled from down the hall. "Take him to trauma room three! *Sandy!* I need you! *STAT!*" Sandy shot out of the break room and saw her best friend, Camila, visibly shaken by what lay before her on the bloody gurney. She tossed her coffee into the nearest trash receptacle and darted toward her hysterical colleague. The cocktail of adrenaline and caffeine rushed through her system. Her heart raced as she pushed open the swinging double doors to the trauma room and was greeted by a scene of ER nurses and doctors barking out directions as they all jostled for position to save a teenager's life.

"One, two, three, lift!" the ER doctor directed before turning his attention to Sandy. "We need you to prep for surgery if we're going to have any chance at saving him once we've stabilized his vitals."

Sandy nodded before darting out the double doors, down the hall past the elevators, and up two flights of stairs where the hospital's operating rooms were located. She hurried through another set of doors that led to a sterile scrub room with a large sink and surgical gowns packaged in tearaway paper bags. She removed her white coat and rolled up the sleeves of her blouse, then stomped on the metal lever under the sink that turned on the water. She ripped open a soap sponge, wet it, and scrubbed every area from her fingertips to her elbows before rinsing them off.

As she shook her arms of excess water the ER team burst through the doors of the operating room. Through the glass wall separating the two rooms, Sandy watched the team feverishly replace an already empty one-liter bags of blood and IV fluid. She rushed through the door connecting the two rooms where a nurse was waiting to assist with putting on her gown and sterile gloves.

"Okay, tell me what we have!" Sandy ordered.

"Multiple GSWs to the torso, one in the arm, and another in the thigh. Both chest wounds are losing a lot of blood. Possible artery damage."

Sandy peered through the crowd to get a glimpse at the patient among the chaos but could see only blood-saturated underwear.

"Jesus! How many bullet holes are there?" Sandy asked.

"Five," the ER doctor responded.

"Patient has been intubated, bleeding has been stopped for all wounds except the two bullets lodged in his chest near his heart. He has a collapsed lung, and you may have to crack his chest, Dr. Darboe. He'll be all yours in five to ten seconds."

Machines designed to monitor the patient's vitals beeped at random; the liter of blood hung only moments ago was half-empty.

The nurse who initially called out to Sandy pressed a round plastic bag pumping air down the patient's throat and into the lungs. A trail of mascara coated both her cheeks.

"Okay, Dr. Darboe. He's all yours," the doctor said, stepping away from the patient, his gown and sterile gloves covered in blood.

Sandy moved into place, quickly surveying the carnage the bullets had made of this young man's body.

All his clothes had been cut off, and if not for his blood-stained underwear and friendship bracelet around his wrist, he'd be as naked as the day he was birthed into this world. Her gaze fixed on the bracelet. A red, white, and blue flag with a large single star in the center.

Sandy's head snapped over to the patient's face. Her mouth and eyes shot wide open. The youth she had to save was her godson. Sandy whipped her head over toward Camila. The sides of her best friend's face were even darker from the mix of tears and mascara. Her two small hands with laser precision pumping lifesaving oxygen into the young victim. Then Sandy saw it. Wrapped around Camila's wrist was her own matching friendship bracelet of the Puerto Rican flag.

Sandy's heart sunk as she watched Camila peel her eyes away from her bleeding, motionless son, Emmanuel, to lock in with Sandy's eyes.

"Please. Don't let him die, San!"

Sandy fought back the tears welling up in her own eyes. She swallowed deeply, clearing the knot forming in her throat, determined to save the life of her best friend's son. Dr. Murphy burst through the trauma room door.

"Nurse Camila! Dr. Darboe! What are you doing?" he demanded.

"Saving a patient's life," Sandy answered.

"Ten blade?" a seasoned ER nurse asked, snapping Sandy's focus back to Camila's son.

"Yes, ten blade—"

"Dr. Darboe, I'm going to insist that both you and Nurse Mercado step aside while other physicians and medical staff attend to this patient. It's against hospital protocol to allow you two to work on this patient. You both are too emotionally invested in the care of this patient."

Sandy, without hesitation and steady hands, sliced through the child's skin, disregarding their boss's orders. "I'm the only surgeon presently on the floor. If you'd like, page whoever's on call, but until they arrive, I'm going to save this child's life," Sandy said while spreading his chest with another surgical device, methodically working her way through his torso in search of the two bullets. She glanced up at the shallow bag of blood.

"I'm not going anywhere," Camila declared. "You can fire me if you want, but I'm not leaving this room. Not while my child is in it."

"Suction and another bag of O neg!" Sandy ordered, putting her scalpel down, and she placed two of her thin, long fingers inside one of the wounds and closed her eyes. Chief Murphy peered at them both before storming out of the trauma room. Sandy never looked up. She'd committed herself to preserving the life of the patient the moment Camila cried out to her. The both of them would have to be dragged out of the chaotic room before surrendering his care to another.

"I can feel one of the bullets. Make that two." She kept a finger in the wound and used her other hand to retrieve her scalpel. She made another small incision at the entry wound.

"Retr—" Before she could complete the order, the same senior nurse placed a retractor in Sandy's hand. After spreading the wound, she looked up and the same nurse had a pair of forceps waiting for her. Sandy removed her finger and replaced it with the forceps. Seconds later she carefully pulled a blood-coated bullet out and dropped it into a metal tray.

The sound of the bullet landing in the metal container seemed so heavy and dense for such a small piece of metal. Her best friend moaned in agony. Sandy placed her finger into the other wound, performing the same technique to retrieve the second bullet before moving on to the young man's legs and arms.

One hour, five bullets, and two empty liters of blood later, Sandy watched the seasoned ER nurse hang a third bag of blood.

"He's still losing too much blood. We're missing something." Sandy took a sponge rinsed in saline and wiped both wet and dried blood away, looking for a wound they may have overlooked.

"Carefully roll him." They moved him onto his side as she

ran her hands down his neck, back, and legs, finding nothing. Horrifying alarms sounded only seconds later, signaling a drop in the patient's vitals.

"God no! Sandy, please!" Camila pleaded as she pressed more air into his lungs.

"Roll him back," Sandy ordered. "Wait!" She grabbed his wrists and raised his arms almost over his head.

"There it is!" Again, she placed her finger into a hole camouflaged by the budding hair in his armpits.

Camila shot a look at the ER doctor who triaged her son. "How did you miss that?" she scolded the doctor.

"Camila!" Sandy yelled. "I need you focused on Emmanuel."

"I . . . I didn't see it. Ca . . . Camila, I'm sorry," the ER doctor said, walking backward into a corner of the trauma room, his head lowered in shame, hands tightly clasped together as if praying his mistake didn't cost his colleague's child his life.

"I can fix this, Camila," Sandy reassured her.

"There wasn't any blood near that shoulder. How can a bullet enter an armpit without going through a shoulder or arm first?" the doctor asked, growing more and more distraught about his oversight.

The senior nurse assisting Sandy slowly shook her head and pursed her lips, and a tear traced down her cheek before she could reply.

"The bullet is in his armpit because his hands were in the air *before* he was shot."

CHAPTER 2

Beneath a clear baby blue sky, a line of trees and perfectly manicured hedges lined the perimeter of a sprawling open field. In the middle sat a large gazebo with fresh, dark cherrywood staining. Red, yellow, and pink flowers spread across the front of the gazebo in the shape of a *U*, and in the center was the cherry-brown casket that held Camila's son, Emmanuel. Under normal circumstances it would have been a beautiful day, but there was nothing normal about parents burying their teenage son on this or any afternoon.

It had been less than a week since Sandy pulled six bullets from her godson's body, inflated his collapsed lung, stitched his shredded flesh, and prayed tirelessly seventy-two hours straight alongside his mother. Despite exhausting all the surgical skills she'd carefully honed over the years, Emmanuel's wounds defied the unlimited resources the hospital showered upon the teenage to save his life. Hours after Emmanuel's second emergency surgery, on September 6, 2016, at 7:09 p.m., Emmanuel Mercado had succumbed to his injuries.

Rows of white plastic chairs were filled with contrasting black suits and dresses worn by Emmanuel's sobbing family and friends. Xavier, Sandy, Camila, and her husband, Hector, lined the front row of the service. Sandy held tight to Camila's hand, consoling her the best she could while fighting back a flood of her own tears.

Xavier fought a unique feeling of sorrow compounded by sympathy and misplaced guilt.

Officer Danny Shore, the cop who shot and killed Emmanuel, also worked at Xavier's precinct. Just two years earlier, Officer Shore had been transferred from a Missouri police department after killing another unarmed civilian just outside St. Louis, Missouri. Within his first year of joining the Southlake, Texas, Police Department, Officer Shore already accumulated more than his share of documented racial-profiling and excessive-force complaints. The same type of complaints he'd received while an officer in Missouri.

Xavier couldn't bear to look upon Emmanuel's makeup-covered face. The members of Emmanuel's family cried out in grief, hunched over, with their eyes buried in their palms. Xavier looked up to the heavens, hoping his tears would fall back into his eyes. Instead they puddled until the overflow forced them out the corners and down his temples.

The Catholic priest who'd baptized and given Emmanuel his first communion approached the podium to take his place at the microphone. His eyes, too, were red from his own tears. He opened a leather binder that contained the sermon he'd prepared.

"Let us pray. Oh Lord our Father, as we gather here today, we praise your name. We pray for a victory in the name of your son, Jesus Christ. We also pray in quiet defiance to honor all the martyrs who came before your young servant, Emmanuel Mercado. In his joyful life, we see your gracious face. We feel your amazing love. Oh Lord our God, how excellent is your name, how awesome is your glory, how rich is your mercy, how inclusive is your grace."

The priest pulled a handkerchief from his pocket to wipe away the evidence of his sorrow. He raised his head to the heavens and shook it in disbelief, then reached beneath the podium and retrieved a bottle of water in his shaking hands to quench his drying mouth. He closed the binder, abandoning his prepared sermon.

"Your faithful servants are tired, Lord. Camila and Hector are tired. Emmanuel's friends and classmates are tired." He paused again, taking another sip of water. His arms and shoulders shook despite his efforts to mask his turmoil.

"I, too, am tired, Lord! As your humble servant, I ask, when will it end?"

The crowd of mourners began to stir.

"When will police officers like Danny Shore see Emmanuel as the promising young man we all did instead of a target for misplaced rage? Emmanuel didn't deserve this, Lord. Emmanuel's family didn't deserve this. Emmanuel's community did *not* deserve *this*!

"Are these the final days you professed in the book of Revelation, Lord? It must be. How else may we comprehend how your faithful servant could be riddled with six bullets? We've all seen the news reports. Man cannot hide his evil deeds from the eyes of the world. Your young, faithful servant Emmanuel's hands were up. He was compliant with the officer's commands *despite* being detained without having committed a crime." The priest's bottom lip trembled, his sorrow morphing into anger.

"Little brown boys and girls can't roam the streets of their own communities without being labeled a suspect, criminal, an illegal, or thug! *Some* police see children wearing hoodies, and instantly they're labeled 'up to no good.' An American citizen speaks Spanish and some citizen's insecurities prompted them to call police followed by threats of deportation. When did wearing a hoodie and speaking a language other than English become executable offenses? What is so broken about America that *some* of its citizens take pleasure in stripping others of their language and culture?

"Is this country so badly lacking in its *own* identity that it feels compelled to strip away another culture's proud traditions? Officer Shore didn't kill Emmanuel—he murdered him! The young man's future was taken from him and his family at the satisfaction of one person's wickedness. Eight times that bigot squeezed the trigger of his weapon. Six of those bullets entered Emmanuel's body for nothing more than walking home with a group of friends. I say it again. I'm tired, Lord!"

"Si! Cansada!" Camila responded, her face no longer wet from tears but red with rage.

Sandy felt Camila's grip tighten around her hand, making it almost go numb.

"We need a victory, Lord. Victory in the form of *justice*! We need these police officers to know they cannot indiscriminately kill our children without meeting your mighty wrath, Lord. I say again, we need a *victory*!

"Law enforcement's brand of justice, when left to police themselves, is a farce. We want no part of corrupt law enforcement systems that encourage incompetent and/or murderous officers to resign from their precinct just so they can relocate, reapply, and brutalize again in another unsuspecting community! Where is the honor in a profession that enables bigots to hopscotch from precinct to precinct, harboring their cultural biases equipped with the power and tools to commit murder? Lord, I—no—*we* need to know that you're hearing us today!"

Camila released Sandy's hand and sprang to her feet with both fists clenched. *"¡Justicia ahora!"* she screamed.

CHAPTER 3

A month had passed since Emmanuel's funeral. Devastated by the young man's murder, Sandy and Xavier had both fallen into a routine of emotional survival. Every morning Sandy would go online, hoping to read better news about the status of the investigation against the officer who murdered her godson.

Because he was in law enforcement, Xavier's hands were tied. No matter how many times Sandy asked, he didn't know what was happening with the investigation. Even if he did, he wasn't authorized to discuss the details without risking his career. They still loved each other, but there was a definite shift in their marital bliss.

"*Xavier!*" Sandy shouted from the den on the top floor of their home.

"*San! What's wrong?*" His heavy footsteps thundered up two flights of stairs. He rushed through the den door, breathing heavy, his department-issued Glock 9mm cocked, his eyes scanning the room.

Sandy recoiled at the sight of the weapon.

"Have you lost your mind? *Put that away now!*" she screamed. Xavier, startled by her response, hid the gun behind his leg.

"You screamed so loud I thought something was wrong," he explained. Sandy dismissed his excuse. Fuming with rage, she cut loose on her husband.

"The only thing wrong in this house *and* this country are police like *you*! Looking for any excuse to come running, gun out, even in your own home! Who do you think you are? Some fake wannabe cowboy ready for a shoot-out at high noon? You think that makes you tough? You think it turns me on? Well, it doesn't. It makes you look like a scared little bitch!"

Xavier, in shock, tucked the gun back into his holster. She was still unsatisfied.

"Xavier, if I wanted you to simply holster your gun, I would have said put it in your holster." She continued, "I said put it away! I don't want to see that weapon in our home *ever* again. Put it in our bedroom safe where it belongs, or you don't ever have to worry about me walking into this house ever again."

Xavier shrank like a reprimanded child before turning to walk out of the den. Shame washed over Sandy as her husband disappeared down the hall.

"Xavier! Baby! Please come back!" she said, getting up from the desk and running after him. The two collided once she turned the corner. Both paused for a moment and clutched each other in the strongest embrace they'd experienced in the last month.

After what felt like forever, she raised her head from the deep cleft of his chest.

She looked up, her eyes meeting his, but couldn't tell if he was angry or embarrassed by her belittling him.

"Xav, I'm so sorry, baby. I shouldn't have said those things.

Seeing the gun just triggered something in me. Please forgive me," she said, perching herself onto her toes to fall back into the nook of his chest she could swear was crafted for her head alone. She wrapped her thin arms around his wide torso, digging her fingers into the muscles in his back.

Xavier felt both the sincerity in her words coupled with the pounding of her heart through her diaphragm. She was indeed terrified. "I know you didn't mean it. It's just—I've never heard you scream for me like that, so I thought something was wrong. I just wanted to protect you. You're right about the gun, though. It should be in the safe when I'm home and off duty." He squeezed her tight with his massive arms, looking down at her tearing eyes and kissing her on the lips.

"Me and you," Xavier sounded off softly.

"Me and you," Sandy responded. They kissed long and deeply before they simultaneously exhaled.

"What happened to make you scream for me like that?" Xavier asked.

A look of surprise spread across Sandy's face. She took a deep breath and a tear fell down her cheek.

"You really don't know what's going on with this investigation, do you?"

"Sandy, spit it out."

"The cop that murdered Emmanuel. The investigation is over. They ruled it a legal shooting. They said the officer f—" Her body shook so hard she couldn't finish her sentence. Xavier finished it for her.

"They said he feared for his life."

Still wrapped tight in his arms, Sandy looked up at him,

dejected. Disappointment consumed her. "I thought you didn't know what was going on?"

"I didn't, San. But I don't have to. It's what we always say . . ." Xavier paused to correct himself. "It's what we're *trained* to say whenever there's an officer-involved shooting. *I was in fear for my life*—"

"What's a grown man to fear from a thirteen-year-old boy from Southlake?" she demanded.

Xavier instinctively shot back. "See! That's what you civilians don't understand. The only time we're called is when something bad is happening. Cops don't have the luxury to enter situations with the mind-set that everything is going to be okay. We handle so many calls you can't count after a while, and of course we realize most of them can be handled peacefully. But we also know it only takes one call out of those thousands for things to go bad.

"It only takes one time for us to treat a suspect like they're *not* a suspect, and BANG!" Xavier fashioned his hand into the shape of a gun pointed at his head. "Then you're receiving a phone call that I'm in *your* hospital fighting for my life, or worse."

Xavier stared Sandy down, showing her how serious he was.

Sandy took a deep breath. Her blood boiled, but she didn't want to yell at him again.

"Xavier, please help me understand. How can a police officer take someone's life so frivolously?" she asked, sincerely hoping the honorable man she'd fallen in love with so many years ago would provide even the most minute reasoning to give her some comfort. Her eyes searched his. She watched him struggling to formulate the right words.

He returned the look, knowing he didn't have a proper answer that would give either of them the contentment they deserved. He equally wished she hadn't forced him to disappoint her with his pending truth. That unspoken, honest, yet brutal truth that only those protected by his blue wall were privy to.

"We're the police, Sandy. Who's to stop us?"

She shoved herself out of his embrace. Her mouth dropped open, her body went limp, and she slid down the wall of the hallway onto the floor.

We're the police, Sandy. Who's to stop us? His words looped in her mind until she could no longer feel her legs. She looked at Xavier, equally sad and disgusted at his response.

So, she shot him a look she hoped would forever etch itself in him like a scar.

His words continued to haunt her. *We're the police, Sandy. Who's to stop us?*

"San, I'm not saying it's right—"

Sandy threw up an open palm to silence him. She turned her head away, unable to look at him.

"How could you say that? How many times have Camila's family been to our home? How many Sundays have she and I tolerated you and Hector drinking yourselves silly watching football, with Emmanuel sitting on the couch between the two of you?

"San—"

"I need you to leave!" Sandy said through quivering lips and fresh tears running down her face.

"What?"

"I don't *want* you to leave, but I *need* you to leave this house before I say something I can never take back."

"Sandy—"

"Xavier," she interrupted, eerie and calm. "Please. Just get out," she demanded, digging her fingers into her chest as if trying to rip out the pain growing inside. Xavier watched as she fell over onto her side on the floor, balled up like an orphan abandoned by her parents. Her mouth hung open to release a cry so excruciating that it failed to make even the slightest sound.

No longer able to witness her in such pain, he complied with her demand and turned toward the stairs. He stopped after taking two steps and without looking back asked, "How will I know when it's okay to come back?"

A deafening silence existed between them for what felt like an eternity.

"Come back when you're the man I fell in love with."

CHAPTER 4

A s Sandy demanded, Xavier left their home. He'd packed a bag, grabbed one of his freshly dry-cleaned uniforms from his closet, and walked out the door. Sandy didn't watch him leave. She remained on the floor, consumed in the resurfaced grief of losing her godson and now, possibly, her husband.

From her fetal position, she heard the sound of Xavier's SUV door slamming shut followed by the roar of his eight-cylinder engine disappearing into the distance. Those sounds hit her like a boxer's one-two punch. Then there was nothing. Except the sound of her sobbing and the shallow echo of her heartbeat filling her head.

Snap out of it, Sandy.

She rolled onto her back and stared at the ceiling of the beautiful home she and Xavier had built together.

Sandy! Get! Up!

The faint, familiar sound of her late father's voice urged her to push herself up from the plush carpet. She rose to her feet and returned to the den. She walked past the desk and peered out the window overlooking the empty driveway where Xavier's

SUV rested moments ago. A fading oil stain sat in the middle of it, taunting her. It reminded her of one of the many characteristics Xavier possessed that had won her heart. He took pride in performing the maintenance on his own vehicle. A faint smile formed as she remembered how he would, without prompting, change her oil and windshield wiper blades, and rotate her tires immediately after he'd first finished with his own.

She turned away from the window, returning her gaze to the computer screen that displayed the article that had ignited their fight. She lowered herself back into the office chair and out of habit opened a new web browser window to check her email. Before she could type the first few characters of her username, a Facebook alert rose near the digital clock at the bottom corner of her monitor.

Curiosity urged her to click on the alert before it disappeared, but she resisted. Her last concern right now was social media. She finished typing her username and password and waited for the page to display her inbox. Before she could read the heading of any of the twenty-three new emails waiting for her, a rapid succession of Facebook alerts fired off again at the bottom of her screen.

She could see they were all associated with the same post. She recognized one of the usernames in the alert as a classmate from medical school. The heading of the post had Emmanuel's name in it. She couldn't ignore it any further. Sandy clicked the alert and saw a post about Emmanuel's murderer not being charged. In just a few minutes over twenty comments had been added to the post.

Sandy scrolled to the top of the post and saw the police

dashcam video of Emmanuel's murder. Her trembling hands maneuvered the mouse past the WARNING notification on the video. She took several deep breaths, contemplating whether she should subject herself to watch the video, before ultimately clicking the play button.

It was the longest, most gut-wrenching one minute and twenty-six seconds of her adult life.

Jacob Milano – I don't see the outrage if there is a reasonable charge against him, teenagers do not have immunity from the law.

Willie Everett – FOH... You don't treat people like that, you especially don't treat an innocent child like that.

Jacob Milano → Willie Everett – AGAIN, if he has been detained legitimately and didn't comply with the officer's orders then he got exactly what was coming to him. From your post description I thought I was going to see a lynching by officers and them dancing on his dead body.

Anna Montlee – The kid was just walking home with his friends. The cop obviously didn't like that the kid didn't get down on his knees to kiss his ass! The kid didn't deserve to DIE! He's a minor, call his parents.

Jacob Milano → Anna Montlee – Kiss his ass? Now that's some hilarious speculation. And let's not forget all that was posted was the encounter. We didn't see video about the cop's reason for stopping him. This is probably just another case of left wing media #fakenews pushing their agenda to paint police in a bad light.

Anna Montlee – Lol...it's been reported on ALL over the news **Jacob Milano** for the last 24 hours by multiple news outlets...how could you not see what this cop did is wrong???

Jacob Milano → Anna Montlee – what i told you remains

true, this is the first I've heard or seen of it, and the clip that **Willie Everett** provided is no way some crazy damning evidence of the worst police brutality I've ever seen.

Tran Nguyen – And you think it's okay how that officer took that kid's life? I guess the police are always justified in your eyes.

Jacob Milano → Tran Nguyen – cops sometimes MUST shoot people who pose a threat. It's in the job description. I personally have an outrage meter. If this is a 10 to you, then what is shooting a kid to death in a park seconds after you roll on scene like they did Tamir Rice? So, in my opinion, this Emmanuel kid being shot is really a 4 or a 5 to me. #ComplyAndYouWontDie

Willie Everett – No. Murdering someone is not in the job description. What you don't get is that these types of encounters happen to Brown and Black motorists, walkers, joggers, BREATHERS, etc. every single day. The disrespect, the aggressiveness, the over response (6 fucking officers) for one teenager, not to mention the lying, and corruption is exactly why relations between law enforcement and the communities they police are antagonistic. And this isn't new. Too many of us live in a police state and all of us are more likely to be abused by police simply for the color of our skin. It's been like this since Emancipation and if you had any empathy at all you would understand why what you view as so small is just one more turd log on the shit sandwich we are fed every damn day. So as per usual your white privilege lets you be ambivalent, and your personality just makes you an asshole.

Jacob Milano – you had a reasonable argument then you had to end it by name calling.

Willie Everett → Jacob Milano – YOU'RE WELCOME . . . ASSHOLE!!!

Jacob Milano – I'm curious how was your argument in any way advanced by your last sentence other than simply to be pejorative?

Tran Nguyen – Because you came into this conversation arrogant and condescending as hell. You behave like a jerk on Willie's page 90% of the time you decide to comment.

Jacob Milano – i talk about the issues and you decide to attack me personally. Shall i then respond by attacking you personally as well? is this how this is supposed to go? if not, why do you go down that path?

Willie Everett → Jacob Milano – I said what I said!

Tonya Day – Yikes! The fact that you see no issue with 6 men being called for one unarmed teenager that resulted in one cop firing six bullets into him and causing his death is ridiculous to me from the get-go.

Jacob Milano → Tonya Day – Is that what i said, or is what i said, "i don't know what he was charged with nor did i see any events preceding this clip of the altercation." How did what i said turn into what you just characterized what i said?

Tonya Day → Jacob Milano – actually what you said was "I DON'T SEE THE OUTRAGE if there is a reasonable charge." I find it scary that you feel that even if that bigoted cop had probable cause to stop Emmanuel (SAY HIS NAME) that he also has the right to murder him like that. Probable cause is not a conviction. EVEN if Emmanuel did something there was no need for him to die. Is the new normal shooting unarmed teenagers even if they are popping off at the mouth? If so, the next time anyone sees little Tyler or Becky call his mom a bitch in the Mall should we all unload six bullets in them?

Lamont King → Jacob Milano – its white privilege embodied. Let me be a cop and your teenage nephew or son mouthed off at me and I shot him. If you tell me that's ok you are America's shittiest uncle or father.

Brian Snow – All of those coward ass cops for that ONE teenager. Those pigs are complete wimps. Typical sucker-built punk thugs in uniforms.

Sandy Darboe – All of you STFU!!! You all have so much to say for an online collective of people who never even knew Emmanuel. I KNEW HIM! I'm the one who baby sat him as a child so my best friend, his mother, could have date night with her husband. I'm the one who attended his funeral and had to catch my best friend after she fainted once they lowered Emmanuel into the ground. I'm the physician who was covered in his blood after pulling six lead bullets out of his teenage body. Emmanuel was a good kid! He NEVER had trouble with the law so any suggestion that he antagonized the police officer that murdered him is reckless and asinine. As for you Jacob Milano, Emmanuel was MURDERED. And if I ever read you speaking ill of his name again I will personally find and castrate you.

●

Sandy didn't sleep at all that night. Between her declaring cyberwar in the comments of social media and her fight with Xavier, her head swirled with uncertainty. She had never fought like that with Xavier, and she had certainly never kicked him out of their own house before. That kind of drama was typical of the reality TV shows they'd both laugh at while snuggled up on the couch together.

She spent most of the night staring at the hypnotic spin of the ceiling fan perched in the middle of their bedroom's twenty-foot ceiling. Her conscience tried in vain to intervene with the anger fueling her stubbornness. She refused to listen to the multiple voice mails Xavier had left for her only an hour after he'd left.

Before she knew it, her alarm had gone off, signaling a new workday. She was exhausted. She swiped the touch screen of her phone, disabling the alarm. At the bottom of the screen, the number five encircled in red notified her of how many missed calls she had from Xavier. Again, she ignored them, placed the phone face down on her nightstand, and climbed out of bed.

"Alexa, play something to make me happy."

"Sure, Sandy. How's this?" The soft artificial-intelligence voice responded before playing a mix of what Sandy categorized as "happy rap" and other uplifting music ranging from popular spirituals from Kirk Franklin to empowering collaborative songs from the king of hip-hop and his queen of R and B. She reached into her shower and carefully turned the knob to the perfect temperature before stepping halfway into the warm, soothing water.

She stood with a bowed head and closed eyes beneath the cascading water as it ran down the top of her head until her long curly saturated hair clung to the middle of her back. She sang along with Kirk Franklin in her head, swaying her torso from side to side. By the second verse she lathered herself with soap from head to toe. Some soap splashed into her eyes. Squinting, she reached for a washrag to wipe away the soap until the sting in her eyes subsided.

The familiar smell of Xavier's shaving cream lingered in the washcloth. In her blind haste, she had grabbed his by mistake. She pressed the rag to her face, covering her nose and mouth. She inhaled deeply, taking in every remnant of his scent. A sense of longing overcame her. She fought back her tears and finished lathering herself with soap. She scrubbed rigorously hoping her pain would also rinse away down the drain near her feet. She wanted it all to disappear—the soap, her and Xavier's fight, and the pain of losing Emmanuel.

An hour later she was dressed, fed, and ready to head out the door. She checked the time on her phone and saw another missed call from Xavier. Finally, she caved and sent him a short text message.

"Headed to work. Still not ready to talk. Not sure when I will be. Sorry." She hit send and quickly locked her phone before she could see the read receipt of the text message. Once out the door, she climbed into her Range Rover and turned on the local radio station morning show. She hoped the hosts had a fresh dose of comedy to take her mind off the last twenty-four hours.

She wouldn't be so lucky. Soon as she adjusted the volume, she heard the comedic trio discussing the dashcam footage of Emmanuel's murder. She hit one of the preprogrammed buttons to change the station but was met with the same discussion by a different set of morning-show DJs. She tried another station. Same results. She violently mashed the power button of the radio with her palm, a tear rolling down her cheek.

"Come on, Sandy, keep it together!" she coached herself out

loud. "You save lives. Focus on that the next twelve hours. You . . . save . . . lives," she repeated until the dashboard rang. The shirtless picture of Xavier appeared. She pressed a button on her steering wheel, sending his call to voice mail even though she wanted to talk to him.

She missed him even more knowing despite having their worst fight ever, he still called for their usual work-commute conversation. Both of their alternating shifts sometimes made it difficult to maintain a regular pattern, but they always kept that tradition . . . until today.

The combined absence of radio DJs and her husband's voice made Sandy's drive dreadful. For the first time in a long time she noticed how many shops and lavish homes she passed now that Xavier's silly banter wasn't entertaining her. Southlake, Texas was a beautiful city accentuated by large, sprawling lawns and mansions that would make anyone envious.

She'd made her last turn and pulled into the hospital employee lot, parking in her usual spot. After grabbing her belongings, she locked her truck and made her way toward the double doors. She checked the time on her phone again and saw more screen alerts for missed calls and new voice mails. She released a large sigh, reluctantly unlocked her phone, and tapped the play button of the first voice mail Xavier left for her yesterday immediately after she kicked him out of the house.

"I know you're angry with me and probably don't want to hear from me right now, but I just wanted to let you know I checked into a hotel for the night. But it's just going to be for tonight. You're my wife and I love you, Sandy, so we're going to talk and work through this, even if it kills me. I can't see my life without you in it. I'm at the Marriott Courtyard, room 108. Just wanted to let you know. I love you."

A fresh tear fell down her cheek as she reached the doors of the hospital. She locked her phone, feeling no urgency to listen to the remaining messages. She wiped her cheeks clean and cracked the slightest of smiles. All she wanted and needed to hear was in the first message. Her man had put his foot down and was coming home to her tonight.

CHAPTER 5

"Sandy! This is the fourth message I've left for you. You need to call me back as soon as you get this. It's urgent!" Xavier's psyche volleyed between frustration and concern. He pressed the volume button on the side of his smartphone multiple times, but the status bar that appeared on the screen displaying the ringer volume level was already at its highest point. He picked up his desk phone at the precinct and called his mobile phone. It instantly rang until voice mail picked up. "Testing, testing, one two three," he recited, leaving himself a message.

Seconds after he ended the call, his mobile phone alerted him he had a new voice mail, confirming his phone could receive both incoming calls and voice mails. He slammed his fists on his desk and leaned back into his chair, his hands resting against his chin.

She can't be this angry with me. She needs to answer the damn phone.

He picked up his mobile phone again, but before he could dial, his captain knocked on his office door. Xavier placed the phone down on his desk and stood at attention.

"Sir."

His captain shut the door behind him and motioned for Xavier to have a seat.

"Any luck contacting your wife?"

"No, sir. Still no answer," he said.

"I'm afraid your time is up, Darboe. If you can't raise her on the phone and convince her to turn herself in, I have no choice but to send a patrol car to arrest her wherever she may be," the captain warned.

"Sir, I've called, texted, and left messages for her. I'm almost sure I'm going to see her tonight once I get home. I'm asking you, as a professional courtesy, give me until tonight to talk with her. Imagine how it'll look for her being arrested at work?"

"The commissioner is already up my ass about the backlash we're already getting from this shooting. Imagine how it'll look if the media catches wind we dragged our feet on a separate arrest because the perp is married to a cop. It'll jeopardize the entire department's credibility," the captain responded.

"Sir—"

"My hands are tied, Darboe. As a professional courtesy you may accompany the officers headed to her job and assist them in discreetly arresting her, but when I leave this office, I will order that she's arrested and brought in for questioning."

●

Moments later, Xavier was alone in a patrol car trailed by another patrol car with a pair of beat cops.

"Siri! Call Sandy!"

"Calling Sandy," his phone responded. Six rings later he was back in her voice mail. He punched his finger at the screen, hanging up the call.

"Siri! Call Work Sandy."

"Calling Work Sandy." The phone rang again.

"Hello. Methodist Southlake Emergency Room. How may I help you?"

"Sean! It's me. Xavier!"

"Heeeey, Xavier. Happy belated birthday—"

"Where's San? I need to reach her—it's important!"

"Is everything okay?"

"I can't go into details right now. I just need you get San on the phone now, please." Xavier snuck a peek at his rearview, hoping the two trailing officers hadn't noticed his attempt to warn Sandy they were only minutes away.

"Xavier, I'm not sure what's going on and it's probably none of my business, but she can't come to the phone right now, but soon as I see her, I'll tell her to call you."

"Goddamn it, Sean! I don't have time to wait. Get her on the phone now!" Xavier heard a long sigh over the phone.

"Look, Xavier. I'm not supposed to say anything, but obviously something crazy is going on today, so if Sandy asks you, you didn't hear a damn word from me."

"Spit it out already," Xavier demanded.

"Sandy's been in our chief of medicine's office since she got here. And the way they called her in there, it didn't look good."

"Fuck!" Xavier said. "Look! I'm about to pull up to the back of the hospital now. If you see Sandy before I do, tell her to go to her office and wait for me or meet me in the back where everyone takes their smoke breaks. It's very important."

"Oh my God, Xavier, you're scaring me."

"I just parked in the back of the hospital now and I'm about to come in. I have to bring Sandy down to the station with me."

"Down to the station? You're arresting her?"

"Don't tell anyone," Xavier ordered before punching his finger at the phone again, hanging up. He flagged the two patrol officers to pull up beside him and roll their window down.

"I'm going to go inside and bring her out. You two stay in the car," he ordered.

"Yes, sir," the two cops responded, but he could see they were both a bit skeptical. Had he not been their superior, his request may not have been received so well. He got out and saw two hospital orderlies smoking near the entrance. One of them perked up and extinguished what he was smoking behind them.

"Xavier?" he asked.

"Hey, fellas. I need you to do me a favor. Sandy left her phone at home and she asked me to bring it to her after she got to work. Can you let me in?" He held up his mobile phone, pretending it was hers. "I'll only be a few minutes." The two of them looked at each other.

"We're really not supposed to let people in this way, Xavier. Can't you go through the front?" one said while small clouds of smoke escaped with each syllable. Xavier walked closer and leaned in so the other couldn't hear what he was about to whisper.

Xavier took two exaggerated sniffs, smelling the orderly's marijuana-contaminated hospital scrubs.

"I'm sure the two of you really aren't supposed to be back here smoking weed either. Now let me in before I arrest you and your buddy for possession and being under the influence of a controlled substance."

The orderly jumped up and swiped his key card to open the door as directed.

"I'll be in and out in five minutes, and I don't want to see either of you back here when I leave," Xavier threatened before entering the hospital to find Sandy. He followed the signs on the wall to get his bearings. It'd been months since the last time he walked these halls.

"Xavier?" Sean's voice startled him. He scanned the corridors of the hospital.

"Have you seen Sandy yet? Is she in her office?" Xavier questioned anxiously.

Sean walked over toward him and whispered, "She's still in that asshole's office. What the hell is going on? When Sandy came in today, her badge didn't work and I had to let her in. Then two of our security guards escorted her to Chief Murphy's office. They've been in there since she got here. I was like, you know, WTF? It's Sandy, y'all. Then one of them took me to their back office and wrote me up for admitting unauthorized personnel in the hospital. Now you're here talking about taking her down to the station like she's some criminal."

"Like I said before, Sean, I can't go into detail. But I need to as quietly as possible talk to her and take her with me out of the hospital without causing a scene." As soon as he finished his statement, Sandy, accompanied by a security guard, emerged from the chief's office. An expression of dejection was spread across her face, and her head hung low.

"Good morning, Officer! Are you here for Dr. Darboe?"

Chief Murphy announced emerging from his office behind Sandy and the security guard, purposely drawing attention from everyone in earshot of his obnoxious voice.

Sandy looked up and saw Xavier in his uniform outside her office.

"You can't be serious. They sent you?" she asked humiliated and disappointed. She raised her head, set her shoulders, and walked resiliently toward him and extended her wrists.

"Go ahead, do your job," she said.

"Sandy—"

"Do it! Arrest me!" Her face flushed red. Her lip trembled, and her eyes pierced an invisible hole right through him. Xavier looked around and stepped closer, pushing her wrists down, shielding her gesture from onlookers behind him.

"Will you stop it? You think I want this? I came so there wouldn't be a scene," Xavier said, shooting a look of contempt at Sandy's chief. "No one is putting you in cuffs. You're going to come with me, and we're going to straighten this out."

"I'm surprised at how nonchalant you are with taking this criminal into custody, Officer Darboe. She threatened to stalk and castrate someone on social media after accusing one of your fellow officers of murder. If you ask me, that officer did us all a favor."

"No one asked you, asshole!" Sandy yelled.

"You better believe I'll be placing a call down to the precinct to let your commanding officer know how nicely you handle criminals when arresting them," the chief taunted.

"Thank you for all your concern, but I'll take it from here," Xavier said through tight lips while lightly placing his hand on Sandy's back to direct her to the back entrance.

"Don't touch me!" Sandy shouted, throwing her shoulder away from Xavier and walking toward the entrance ahead of him.

"Just an FYI, Officer. Dr. Darboe has been placed on a six-month *unpaid* leave of absence as a result of her unsavory social media activity. This hospital will not tolerate its employees making disparaging remarks about our police officers or any law enforcement entities. If it is determined no charges will be brought against Dr. Darboe, we will consider bringing her back as an employee. Good day to you, Officer," the chief concluded before heading back toward his office.

Internally, Xavier fumed as he rushed down the hall to catch up with his wife. By the time he reached the exit, it was too late for him to explain what was happening. She had already seen the squad cars. The two officers that accompanied Xavier jumped out of their car once they saw Sandy unescorted.

"Six police officers for thirteen-year-old, Emmanuel. Three officers for little ole me." .

"It's not like that, San—"

"Everything okay, sir?" one of the officers asked, his left hand positioned on his holstered taser.

"Everything is fine. You can return to your vehicle. She'll be riding with me in my car," Xavier said.

"Should I cuff her, sir?" the officer questioned.

Sandy snapped her head at Xavier.

"No! Now, return to your vehicle and follow me back to the station. That's an order."

"Yes, sir," the officer responded, sarcastically smiling at his partner before returning to their car.

"I don't think so, Officer Darboe. I won't be riding with

you," Sandy exclaimed, shooting a wicked glance at her husband before walking toward the two officers with her wrists extended.

"Sandy! What are you doing?" Xavier questioned.

"Fuck you, Xavier Darboe! You're no better than the rest of them."

CHAPTER 6

O verrun with helplessness, Xavier confined himself to his office. Rocking back and forth, he listened to his worn, cushioned chair squeak to the rhythm of his anxiousness. He stared through the glass wall, watching his fellow officers strategically enter and exit the interrogation room holding Sandy. Because he was her spouse, the conflict of interest was obvious, thus barring him from intervening. His captain promised Xavier that Sandy would be extended every courtesy owed to him via the blue wall's code of conduct. However, Xavier was still uneasy.

He'd watched this scene hundreds of times. As their training dictated, detectives rotated from the interrogation room to the adjacent observation room with its one-sided mirror. The psychological game of investigative roulette was a tactic he'd also played himself on suspected perpetrators. Each session was purposely designed to pinpoint their suspect's weakness for exploitation. For investigators, all that mattered was securing an admission, documenting a confession, and ensuring a conviction. Regardless of the tactics.

Endless questioning to exhaust you, denying basic needs such as water and the bathroom, delaying access to legal representation, and even lying about the facts of the case to suspects were standard practices. Keeping the scales tipped in the detective's favor meant a higher investigative clearance rate. Whether or not the accused was innocent was of no consequence once you entered the precinct's doors. Advancement in detectives' careers paralleled the successful frequency they were able to charge and convict the suspects they arrested. If that meant innocent men, woman, and even children went to jail because of their ambition, so be it.

Xavier knew this and, as such, made it a point to coach Sandy how to survive police encounters after he'd graduated from the academy.

Rule #1: Keep your mouth shut! The only exception is requesting your phone call to Xavier or their attorney. Until he or their attorney arrives, don't say a word!

Rule #2: Invoke your Fifth Amendment right to be silent. Repeat, repeat, repeat until they acknowledge it, and then you wait for your legal counsel to arrive. While you wait, keep your mouth shut!

Rule #3: Mentally prepare yourself to be detained for up to seventy-two hours. That's the legal limit police can hold you before they must either charge you with a crime or release you without a charge. If you must, count the cracks on the walls to pass the time. While you count, keep your mouth shut!

Rule #4: Don't talk to other detainees, guards—not even the roaches and mice—about why you're detained. No one there is your friend, and what might seem to you as the most unimportant comment could contribute to you being charged with a crime. In other words, keep your mouth shut!

Despite his tutelage, his mind still played out all the possible scenarios and why her questioning over a social media post was taking so much time. Xavier knew the longer the interrogation, the greater the likelihood Sandy would say something she'd eventually regret. Xavier couldn't stand on the sidelines any longer. He walked out of his office, slowing his gait as he passed the interrogation room, hoping to overhear what was happening.

He continued into the kitchen area, poured a large cup of coffee, and lingered there. He hoped he would stumble across casual conversation that would give him more insight on her status. His attempt didn't go unnoticed. A group of officers saw him, smirked, and quickly changed the subject of their gossiping before exiting the room.

So much for the blue wall. Xavier posted himself in a corner of the kitchen, pondering his next move while blowing air across the top of the steaming cup of coffee.

"Did you see who patrol brought in for questioning about an hour ago?" a voice familiar to Xavier asked from the corridor leading toward the kitchen.

"Affirmative! Magglio said Sarge's wife is in there for some anti-cop social media post. She's hot, though."

"Ten-four! That's one mongrel I wouldn't mind race mixing with," the familiar voice quipped.

"Maybe you should take a run at her. See if she wants something else besides nigger cock in her."

"Hey now, easy. Don't say that," the officer corrected. "Sarge isn't a nigger. He's from some shithole country in Africa. That makes him worse than a nigger."

Fuming, Xavier shot out of the corner of the kitchen and

purposely collided with the familiar-voiced officer, who was also the bigger of the bigoted cops. He locked eyes with Officer Shore, the same cop who'd murdered Emmanuel. Xavier let his hot cup of coffee spill down the front of the cop's pressed uniform.

"What the fuck!" the officer shouted, pinching the fabric at the front of his shirt and flapping it, trying to alleviate the burn running down his chest and stomach. Xavier eyed them both from head to toe, widening his stance to impede their path, daring them to engage him in an altercation. The soiled cop mirrored Xavier's posture, still grimacing from the spill but refusing to back down. The smaller officer stepped in between them.

"Apologies, Sarge. We *obviously* didn't see you."

"Obviously." Xavier replied.

"No offense, Sarge. Just a couple cops engaging in harmless locker-room talk. You know how it is. Right, sir?" He prompted his larger partner, throwing him an elbow to snap him out of his angry gaze. "Sure, didn't mean anything by it." he said again, forcing an insincere response.

"Right. We're all on the job, right? All part of the same family," Xavier said. "But you meant to say, 'you didn't mean anything by it' *what?*" Xavier demanded.

"We didn't mean anything by it, *sir!*" Officer Shore replied sourly.

"Riiight. Get out of my sight," Xavier ordered, maintaining his stance, forcing the two subordinates to respect his wide berth and walk around him. He heard them snicker as they turned into the locker room. The exchange pushed Xavier to a boiling point. He stormed through the precinct and burst into the interrogation room.

"This interview is over," he announced.

"Says who?" the detective sitting across from Sandy challenged.

"Me!" Xavier responded.

"You're out of line here, Sarge, and you know it!"

"Dr. Darboe, have you been Mirandized?" Sandy looked at her watch, then her husband, and rolled her eyes.

"I've been here for over an hour, and now you waltz in questioning if my rights have been violated or not?" Sandy shooed him away and turned her attention back to the detective, who returned a smile.

"We were about to take a break anyway, Sarge. How about we give you two a few minutes? You know, as a professional courtesy," the detective said, motioning toward his partner to leave the two alone. As soon as the door shut, Xavier turned his attention to Sandy.

"Look, I know you're angry at me, but I'm trying to help you, Sandy!"

"Hmph," she scoffed. "Help? You want to help? Here's how you can help, Officer Darboe. Storm out of here the same way you came in. Only this time barge into the Internal Affairs office and share with them all the disgusting stories you've vented to me over the years after you've finished off a six-pack. Tell them you've witnessed your fellow officers routinely violating citizens' rights.

"Tell them how you've lost count of the instances you've overheard them call people who look like you and me monkey, mulignan, and nigger. Explain to IA you 'good cops' are no longer content with sharing squad cars, playing poker, and drinking beers until you're vomiting with bigoted cops who don't even respect you enough to hide the fact that they're bigots and racists." She shook her head.

"How dare you barge in here as if you're not complicit. You're not innocent, Officer Darboe! *Your* job, Officer Darboe, is to uphold the law and protect the innocent from those who wish to do them harm. So, every time you 'good cops' turn a blind eye to your fellow cops violating someone's civil rights, you're *not* upholding the law. Every time you're silent when witnessing your fellow cops rough up someone, submit a false police statement, pull their weapon to intimidate, or, heaven forbid, shoot someone who isn't posing a threat, you're not protecting the innocent. Instead, you're enabling the criminal behavior of officers who've sworn to protect us.

"You fucking cops and your blue wall." Sandy hesitated for a moment, contemplating if she should continue her tirade. Then she turned in her chair, arms folded, to face her husband. "What if your uncle had been a cop? Would you have allowed your blue wall to protect him and cover up what he'd done to your sister?"

Xavier's complexion paled and his stature shrank.

"H-how c-could . . . ," Xavier stuttered before pausing, closing his eyes, and taking several deep breaths to gather himself. "How could you say that to me?" he questioned through eyes that increasingly grew watery with every word. "You know she committed suicide because of what he did to her, Sandy."

Sandy stood her ground despite how hard it was to speak of it.

"I know it's an unpleasant question," she conceded. "But it's an equally fair question if that's what's required to finally bring your morality back into focus, Officer Darboe. Where and when will you 'good cops' finally draw the line? Had your uncle been a police officer in this precinct, would you have allowed your blue wall to protect him? Or would you have arrested him, charged him, and let a jury of his peers decide his fate?"

"That's not a fair question."

"How the hell is it not fair? You're a cop, right? Every working American citizen is required to pay taxes, and those taxes pay *your* salary, right?" she yelled. "And in exchange for your salary, your job is to ensure people like your uncle, who prey on the innocent, are arrested and tried for their crimes, right?" she scolded. Xavier broke eye contact. "Answer me when I'm talking to you!" she demanded. Xavier's shame was replaced by anger.

"Yes! Had I been a cop when we found out what he'd been doing to her, I'd been the first to arrest him, beat him until he was bloody, and charge him for everything he did wrong."

"Finally, a breakthrough," Sandy said sarcastically. "So answer this nonrhetorical question. Why don't you arrest, bloody, and charge all the timorous police officers you've worked with the last seven years? Why do they get a pass . . . every . . . single . . . time they break the law?"

"That's not fair, San—"

"Fair? There's video of cops beating and gunning down innocent citizens almost every week. Then they're rewarded with paid vacations. After that, the same department responsible for committing the crime launches some faux investigation that vindicates these vacationing officers the moment they regurgitate how they were in fear of your life. If you're a civilian like me, there's no such thing as justice if our perpetrator is a cop.

"We've watched the repeat of this show soo many times we already know the ending and we're sick of it. This wicked show needs to be canceled. But let's be honest. That's not going to happen. Meanwhile, citizens are left to wonder, who's to keep us safe when the police are the ones preying on us? Can you comprehend the level of distress caused by knowing that we citizens are literally financing our own murders via our tax dollars? It's enough to drive a person insane—"

"Do you know how fucking hard it is being a cop?" Xavier demanded.

"Aww, the baby needs his diaper changed," Sandy replied.

"Sandy! Don't do that!"

Sandy again slowly shook her head at her husband, then sat forward in her chair, unfolded her arms, and rested her elbows on the table in front of her. She interlocked her fingers, folded her hands, and in a measured tone responded.

"Xavier, you're my husband and I love you. But you're also a grown man who needs to hear me and hear me well," she chastised. "And with that said, fuck you and any other cop's feelings who's looking for anyone to host your pity party!

"There's no government-issued executive order mandating any of you to become police officers. No one forced you to apply for a career as a cop, and no one forced you to endure months of training in the police academy. So don't you dare fish for sympathy for a career path you *all* made.

"Where do you cops get your misguided audacity? We have men and women who've volunteered to serve in our military who have *never* complained about how *hard* it is going to *WAR!*

If you or any of your colleagues find the rigors of your profession too difficult, then *resign*. Then, *choose* another career. And *shut the fuck up*! You collection of whiny. . .little. . .bitches!"

CHAPTER 7

our hours after Sandy's arrest and interrogation, she was reluctantly released without being charged for a crime. She rode home with Xavier, present in body but absent in spirit. She stared aimlessly out her passenger-side window, hypnotized by her city's picturesque beauty. Majestic photographs developed in her mind after every shuttering blink of her eyes captured a landscape that could rival breathtaking works of art.

In those fleeting moments she'd carved a small, peaceful nook to shelter her from the turmoil of the last few weeks. That was until the speed bumps of their gated community betrayed her fanciful musing and snatched her back into reality. She jumped from Xavier's SUV, leaving him behind before he could turn off the ignition.

When Xavier finally made it inside, he headed directly to his man cave, grabbed a few beers, and settled into his worn leather couch. He heard the water from Sandy's shower upstairs end in the pipes of his basement sanctuary. He raised the can in his hand to sip his ice-cold beverage and contemplated the last twenty-four hours. He was officially in the captain's doghouse after interrupting Sandy's interrogation and Sandy's declaration on social media made him precinct pariah. The blue wall he coveted so desperately would no longer shelter him.

Not only did Emmanuel's murder set off a rapid succession of events in their community but also in their marriage. How he and Sandy saw each other as individuals had now forever changed. Suddenly, the water tracing the pipes upstairs to the basement stopped. After a few moments of silence Xavier heard the door of their master bedroom slam shut.

I can slam shit too! He threatened to himself before downing what remained of his beer, popped the top of another, downing it in one long gulp, and belching obnoxiously. He stretched out on the couch and pulled his favorite gray fleece throw blanket up to his chest. That night they decided to sleep alone, without permission or provocation from the other. His second beer multiplied into four, then six, and then finally at seven and a half he'd reached the drunken solitude he subconsciously longed for.

His inebriation eventually betrayed his solitude when his mind replayed every word of Sandy's condemnation of his character, profession, and honor until he finally broke down sobbing. So much had occurred over the last few weeks he didn't know if the tears he shed were for Emmanuel's death or the pending death of his marriage. Questions swirled in his mind, forcing him to contemplate whether he was guilty of all that Sandy charged him with. Naivete, complacency, dishonor, cowardice, even stupidity. The list of insults was extensive. Her verbal barrage so unrelenting he knew there was no way he'd comprehended it all. What he could recall, though, stirred his pride and ego.

She's got a lot of nerve talking to me like that. I didn't create the justice system. And I for damn sure didn't break it. How does she expect me, one cop, to fix it all by myself? Fucking civilians! They watch a few cop shows on television, and as soon as one of us does something stupid, they think there's some grand conspiracy against them. Everyone's suddenly an expert on policing after binge-watching Law and Order *reruns. God damn know-it-alls!*

Xavier emptied the rest of his beer can into his mouth until his cheeks reached capacity. In exchange for the beer polluting his body, tears were released attempting to cleanse his soul of guilt. Then he finally admitted it.

Sandy was right. I haven't been a good police officer since my first year as a beat cop.

Xavier recalled his time before he was promoted. He remembered his junior year in high school when he decided to become a police officer. It was the evening of March 3, 1991, when video broke of Rodney King being beaten by the LAPD. Then he remembered how he beamed with pride after graduating the academy and little boys and girls saw him in his uniform.

He promised himself he would not be like *those* cops that beat Rodney King. He promised himself never to be *that* type of cop. He would instead be *that* cop who would inspire other black and brown children to want to wear the uniform instead of fear it. He pledged to always be *that* cop who made a difference. The one not afraid to show communities that at least one of them was good and on their side.

He'd learned most of the names of the residents on his beat. He volunteered for The Police Athletic League and other mentoring programs to foster a collaborative community and police relationship. Although it was not his intention, his connection with the community helped his quick ascension through the ranks. However, the pledge he took dissipated with the accumulation of stripes and accommodations he earned.

His ambition methodically made allowances for unsavory behavior by his fellow officers. Like many before him, being well liked facilitated more stripes, and no one likes the cop who rocks the boat.

Tonight, lying on his worn college couch, Xavier was faced with judging the choices he'd made in his profession. He reached for another beer, fumbling, and knocking over the collection of empty cans. He didn't want to think about it anymore. He wanted more of the bitter carbonation to wash away his conscience. He wanted to disrupt the steadying needle of his reemerging moral compass.

More! I need more alcohol!

He threw off the gray blanket, jumped up from his couch, and headed back toward his basement bar. He pulled open the refrigerator, but it was empty. Next he turned to the wooden shelves surrounding the refrigerator and scanned the bottles. After grabbing a double shot glass in one hand and his favorite Irish whiskey in the other, he poured until the overflow ran down the sides of the glass. He tossed back the contents of the glass onto the length of his tongue and swallowed.

He exhaled as the spirits slid down his throat and warmed his stomach. He poured one more before returning the bottle to its shelf and collapsing back onto the couch. The calming effects of the whiskey began to take hold. A long and deep shiver ran through his body.

Whew! That's better!

He rejoiced, feeling the pressure of his concerns getting

lighter by the second. Staring at repeats of SportsCenter on the muted television flanked by wedding photos, he smiled for the first time he'd been home. He reflected on his marriage prior to Emmanuel's murder. He and Sandy could never stay angry with each other very long before one of them caved and apologized. Regardless of who offered up the apology first, the hours that followed would be consumed by lovemaking all over the house.

You know Sandy's right, Xavier. Now, don't be wrong and stubborn. Take your ass upstairs and apologize. She gave you the kick in the ass you needed to square yourself away. Let her know you see what mistakes you've made. Then make good on the oath you took as an officer and a husband.

Xavier launched himself from the couch and darted toward the stairs, knowing what he needed to do. Midway up the staircase he lost his balance. He shook his head and placed his hands on either side of the wall to gain his bearings.

Shit! I drank too much too fast. Don't let her see you're drunk. You don't need that fight right now.

He sat down on the stairs, taking deep, deliberate breaths to gather himself, but the dizzying feeling remained.

Breathe, Xavier. In through your nose and out through your mouth. Damn! I'mmm druuunk.

●

"Xavier! Wake up! Wake up. Xavier! Can you hear me?" Sandy said, lightly rubbing Xavier on his cheek. "Are you okay?"

Xavier snapped out of his drunken slumber. Drool coated his lips and cheek. His vision was hazy, and his head was pounding. Dazed and confused, his eyes finally focused on Sandy's gray almond-shaped eyes. He wiped his face with his large hands and groaned.

"What time is it?"

"It's a little after ten a.m."

"Shit! My shift started at eight a.m.!" Xavier said, rolling off his back to crawl up the basement steps on his hands and feet. His tongue was dry as cardboard, and his stomach performed somersaults, begging him to make a stop in one of the bathrooms.

"I can't believe I slept through my alarm." He pulled his phone from his pocket, placed his thumb over the home button to open it, and tapped his clock app.

"Fuck! I didn't even set it," he scolded himself, wiping the accumulated crust from his eyes and the corners of his mouth.

"I picked a hell of a time to miss roll call. My captain is going to write me up for sure, if he doesn't take my stripes." He rushed over to the sink, turned on the faucet, and hastily squeezed too much toothpaste onto his toothbrush. He shoved the brush into his mouth, feverishly scrubbing his teeth and tongue. He brushed hard and accidentally too far, hitting the back of his tongue, igniting his gag reflex.

Liquor-laced vomit filled the sink basin as his body evacuated the contents of his stomach. Xavier looked at himself in the mirror through the sparkle of stars dancing to the ringing in his ears.

Uhhh! I feel so much better now.

He rinsed with water and then Listerine until his mouth burned, hoping to erase as much evidence of the previous night's binge drinking. Sandy appeared in the bathroom behind him and placed a freshly dry-cleaned uniform, socks, and shined shoes on her vanity. His heart warmed for a moment, and his gross tardiness wasn't as important anymore.

"Thank you, San!" He beamed.

"Anytime, Xav," she said before walking over to him and kissing his toothpaste-stained lips. She recoiled when he tried to kiss her back.

"You might want to rinse your mouth again, baby. I can still taste the whiskey."

"What would I do without you?" he teased.

"Be late more often, order more takeout, and have to jerk off way more than you'd prefer," she said with a sly smile.

"Someone has jokes this morning."

"Sorry, babe. You walked right into that one," she quipped, but Xavier didn't mind at all.

"You know I love you, right?" he said.

"Yes, baby. And I love you too."

"We're going to be okay, aren't we?" he asked, throwing on his uniform, socks, and shoes, skipping his shower.

Sandy walked over to her husband, helping him put the finishing touches on his tie. "Yes, baby. I guess we've spoiled each other, never really having a blowup like this before. And we've never lost someone so close to us like Emmanuel. Then the *way* we lost him. It was just too many emotions to process and manage properly," Sandy said.

"Yeah, I can't remember the last time I slept without you next to me," Xavier said.

"I was mad at you too. I still may be, a little," she admitted, "but I missed you more than I could ever be angry with you. I learned that about myself last night."

"Just us?" he asked with a smile.

"Just us!" she responded matching his smile.

Xavier parked his car in the precinct lot and hurried into the building. He breached the doors and saw there were barely any officers to be found except for the few responsible for staffing the booking desk.

"Good morning, sir!" one officer announced loudly. "Rough night?"

"I think I'm coming down with something. I'll be okay, though. Where is everyone?" Xavier asked. The two officers stationed at the desk looked at each other peculiarly, then back at Xavier.

"You haven't heard, sir?"

"Heard what?"

"Sergeant Darboe! My office! Now!" Xavier's captain ordered from the threshold of his office door. The two officers snickered and went back to work as Xavier hustled around the desks, past the drunk tank where he probably belonged, and into his captain's office. He stopped to close the door.

"Leave it open," the captain ordered. Xavier stood at attention in front of the captain's desk.

"You look and smell like shit! I see now why you missed roll call."

"Sir—"

"If you're about to give me an excuse, Sergeant, you might as well stow it. I'm writing you up for missing roll call, and if it happens again, you'll be suspended without pay for at least two weeks. Is that understood?"

"Yes, sir!" Xavier responded.

"Good." The captain stood up, walked around his desk, and inspected Xavier's uniform, shaking his head. "All the mouthwash in the world can't mask the whiskey seeping from your pores. I could smell it soon as you entered my office."

"Sir, I only had two drinks last night, but I forgot to set my alarm. It won't happen again, sir."

The captain smirked. "I commend you for your honesty about drinking contributing to your lateness."

"This was a onetime occurrence, and it won't happen again, sir."

"I'd be remiss not to take notice of your level of insubordination as of late, Sergeant. First, you interrupted a suspect's interview yesterday. One I'd specifically ordered you to steer clear of. And today you admit to alcohol contributing to your tardiness. I always liked you, Darboe, but you leave me with no choice but to place you on suspension for thirty days pending your completion of the substance abuse program."

"I don't have a substance abuse problem, sir!"

The captain snarled at Xavier contradicting his decision.

"Silence yourself, Sergeant! When it's your turn to speak, I'll tell you to speak." Xavier bit his lip and growled his response.

"Yes, sir."

"Further, your suspension will be unpaid with full reinstatement authorized only after successful completion of that substance abuse program. You will be required to provide routine progress reports to the department counselor, and if everything checks out, you'll be back on the job in no time. Any questions?" The captain paused for a few seconds. "Now you may speak, Sergeant.

"Sir! I'd like to respectfully go on the record that I do not agree with this decision and am in no way in danger of being an alcoholic. I'd like to respectfully request you reconsider and grant me permission to continue my duties."

"Your request has been noted and denied, as I'm sure if I Breathalyzed or pulled blood right now, I'd find sufficient cause to uphold my decision. However, if you decide to pursue this matter officially, when your Breathalyzer results come back positive, I will recommend your suspension be three months instead of a couple weeks, and any slipups during that time will result in your immediate termination.

"As upholders of the law, we must ensure our officers are held to the highest of standards so that our character can never be called into question." The captain paused again, only this time checking his phone and multiple emails before pointing at Xavier, signaling he could respond. Xavier was trembling with anger.

"I'll report to counseling immediately, sir. Reports will be in on time and without incident. I look forward to returning to my duties in thirty days."

"Now that's more like it, Sergeant. You're dismissed."

"Yes, sir." Xavier pivoted 180 degrees and exited the office. He saw the two officers at the booking desk, who were still whispering between themselves. He marched past them as quickly as his feet allowed him to move. Once he turned the corner, he crashed into a forensics officer he'd been in the academy with.

"Whoa! What's the rush, Sarge?"

"No rush, Shelborne. I just need to get out of here."

"Yeah, me too. I'm headed down to the crime scene now. It's going to be a shit-show around here. Cap is already getting requests from the press. The commissioner is planning a press conference by the end of today."

"Press conference? What the hell did I miss?"

"Have you been under a rock the last twelve hours? How have you not heard?"

"Heard what, Shelborne?"

"You remember that Florida case? When little homey was murdered by some cop wannabe, right?"

"Of course," Xavier responded.

Shelborne looked around, making sure no one was eavesdropping. "Well, somebody popped that punk, Michael Drawoc, last night. That motherfuckah is dead."

"Are you serious?"

"As a heart attack. Apparently, that little bitch has been living in Texas ever since." Shelborne placed his hand on Xavier's shoulder, lowering his voice to a whisper.

"Our little homey finally got the justice he deserved."

CHAPTER 8

A few days had passed since the Darboes' fairytale marriage took a whirlwind spin that ended with a double tap of professional suspensions. Sandy was comfortably seated on the passenger side of Xavier's SUV with her bare feet resting on the dashboard. The rhythmic hum of the engine on cruise control lulled her into a peaceful trance she hadn't experienced in months.

She took in the beautiful, untouched landscape of the Texas open road while Xavier calmly maintained their course past Houston on their way to Louisiana, per Sandy's suggestion. With his left hand secure on the steering wheel and his right interlocked in Sandy's fingers, they'd found the peace of mind that evaded them both since Emmanuel's murder. It had been years since they'd taken a road trip together.

Not since their meager days as undergraduate students were these two able to shut out the rest of the world. Almost a decade removed from cramming for exams, spring breaks, and tossing their tasseled caps into the air, they were now free of occupational obligations. Seizing the moment, they'd packed a few bags and set a course for New Orleans to rekindle the love that brought them together so many years ago.

"I just want to go on the record," Xavier said, "for someone who's been suspended and ordered to complete a substance abuse program, New Orleans might not be the best choice for our destination."

Sandy shot a sly side-eye at her husband and pursed her lips, giving him faux attitude.

"Ha ha. I'm just saying, babe," Xavier reiterated.

"Well, I guess we better not tell anyone we're going to Nawlins then, huh?" Sandy replied. "We'll make a stop in a few random cities, take a bunch of pictures for the 'Gram,' and conveniently forget to take more once we hit Bourbon Street. Deal?"

"Ha ha, deal," he agreed. "I still can't believe we managed to get suspended at the same time. But you know what? To hell with them—we needed a vacation anyway."

"That's right, Xav—to hell with them. And who the hell do they think they are, anyway? Telling my man how to live his personal life? They must not know my baby does some of his best work after a couple drinks." Sandy was sporting the most devilish of grins he'd seen in months.

"I'm putting you to work the moment we hit Nawlins," she warned.

"Promise?" Xavier asked.

Sandy leaned over the armrest, grabbing a handful of what lived between Xavier's thighs. He groaned, the car slightly drifted, and one of the vehicle's safety features alerted they were crossing over into another lane. Xavier pulled the vehicle back steady.

"Focus, Xav. First, you have to get us there safely. Then I'll put what's in my hand down my throat."

Eight hours, two bathroom breaks, and one impromptu quickie in the back seat of Xavier's SUV in Shreveport later, Sandy suggested they find a hotel in Baton Rouge. Their little Shreveport romp reminded them of their study sessions together in college that usually morphed into them finding the quietest corner in the university library to satisfy the urge of their teen-aged hormones.

After finding a hotel that met Sandy's standards, they pawed at each other. Taking turns being discreetly inappropriate, they became so distracted that the hotel receptionist had to repeat herself multiple times to get all the necessary information to confirm their booking.

Once they entered their room, they dropped their bags and round two ensued. An hour and a shared shower later, they smiled at each other while they put on fresh clothes. They didn't have any specific big plans. They were just happy to be away from Texas and together. They headed back downstairs for dinner at the hotel restaurant followed by drinks at the bar.

As usual, Sandy's bubbly personality earned her instant friends from the bartenders and other couples who were also visiting from out of town. Xavier marveled at how easily she could befriend the most diverse collection of strangers. By the end of the night they all would love her, but not as much as he did. Once again he knew he was hers and she was his, unconditionally.

"You're one lucky man, Xavier!" sounded off both men and women alike wherever they socialized.

"Final call!" the bartender warned, and all the customers at the bar fired off their last drink orders. Sandy requested two more drinks to carry back to their room. She meant what she had said about putting Xavier to work and what better way to spice things up than with some liquid courage. Sandy and Xavier said their last goodbyes to their hotel neighbors before making their way to the elevators.

"That North Carolina couple was so nice, Xav," Sandy said.

"A little too nice. If I didn't know any better, I'd think they were trying to convince us to swing with them, San," Xavier joked. Sandy placed one of the drinks in Xavier's hand and reached into her clutch purse.

"The wife slipped me their room key and said if we get bored tonight, we should pay them a visit," she said, waving the plastic key card in the air.

"Wooow!" Xavier said, pressing the up arrow to summon the elevator. They both leaned into each other drunkenly and laughed.

"Of course, I told her thanks but no thanks. She refused to take the key back, so I held on to it just to be nice," Sandy said with a seductive giggle.

"My baby still got it." Xavier bit his bottom lip and danced a modest two-step for his wife to enjoy. "I can't blame them, though. Seeing you in those pumps and that tight skirt . . ." Xavier kissed Sandy deeply a few seconds before the elevator dinged signaling its arrival.

"Xav," Sandy moaned, tilting her head back and swallowing the mixed drink in her hand all at once.

"Yes?" he replied, devouring the drink in his hand the same way.

"I want you so bad right now."

He pulled her into the elevator and pressed every button in between the lobby and the twenty-fifth floor.

"What are you—" Sandy questioned.

"Shhhh. Close your eyes," Xavier ordered while turning her toward one of the corners of the elevator. He grabbed the glass from her hand and placed them both on the elevator floor. She followed his lead and hurried into place as the elevator door closed. Xavier pressed himself up against her, laid his hand in the center of her back, and eased her forward. She panted as the height of her heels forced an arch in the small of her back. Sandy placed one hand against the wall while the other reached back feeling for the bulge growing in her husband's pants.

Xavier pulled her skirt up over her hips and dropped down to his knees so he could run his tongue along the trail where her underwear would have been had she worn any.

"Xaaaav!" She moaned as his tongue stretched to swipe the full length of her labia from behind. The elevator dinged.

"Xav, someone's going to see us."

"Maybe, maybe not."

The doors opened after reaching the second floor. Xavier focused on his wife. After a few seconds the elevator dinged again just before sliding shut. Relieved, Sandy released a large sigh mixed in with a moan. He reached in between her thighs and ran his hands methodically around her labia. Her legs began to shake. His thumb and index finger were saturated.

The elevator bell sounded again. She turned her head for only a second before Xavier rose from his knees, grabbed a handful of her curly hair, and turned her head back to the corner.

"Just surrender," he whispered in her ear.

Sandy's panting increased until she finally gave in. "Give it to me, please?" She reached behind her to find Xavier had already unzipped his pants and had a handful of himself ready to enter her. The elevator dinged again. Xavier thrusted himself inside her.

"Yeeeeeess, my love," she sang, competing with the hot panting of Xavier's whiskey breath. The elevator chimed; doors opened and closed for ten more floors without interruption.

"Put a baby inside me, Xavier."

Sandy's request pushed Xavier to climax. He dug his toes into the soles of his shoes, his fingers forcefully gripped both sides of her hips, and he released a roar that sent both of their legs shaking in harmony. Sandy looked back over her shoulder, lips parted and tongue extended to meet Xavier's. Their tongues danced while another ding of the elevator came and went. She slowly turned, wanting to face him.

He pulled out of her as she turned until it fell and slapped against his thigh. He slid her skirt back down into place as she grabbed a handful of him and carefully placed it back through the zipper of his slacks. The elevator chimed again, but it didn't break the sensual, deep kisses they shared.

"We know what you two will be doing once you get back to your room," an older man accompanied by his wife with a matching Hawaiian shirt and Crocs said as they shuffled into the elevator with smiles on their faces. Sandy's and Xavier's childish giggles broke their kiss.

"Me and the misses love seeing young love, and you two have it. We can tell," the older gentleman said.

"Mmmhmm," his wife concurred. "I still can't keep my

hands off this one." The older lady ran her fingers through her husband's thinning hair, planting a kiss on his cheek. She finished off her flirtations with a playful pinch on her husband's flat butt as the elevator doors shut with the four of them onboard.

"Oh, sweetie. This is going up, not down," she said after feeling the elevator rise.

"That's fine. We'll get to where we're going eventually," her husband responded. His wife paused once she saw all the floors between twelve and twenty-five were pressed. She looked back at Sandy and sized up Xavier.

"Ezel, we'll get off at the next floor and catch the next elevator going back down," she said before winking back at Xavier and Sandy.

"Okay, love," he responded simply.

Sandy and Xavier laughed to themselves, a little embarrassed they'd been figured out. Sandy reached around Xavier's waist and held him tight; placing her head in the middle of his back, she could hear his heart beating. The elevator dinged again.

"You two have a good night," the older man said as he prompted his arm in the air for his wife's hand to wrap around his biceps.

"Thank you. You two as well," Xavier responded. The doors slid closed, and Sandy playfully plucked the back of Xavier's ear. He looked back at her and smiled. She perched herself onto the tips of her toes.

"Hey," she whispered, "sorry to tell you this, but it feels like we lost some of the babies you just put inside me. You're going to have to replace them when we get back to the room," she teased.

"Okay, love."

CHAPTER 9

The next morning Xavier's head was pounding. He rolled over halfway and reached for Sandy but found disheveled sheets instead of his wife's curvaceous frame. He scanned the room through squinted eyes, his head flooded with flashbacks of last night's escapades. He scanned the room; his memory was blurry and fragmented. Eventually, he filled the gaps, seeing the littered path of discarded clothes leading from the door to the bed. Followed by a quick chuckle inspired by two empty bottles of wine on the nightstand.

Yup! That's how the love seat ended up on the balcony.

He smiled and rubbed his eyes, refocusing them to find the hotel alarm clock read 12:37 p.m. He grabbed his watch from the nightstand, knocking one of the wine bottles to the floor, and confirmed the time. He heard the shower running.

"Sandy?" he yelled, but the smacking of his dry mouth seemed louder than his actual voice.

"Who else you expecting to be in here?" she joked. "I'll be out soon."

Xavier rolled back into the dent he made in the hotel's memory foam mattress. His nose detected the stench of alcohol on his breath through his cheeks and closed lips.

I need to slow down. These hangovers are getting worse. Maybe I did need that suspension and this substance abuse program more than I realize.

He finally rolled out of bed and headed straight for the minibar. The assortment of the beer and miniature bottles of gin, vodka, and whiskey both enticed and nauseated him. He grabbed an overpriced twenty-ounce bottle of water. In one breath he swallowed its contents before falling back onto the bed. He released a monstrous belch and stared up at the ceiling, content with waiting for his turn in the bathroom.

The memories of round three kept him company while Sandy's hair dryer sounded from behind the closed bathroom door. He recalled Sandy's toned thighs walking toward him, sporting a black garter belt. His heart rate had instantly increased seeing her long legs perched atop five-inch platform stilettos. She had planned last night perfectly.

First, she'd dangled the blindfold and an oversize black feather in her hand before slipping the blindfold over his eyes. Then she'd treated him to a sensory overload of pleasure. He recalled the first few moments, anticipating the unknown and then rejoicing when countless carnal desires overran him. After those initial moments all that remained were a foggy haze of eroticism.

Moments later Sandy emerged from the bathroom, wrapped in a white towel. She giggled at her husband's defeated posture sprawled out over the bed.

"You were in rare form last night. I don't even remember how it all ended or even falling asleep," Xavier admitted.

"Good," she said with a wink as she walked past him toward her bag, from which she retrieved her body lotion.

"You were an animal. Was it your idea to move the love seat onto the balcony or mine?" he asked, prompting Sandy to roll her eyes.

"That was definitely mine. Don't try and steal my thunder," she said, rubbing her palms together, spreading the lotion evenly in her hands before applying it to her body. "You know we're going to do it all over again when we get to New Orleans, right?"

"Soon as we check in, I got you."

"Good, because I have a few more surprises packed away for you," she warned. Sandy bent over and ran her hands down both her legs and arms, coating them in the scented lotion. The aroma floated across the room.

"Baby? Are you okay?" she asked, loosening her towel and working her hands around her torso and the small of her back.

"Uh-oh, watch out!" Xavier warned before rolling off the bed and darting into the bathroom.

"Aww, my baby's getting old," she teased, walking into the bathroom to check on him.

She took in the sight of Xavier's long legs and massive body sprawled across the tile floor. His hands had a death grip around the toilet bowl, and half his bald head disappeared below the rim.

"Don't worry, Xav. I already called down to the front desk and told them we'd need a late checkout, so you have another hour to get all that out your system and showered. I'll pack up our things and lay something out for you. You want breakfast?"

More gut-wrenching vomit erupted from his mouth.

"Ohhhkaaay. No breakfast for you. Got it!"

Xavier, exhausted and panting, shot a playful sneer at his wife while resting his head on the rim of the cool toilet bowl.

"Come here. Give me a kiss." He puckered his dry lips and smiled the best he could.

"You wish. How about you focus on your vomiting, old man. We're on vacation, remember? Next stop, Bourbon Street!" Xavier's back arched again, and another eruption of wine-inspired vomit evacuated his stomach.

Four hours, a cup of coffee, three Advil, and a thirty-two-ounce Gatorade later, Xavier was feeling closer to his normal self. The WELCOME TO NEW ORLEANS sign prompted a large smile from Sandy. She reached over the armrest and grabbed a handful of his thigh, then started rubbing it.

"You feel better, babe?"

"Better? I feel great! If you pull over, I'll show you."

"Easy, cowboy, let's get some food in you before we hit these Nawlins streets," she quipped. "Once we're checked into our room, we can ask the concierge where the best hangover food is."

"I'm salivating for a po'boy right now," Xavier said.

"Yes. You read my mind. No wonder I love you," Sandy replied, pulling up to the front of their hotel. The valet standing at the podium had his face buried in his phone and didn't notice their arrival. She turned off the car and popped the trunk. The valet finally pocketed his phone and sprang into action. He bolted around the car, opening Sandy's door first, and took her keys. Then the doorman hurried over to open Xavier's door.

"Welcome to the InterContinental, sir. What brings you to New Orleans? Business or pleasure?" the doorman asked.

"Pleasure. My wife and I are road-tripping and making memories."

"And maybe getting into a little trouble along the way," Sandy added. Xavier noticed her devilish grin and nodded his head in agreement. Sandy bit her lip, then turned to the valet.

"Did I read your website correctly? You guys have a rooftop pool and jacuzzi?"

"Yes, ma'am! It's open until eleven p.m. every night," the valet responded before looking over to make sure the doorman wasn't eavesdropping. "They don't always make people leave or lock the doors. If you're quiet and not bothering anyone, guests have stayed up there until sunrise. Just an FYI."

"Thanks for that little gem," Xavier said, squinting to read the valet's name tag. "Uh, Joshua." He reached into his pocket, peeled off a ten-dollar bill, and passed it to his new friend.

"Thank you, sir! Also, if you have any questions, feel free to ask me. I know we have concierge services for general questions, but I'm also here if you have any *unconventional* requests," Joshua said with a wink before handing Xavier the claim ticket for their car and jumping in the driver's seat.

A young bellhop rushed through the hotel doors toward them with a wheeled cart. He grabbed their bags and loaded them onto the cart. He ushered them to the check-in counter, then positioned himself off to the side, pulling his phone from his pocket to occupy himself. Xavier took in the design of the lavish lobby before noticing the bellhop smiling brightly and nodding his head in agreement to whatever he was reading.

"About time!" the bellhop mumbled a bit too loudly.

"You win the Powerball?" Xavier joked, prompting the

young man to lock his phone and shove it back in his pocket.

"Sorry, sir—"

"Come on, man," Xavier said to set him at ease. "No need to apologize. Seriously, though, what am I missing?"

"Are you on Twitter or Facebook?" the Bellhop asked.

"Of course."

"Log on and check it out. It's all over social media," he instructed.

Xavier retrieved his phone, unlocking it with his thumbprint.

Sandy slid next to him, wrapping her arm around his waist so they could both read. Soon as his Twitter app loaded, he looked to the left-side menu. The bellhop was right. A new hashtag, #AOBTD, was trending. He opened his Facebook app and saw the same hashtag on almost all his friends' newest posts. A best friend from college was in a full-scale cyberwar with commenters trolling him.

Paragraph-long responses accentuated by red angry-faced emojis and profanity-laced replies in all caps were being lobbed back and forth like grenades. Xavier scrolled up to the muted video in the post. He increased the volume so he and Sandy could hear a Baton Rouge news reporter deliver the latest in front of a backdrop of police tape around a modest crime scene near an alley. At the bottom of the video screen, a news report ticker tape told the story. Xavier and Sandy finally understood what spurred the bellhop's excitement.

"Former Baton Rouge, Louisiana police officer Shane Tumaini, who came under scrutiny after shooting Alvin Gold at close range while attempting to arrest Mr. Gold, was found dead from multiple gunshots to the head." Xavier muted the volume.

"AOBTD?" he questioned.

"Another One Bites the Dust, sir."

CHAPTER 10

Almost a year had passed since Emmanuel's murder. Two hundred seventy days since a cascade of events instigated Xavier and Sandy's month-long recess. A recess that reignited the fuel that drove their love for each other. They'd methodically crisscrossed the country, checking off countless national treasures from their traveling bucket list. The product of that rekindled passion brought them both to the bright lights of a sterile Southlake, Texas, hospital room. The messy bun Sandy tied atop her head rivaled the leaning trajectory of that famous tower in Pisa, Italy.

Ten hours into labor, Sandy's hospital-issued gown was saturated in sweat as she bore her chin down into her engorged bosom. Between contractions she burned imaginary holes through Xavier's towering frame as a superhero would an arch nemesis. Her entire body screamed at Xavier for his role in planting such a large child inside her.

Xavier stood at her bedside, coaching her through the breathing techniques they'd learned in childbirth class. Periodically, he'd look down at his numb hand lying trapped in Sandy's merciless grip. He was equally excited and nervous the moment Sandy's doctor finally announced they were in the homestretch.

"The baby's crowning!" the doctor exclaimed.

"Thank God!" Sandy said.

"Sandy, you're doing great," the doctor reassured. "Now, I just need you to give me one more big push and it'll be over. I promise." Sandy cut her eyes at her obstetrician before closing them. Squeezing Xavier's hand once more, she released an agonizing war cry.

"Aaaahhhhhh!" Sandy sounded off to reclaim ownership of her own body.

"Okay! He's out!" the doctor announced, then cleared the child's sinuses and mouth with an aspirator. The bright lights and colder air catalyzed the newborn's announcing his arrival into the world.

"He! You said he!" Xavier cried out, craning his neck and leaning over the blue, sterile partition impeding his sight. "It's a boy?"

"Yes, Mr. Darboe. Congratulations! You both have a healthy baby boy." Xavier looked over at an exhausted Sandy. She was slumped back on the hospital bed, spent, and gasping relatively pain-free air for the first time in half a day. The nurses hurried the child off to the side, cleaning and wrapping him in the standard red, white, and blue hospital baby blanket.

"San," Xavier said, shaking his semi dead hand by his side to expedite blood flow. He softly kissed her damp, salty temple. "Thank you! This is the greatest gift you could have ever given me." Sandy managed an exhausted smile and rolled her head over to lock eyes with him.

"Where's my phone? I need to record what you said for evidence," she joked.

"Forever the comedian."

"You just wait and see. After ten hours of pushing that big-head baby out of me, you're going to be at my beck and call for weeks." Xavier laughed in response, but Sandy's expression told the tale. She was not kidding.

"Foot rubs, back massages, sponge baths, and don't you think I'm going to be the only one getting up when he starts crying. Oh yeah, you just wait and see what I have in store for you." She puckered her lips and blew him a kiss.

"Mmhm. Love you too," Xavier replied to her threats.

"Here he iiiiis," the nurse sang, placing the newborn on Sandy's chest. She kissed their chocolate, curly-haired son's forehead, and tears fell down both parents' faces.

"Have you two decided on a name?" the doctor asked. They both smiled at each other, proudly nodding their heads but did not speak it out loud per Xavier's ancestral tradition. Xavier kissed Sandy once more and reached out for his son. He engulfed the newborn in his large, dark hands and turned to find a space in the room less busy than the delivery bed.

"Xavier? You're going to do it, here? In front of all these people?" Sandy questioned. Xavier stopped and turned to face his exhausted wife. His back was straight, shoulders broad, chest protruding, and his head held slightly higher than usual. Pride emanated from him like a celestial glow.

"*Our* traditions," he stressed, "are *nothing* to be ashamed of." The pediatrician and nurses attending to Sandy exchanged questioning glances at one another amid the couple's veiled conversation.

Xavier could already feel the hypnotic rhythm of ancestral

drums stirring the spirits of his lineage to rise from their celestial slumber. He smiled recalling the memory of the last naming ceremony he'd witnessed as a child in Gambia before they migrated to America.

Xavier stood next to his mother, who was dressed in her best ceremonial garb eight days after his sister's birth. His father had just picked his sister up from their mother, her small head was cradled in their father's palm while the rest of her little body fit across his wide forearm. His mother shuffled into a choreographed dance circle with other women, barefoot, and with colorful head wraps like the crowns of their ancestors.

With a subtle bounce in his step, their father slowly turned away, maneuvering toward the front of the villagers who had come to witness the naming of their village's newest member. The intensity of the drums increased. Women danced enthusiastically while the men marched from side to side, a spear in one hand and a shield in the other. Birds hovered above; some of them sang out announcing to the other fowl that a new child had entered this existence.

Xavier's father looked down at his daughter, equally proud and scared for what this world had in store for her. He studied her full thick head of hair. Xavier momentarily lost himself imagining the young warriors he would have to wrestle once she was of age and able to receive suitors.

"Heavy is the head that wears a crown, my daughter," their father said. "I will not lie to you. You are a blessing that many will not instinctively embrace. Ahead of you lie many unforgiving days. Your blessings will be mistaken as targets for your enemies' arrows.

The wicked will pit their ignorance against your grace. They will challenge your rightful place in this world. Do not fear them. Do not cower from their unwarranted persecution. Cover yourself in the protective shroud of family and community. Be fair and embrace only those who will embrace you equally in genuine love." He kissed his daughter's forehead before continuing.

"As for those who bend bows and take up arms against you, stand unafraid and in defiance of them. Stand ready to smite those who wish you or your loved ones harm."

Xavier watched as his father exposed her naked body to the heavens. Cradling her head, neck, and shoulders with one hand and her backside and thick legs with the other. Xavier's father carefully raised his daughter toward the blue sky. Then he recited her name followed by words their Gambian tradition demanded.

Back in the delivery room goose bumps formed over every inch of Xavier's body. He carefully picked his son up from Sandy, the baby's small head cradled in his palm while the rest of his long, thin body fit across Xavier's forearm. Xavier carefully raised his child toward the heavens and spoke the same words he heard his father speak decades ago before finally announcing his name.

"Jason Alexander Darboe, behold! The only thing greater than yourself." Presenting his child to God just as he had watched his father on the days his younger sister and two brothers were born. He lowered his son safely back to his arms, closed his eyes, and bent his head forward, inhaling his son's scent.

"I promise to always keep you safe."

CHAPTER 11

Jason's conception during his parents' road trip and subsequent birth nine months later set their rekindled love ablaze. It ran hot, consuming all the ill will and stress their suspensions initially caused. During the pregnancy they plotted a course to reset their lives to complement the reboot of their love. Only a month after the birth of Prince Jason, they sold their house, said goodbye to their Texas friends, and headed east with their eyes set on Washington, DC. The DMV, a term used for the tristate area comprising DC, Maryland, and Virginia, would be their new home.

After months of playing the role of reformed and compliant employees at their Texas jobs, they secured new employment within their respective professions. Xavier transferred to the Metro Police Department in DC and Sandy accepted an offer to continue as a surgeon at the prestigious George Washington University Hospital. With the help of a veteran's mortgage loan discount and their combined incomes, they were able to secure a plush two-level, two-bedroom condo on New York Avenue in the heart of Northwest, DC. The two instantly fell in love with "Chocolate City." The diversity, culture, and history of the district had won them over during one of their stops on their month-long road trip.

Tending to Jason was the only reason they weren't out half the nights discovering new restaurants and venues to hear live music, or cheering on one of the many local sports teams, unless they were matched against the Mavericks, Atros, or Cowboys, of course. Sandy and Camila promised each other to remain the best of friends despite her moving away. But the prospect of the two new parents setting off on new beginnings gave them a sense of relief they had not felt the last year in Texas.

With renewed focus and only one more month of maternity leave remaining before starting at George Washington Hospital, Sandy sat comfortably on their new navy-blue suede couch. Xavier was already two months into his probationary period at his new precinct and drinking significantly less. He decided he would indulge only on the weekends, leaving him sober during the weekdays. His commitment to better manage his sobriety was the cherry on top of their new cake of refreshed marital bliss.

Meanwhile, Sandy's day typically revolved around caring for Jason. Diaper changes, breastfeeding, naps, and repeat. But that schedule would be interrupted today. It was a tumultuous time for America. Smartphones partnered with the viral effect of social media gave birth to a never-ending stream of vivid and violent evidence of America's sins against its own citizens.

What seemed like every week, new video footage documented the murders of minorities at the hands of corrupt police officers. America could no longer deny the glimpse of bigoted violence Rodney King had endured in 1991. King's beating video was merely a drop in the cesspool of systematic racism perpetuated by deep-rooted American white supremacy. Nonminorities who took to their platforms to claim that the 1991 L.A. assault had been merely an anomaly occurrence of police brutality were forced to eat crow in this new millennium.

The United States of America could no longer honestly deny the unsettling truth minorities had been warning nonminorities about for the last 150-plus years. Police departments were havens for conniving bigots set on infiltrating law enforcement. Once officers received their badges, the power it bestowed upon them translated to suffering and oppression for minorities in the communities they policed. That power, the blue wall of silence, and the political power of the Fraternal Order of Police created a system that gave those who wished to abuse it free rein to hunt minorities like prey.

Sandy settled into her couch, nestling Jason, watching *Time: The Kalief Browder Story* on BET. The critically acclaimed documentary was produced by hip-hop mogul Shawn "Jay-Z" Carter. The six-part series highlighted how the criminal justice system tragically failed sixteen-year-old Kalief Browder, who spent three years in Rikers Island Jail awaiting trial—two of those years in solitary confinement—after being falsely accused and arrested for stealing a backpack.

Sandy felt suffocated by the tales of Kalief Browder's misery. She turned the channel, wanting to escape, but the next network displayed coverage of a prayer vigil in Baltimore, Maryland. A gathering of West Baltimore residents sang songs and consoled one another at North Mount Street outside the large mural dedicated to the memory of another martyred young man. This mural, however, wasn't inspired by drug or gang-related violence.

Today marked a year passing since this young man lost his

life while in the custody of the Western District Baltimore Police Department. The results of the coroner's report concluded a severed spinal cord was sustained by the victim during his illegal arrest. As a result of the brutal nature in which the young man died, his death was ruled a homicide.

The young man's murder catapulted the citizens of West Baltimore into a state of civil disobedience and protest. For an entire week news helicopters captured in real time how West Baltimore unified and resisted the Western District "way." This "Western way" served merely as veiled and coded language of the Western District's overuse of force and blatant brutality under the guise of "being tough on crime."

CHAPTER 12

The next day Sandy and Xavier were enjoying a lazy day in bed with Jason. The television was muted. The usual barrage of mindless television shows was no match for Jason's smiling and cooing. Then the local DC news channel flashed the words BREAKING NEWS across their screen, catching Xavier's attention. He grabbed the remote from the nightstand and turned up the volume.

"We interrupt your regularly scheduled Saturday afternoon programming to bring you the following breaking news out of Washington, DC. Last night we reported on a vehicle explosion that left all six passengers dead. We've just confirmed from the Metro Police Department in DC the explosion was in fact intentional, and investigators are treating the event as a terrorist attack. The targets were six Baltimore police officers celebrating absolution of charges in the murder of a twenty-five-year-old West Baltimore resident one year ago," the anchor announced.

Sandy and Xavier exchanged matching looks of shock.

"A bomb in DC? The Feds are going to be all over this," Xavier said. "Don't be surprised if there's a curfew too. Whoever did this better pray they're never caught because if they are, they're never making it back to the precinct. Not alive, anyways,"

Xavier confessed, prompting Sandy to punch him in the arm.

"Don't speak that wickedness into existence!" Sandy said, staring at Xavier, who simply looked at her with the most serious face.

"I'm serious, San. They're going to lock this city down until they find whoever did this," he said as the news story continued.

"Based on preliminary information we've gathered thus far, the six Baltimore police officers were at a popular cop bar in Northwest, DC. At the end of the night the officers boarded a party bus rented for them by the Fraternal Order of Police. At approximately one forty-three a.m., only three blocks from the bar, the party bus exploded, killing all six officers." The news stopped in the middle of the report.

"One moment, I'm getting new information. We have just learned that the ATF, the Bureau of Alcohol, Tobacco, Firearms, and Explosives, will be assisting the Metro Police Department in the investigation. They have already identified the explosive device that destroyed the party bus as an IED, improvised explosive device. The ATF and the Metro Police Department's bomb unit are still scouring the crime scene for evidence to identify the materials used to construct and detonate the bomb. The mayor of DC has scheduled a press conference along with the chief of police. Stay tuned for more information as it becomes available," the anchor concluded before Xavier lowered the volume.

"Whoever did this is going to die in prison but only because DC outlawed the death penalty," Xavier said nonchalantly.

Sandy's mood shifted. "Do you even hear yourself?" she questioned.

"Sandy, this is vigilantism. You can't think blowing up cops is the right answer?" Xavier questioned.

"I'm not saying it's right, Xavier, but people are fed up watching videos of cops brutalizing and murdering people. Don't you guys get it? We feel under attack. Do you all even care?" Before Xavier could answer, the television interrupted once more.

"We interrupt this regularly scheduled program to bring you this breaking news story." This time it was obvious the DC news anchor was visibly shaken.

"We've just confirmed that NBC Washington has received, along with other news outlets, a vigilante manifesto. We are warning our viewers this manifesto is not intended for the faint of heart, and if any children are present in the room, you may not want them to view this report," the news anchor warned before retrieving a few pages from one of her news producers.

"Copies of the manifesto have been given to law enforcement, and they have authorized us, as a matter of national security, to broadcast this message to the American people. The vigilante manifesto reads, *unedited*, as follows."

"I'm going to be frank. If you're a racist, bigoted, or culturally insensitive police officer, I hate you. You should all be corralled like cattle and slaughtered. If you're a cop and what I've said angers you, makes you uncomfortable or feel under attack? Good, you're probably one of the cops who should be executed.

"For all the honorable police officers who wear the uniform, badge, and holster a weapon with hopes they'll never have to use it, we sincerely thank you. The career you've chosen is not an easy one, and we're grateful you've chosen to serve honorably. But more of you 'good cops' need to weed out your dishonorable colleagues who've snuck under your wire. Your habit of turning a blind eye to all your

fellow officers terrorizing American communities ends today.

"I'll say again. To all honorable law enforcement professionals, you are not my enemy. However, for those who have abused the badge and the power it wields, you ARE my enemy and will be treated as such. We've grown weary witnessing corrupt police officers preying on and murdering the people they swore an oath to protect.

"This point forward, you are now the hunted. We will not pardon nor forgive your sadistic behavior any longer. You will not be allowed to return to your home and enjoy salaries funded by our tax dollars. Saint Augustine of Hippo once famously said, 'An unjust law is no law at all,' and we are living in times of both unjust laws and law enforcement.

"My fellow Americans citizens, it's important that you understand the contempt I possess for criminal police officers did not develop impulsively. Nor am I experiencing a breakdown of my mental state. Our most basic right as human beings is to live. Self-preservation is coded in our DNA; therefore, we choose to survive. The once naive citizen penning this declaration of war against rogue police stands before you a true patriot, unremorseful and defiant. I am resolute in my civic duty to resist injustice, whether it be by violence or peaceful civil disobedience.

"Today, I no longer choose to practice the latter. America's laws and justice system have failed to protect its citizens from the murderous intent of racist and bigoted police officers. You have left us no other alternative but to proactively protect ourselves by eliminating those who wish us harm."

"And there you have it ladies and gentlemen," the news anchor continued, "the vigilante manifesto that government officials are treating as a terroristic threat against law enforcement due to the message's intent to intimidate and coerce American citizens. Lawmakers on both sides of the aisle have condemned what they've called a 'declaration of war on police,'" the news anchor said before a long pause. Sandy and Xavier could see the anchor's unblemished brow wrinkle, contemplating her next words.

"I've lost count of how many reports I've done about unarmed citizens losing their lives at the hands of police officers. I'll confess that this concerns me. I have family who are law enforcement and if I'm forced to report on the deaths of one of my family members due to this vigilante's actions, I could never live with myself. But the blame doesn't fall on the victims of police brutality or even this vigilante. It ultimately falls upon us.

"We need to take a hard look at ourselves in this country and start speaking the truth. Or, are we so bereft of civility and honor that we cannot sensibly agree, as a nation, that the frequency of police shooting unarmed citizens is a glaring symptom of our broken law enforcement system? I don't agree or support this manifesto, but I'm going to admit a difficult truth. We've brought this vigilante upon ourselves." The news anchor, disgruntled, yanked her earpiece out and discarded it on the desk in front of her.

"Countless reels of brutality and murder at the hand of bad cops are routinely broadcast to high-definition flat screens across America. But the victims aren't rich, famous, share my or my producer's skin tone, so we tend not to care as much as we ought to. We need to be honest and admit that's why so many of us are so silent. *Our* privilege is the festering open sore that has perpetuated our complacency since birth. However, our complacency can be cured.

"Like many ailments, curing oneself first requires the acknowledgment of a sickness. Followed by treatment, and in some cases rehabilitation to remove all traces of the affliction from a person's life—" Suddenly the television in Xavier and Sandy's home abruptly switched to a children's cereal commercial.

Sandy picked up the remote to mute the television, then looked at Xavier.

"Looks like you're the ones being hunted now."

CHAPTER 13

t was 6:00 a.m. at the Metro Police Department's Third District assembly room. Xavier maneuvered his way into an empty seat toward the front of the room, closest to the podium. Over the last couple of months, he'd met most of the officers in the precinct, but he would periodically catch one or two eyes giving him the typical "who's the new guy" stare as he settled in. By now, he knew the routine: some would be warm and welcoming while others would be purposeful jerks itching to haze the new guy.

He'd done the dance and had already won over a few new friends after he dropped off three dozen doughnuts and a box of fresh-brewed Dunkin' Donuts coffee in the kitchen area. Those who weren't aware of his generosity looked at him the hardest, trying to get a read on him.

"Ten-hut!" the commanding officer called out. His white shirt accentuated by sergeant stripes on his arm contrasted with the light-blue shirts of the officers who reported to him. All the officers in the room stood at attention as he looked them over while walking down the center aisle toward the podium.

"As you were," he barked, allowing the freshly shaven men and impressive women in the room to take their seats.

"Good morning, Third District."

"Good morning, sir!"

"As you are all aware, we have multiple federal agencies partnering with us to investigate the vigilante threat. Based on the newest information I've received; this apparently isn't as new a threat as we've thought. The Feds have been able to track this person or persons activity back a few months. So far yesterday's incident was only the first within our district specifically, and it will be our job in the coming days and weeks to ensure it stays that way. Isn't that correct, Third District?"

"Yes, sir!" they all responded in enthusiastic unison.

"If any of you aren't up to speed on what's occurred thus far, there are briefs available that will fill you in. In accordance with our standard police protocols, everyone keeps their mouth shut when they encounter the media. This is now a federal investigation, and we are here in a support capacity, and I don't want any fuckups. Is that understood?"

"Yes, sir!"

"No one is to talk with the press! I don't want *any* posts on social media. No pillow talk with your wives, girlfriends, husbands, or boyfriends about this investigation. Is that understood?"

"Yes, sir!"

"If anyone asks you any questions, what is your response?" the sergeant asked.

"No comment, sir!"

"That's correct. All questions from the press should be referred to our precinct public relations department, and they will make all necessary statements pertaining to this investigation. Is that understood?"

"Yes, sir!"

"Now, on to our next set of business. Officer Kamara, you will be riding with Officer Darboe this week as he continues to orient himself to the Third District's way of policing. He's a transfer from Texas, and whoever was his previous commanding officer brought him up right because he rarely comes empty-handed when reporting to duty. Thanks for the doughnuts and coffee, Darboe."

"My pleasure, sir."

"Darboe?" an officer questioned. "Your family, they're West African?"

"We're Gambian—"

"Kamara, you recruit one of your tribesmen to the precinct?" a stringy light-haired officer commented, elbowing the snickering officer next to him. Xavier peered at the teasing officer, trying to decipher if the comment was simply insensitive or purposely malicious.

"My family is from Sierra Leone, Furrman. Try reading more books instead of watching porn and you'd know the difference," Officer Kamara shot back, prompting soft laughter from the rest of the room.

"Okay, that's enough," the sergeant ordered. Xavier looked over at Officer Kamara and returned an appreciative nod.

"Further, this weekend there will be a rally by several alt-right groups in Alexandria, Virginia. The groups are gathering to protest the removal of the Appomattox statue. Considering the size of the crowd they're expecting and our proximity to Alexandria, the police chief there has asked we provide additional officers to assist in security and crowd control. Those who wish to volunteer, there will be a sign-up sheet posted on the bulletin board after roll call. We need the names by end of shift today."

"Count me in, Sarge!" Officer Furrman volunteered.

"Glad to hear it, Furrman. That is all. Be safe out there today. Dismissed!" the sergeant concluded before stepping down from behind the podium. Xavier gathered his gear and headed toward Officer Kamara. The two shook hands.

"Welcome to the third," Kamara said. A few other officers shook Xavier's hand, welcoming him, taking notice of his sergeant stripes.

"Thanks, Kamara. Transferring here has been a pleasant surprise. My old precinct in Texas? I wasn't used to seeing so many of *us* at roll call."

"Welcome to chocolate city, *bruh*." Kamara turned his forearm over to reveal a branded scar of the Greek letter Ω. Xavier smiled seeing that it matched the brand sneaking out from under his short-sleeved uniform.

"You'll find plenty of friends here in the third district, so we'll make sure to take care of you," Kamara said before the two drew nigh, embracing close enough so the surrounding officers couldn't make out their words. At the conclusion the two colleagues exchanged a concealed handshake only those in their fold would recognize.

"You two going to kiss next?" Officer Furrman jabbed before slapping another officer on the back before heading over toward the bulletin board to volunteer for the Alexandria detail.

"Is he the precinct comedian?" Xavier asked.

"The precinct asshole would be more accurate. He's 'on the job' but he's not on 'our' team. You follow me?"

Xavier nodded before following suit and heading over to the bulletin board to also sign up.

"You sure about that, Sarge?" Furrman questioned after Xavier signed his name a few lines below his.

"DC is way more expensive than what the wife and I are used to back in Texas. The overtime will come in handy. Especially now we have a new addition to the family."

"A new crumb snatcher, huh? Congratulations, sir. My family's originally from Old Town Alexandria. I can trace my lineage back a few generations. If it gets hairy out there, you come find me and I'll let the locals know you're a good ol' boy. Hell, if we go back far enough, I'm sure my people crossed paths with yours at some point," Furrman said with a sinister sneer.

CHAPTER 14

"Blood and soil! Blood and soil! Blood and soil! White lives matter! White lives matter! White lives matter! You will not replace us! Jews will not replace us! Jews will not replace us! Sieg heil! Sieg heil! Sieg heil!" The repetition of white supremacist chants followed by the German Nazi salute flooded the air of Alexandria, Virginia.

Once-beautiful collages of tweets and chirps performed by choruses of cardinals, robins, and blue jays were now drowned out by words of hate. Counterprotestors within earshot of the swarm of proud bigots corralled themselves around the Appomattox statue. In accordance with their brainwashing, the white supremacists spewed their collective chants of hate, polluting everything their wicked words touched.

Xavier and his fellow officers had taken up early posts near the protest's destination point. He was there to maintain a fragile state of peace that was slowly unraveling before his eyes. Within moments of beginning the demonstration, it became apparent how prepared the white supremacists were. Almost half of the men were dressed in tactical gear including helmets and full-body shields. Xavier's trained eyes noticed the matching bulges beneath their shirts near their waistlines and near their ankles where the supremacists concealed their firearms in accordance with Virginia's concealed-carry gun laws. It was clear the racists weren't only here to protest but also to instigate, engage, and if ordered to by their leaders, to kill.

Xavier's blood boiled, but he tempered his frustration, reminding himself of the oath he'd taken to perform his duties without prejudice or bias. But he couldn't help but scoff at the irony of that oath as he steadied himself, ready to protect those whose sole purpose today was to enact prejudice, perpetuate culture bias, and xenophobia.

"Hey, you . . . nigger!" a slovenly dressed white supremacist yelled at a melting pot of young Alexandria counterprotestors. "Go back to Africa!" he said, hoping to incite a reaction.

"I'll go back to Africa when you return to the caves of Europe, you Caucasoid Hamite!" a counterprotestor fired back, igniting a roar of laughter targeted at the white supremacists. Had the young racist not been holding the hate group's full-body shield, a passerby could have easily mistaken him for your everyday khaki pants, polo shirt–wearing university student.

Xavier kept his head on a swivel and closed ranks with his fellow police officers. Some in uniform, others in riot gear, and a covert few in plain clothes to blend in. With every passing minute he could feel the tension thickening like a cloud of smoke in a smoldering home.

"Die, faggot! Race traitors! Nigger lovers!" The racists yelled at Caucasian counterprotestors who rebuked the white supremacist platform in their words but most importantly, their actions. For Xavier, these young millennials were a glimmer of hope that all humanity was not lost. It signified that righteousness would find representation by *all* and not just the oppressed.

But the white supremacist's words continued to cut into Xavier like a small blade, leaving him more damaged with each slur hurled his way. He recalled his training, imploring himself to de-escalate his own feelings of disdain for the same group he was on duty to protect. He scanned the crowd from left to right. When a few scuffles broke out they were quickly dispersed without incident or arrest. Then suddenly off to Xavier's right, a circle of counterprotestors around the Appomattox statue grew larger, its members chanting with interlocked arms.

"Love, not hate! Love, not hate!"

Xavier grabbed and pressed the button of his shoulder-mounted walkie-talkie.

"This is the Metro Police Department of DC to Command. We have a situation developing at the Appomattox statue."

"This is Command, go ahead."

"Alt-right protestors with full-body shields and riot gear are marching in formation toward peaceful counterprotestors at the Appomattox statue. Requesting a crash team to intercept."

"Affirmative. Metro PD team one, rally there and await instructions."

"Ten-four," Xavier responded into his walkie-talkie, but the situation had already escalated.

Counterprotestors in the front of the statue were being pepper sprayed while others along the side were being rammed by the shields of the white supremacists, breaking their interlocked-arm chain. Frightened sounds of men and women who'd fallen to the ground flooded the air. Some pulled their toppled comrades away from the melee while others continued providing cover for another counterprotestor who'd successfully scaled the Appomattox statue. The counterprotestor retrieved a spray can from his back pocket to tag a peace symbol across the folded arms of the statue.

The defacing of the statue sent the white supremacists into a frenzy. More rushed over to the statue to join them. The white supremacists engulfed the outmatched counterprotestors until only the uniforms of the white supremacists were visible. The counterprotestors disbanded in all directions, screaming, choking, and pulling their wounded away to avoid further harm.

Eventually, the white supremacists pulled to the ground the protestor who scaled the monument and pummeled him with the heel of their boots. When Xavier's team of officers finally arrived at the scene he grabbed one of the white supremacists assaulting the counterprotestor to arrest him.

"Stand down, Sergeant!" his commanding officer ordered a few feet behind him.

"Get your filthy hands off me!" the white supremacist shouted.

"Alexandria PD is on its way. They will disband this group and make the appropriate arrests. Close in our ranks here and wait further orders," Xavier's commanding officer ordered.

Xavier stared down the raging white supremacist and then his other fellow officers, all of them standing firmly, batons in hand, displaying a faux formidable presence. He locked eyes with Officer Kamara, who motioned for Xavier to join their ranks as ordered. Xavier stole another look at the white supremacist, who was now shooing him away with the largest of grins.

"Go on now, boy. You have orders to follow."

Xavier clenched his jaw. He found a space next to Kamara

and exhaled in frustration. His heart pounded so hard he could feel it in his throat. His mouth was bone-dry, and beads of sweat raced down the center of his back. He reset his feet and scanned the crowd closest to them, noticing it had swelled twofold. On one side were the white supremacists and on the other a rivaling faction of counterprotestors who were set to retaliate after their peaceful protest was met with violence.

"Come on! I got something for you, monkey!" a voice yelled, followed by the tossing of bananas. The bananas were hurled back at the white supremacist. One of the returned bananas hit a middle-aged supremacist, with a US-flag bandanna, black cargo pants, and tactical vest, in the face. He snapped around, face red and enraged. A cameraman from the local news only a few feet away captured the supremacist pull up his shirt to retrieve a semiautomatic sidearm from its holster. "Hey, nigger!" he shouted.

Xavier jumped forward, grabbing his weapon, ready to announce himself.

"Po—"

Officer Furrman dashed past Xavier, shouting, "Hey, Brother! Whoa! Whoooaaa! Don't do it!" He placed his body between Xavier and the gun-wielding white supremacist. Xavier took one step forward, his hand firmly holding his weapon. He saw Furrman flash a hand gesture the supremacist recognized. The supremacist extended his hand to Officer Furrman, who slapped it away before yelling and shoving the angry supremacist forward, away from the direction of the counterprotestor who'd hit him with the banana. Furrman turned back toward his fellow officers.

"I got it, Lieutenant! Everything's under control!" he shouted. Xavier, hand still on his weapon, locked eyes with Furrman. They exchanged glares. Furrman wiped his brow and smirked at Xavier.

"Sergeant! Holster your weapon and return to formation," the lieutenant ordered. Xavier returned a perplexed expression to his lieutenant. "Back in formation! That's an order!" Xavier flipped the safety back on his weapon and slowly slid it back to its holster.

He looked over at Kamara. "Did you see that?"

"Yes, I—"

"Look ouuuuut!" someone screamed off in the distance, followed by the screeching of tires against the asphalt. Xavier bolted without the consent of his lieutenant toward the screams. His boots beat the pavement down a street that was previously filled with peaceful counterprotestors. Now the crowd had parted; what remained of the protestors crammed the sidewalks with terror, tears, and the wounded. In front of him was the back of a Dodge Charger amid the broken and battered bodies the driver had just plowed down.

Protestors who'd managed to avoid being hit pulled out their smartphones to record the car, driver, and the injured. Others pounded the vehicle with their bare fists and their protest signs. The smell of burning rubber filled Xavier's lungs as he sprinted through the trail of white smoke. His peripheral vision caught glimpses of brown and white bodies sprawled along the ground.

His senses sharpened as he burst through the remnant of tire smoke only to see more carnage. Broken bodies writhed in pain. The asphalt was stained with fresh blood spatter. Broken phones, baseball caps, and tennis shoes were scattered randomly yards away from their owners.

Then, there it was. The white reverse lights of the charcoal-colored Dodge Charger glared at him like the eyes of a savage beast pouncing towards its next prey.

"She's not breathing! Somebody, help!" a man screamed, holding a young woman's bloody head beneath his trembling hands. Xavier slowed his gait, retrieved his weapon from its holster, and took up a position on the sidewalk closest to the driver.

"Police! Stop the car, now!" he ordered at the vehicle, but the driver didn't comply. The car continued to reverse from the direction it came, dragging its broken fender and the torn clothes of one of its victims along the way. Tinted windows prevented Xavier from seeing the perpetrator. The driver accelerated past Xavier's position. The car's wheels screeched again.

"Police! Stop immediately or I'll shoot!" Xavier ordered again as his reflection in the driver's window came and went. He focused his aim where he envisioned the driver's torso would be positioned. He held his breath and squeezed the trigger of his weapon four times.

The first bullet shattered the glass of the driver's side window. Xavier saw the driver jerk in his seat as his next three bullets found their mark. The car swerved, slowed momentarily, then the engine revved again, continuing its retreat. Xavier moved into the middle of the street, taking a new position before squeezing off three more rounds. The car swerved once more before the engine finally died down and the car crept to a halt.

With his weapon still extended, he methodically paced toward the idling car. From the opposite side of the street, Officer

Kamara closed in on the car with his weapon drawn.

"Hands! Show me your hands!" Xavier shouted at the slumped-over driver. Officer Kamara pulled the door handle of the passenger side, and it swung open. He peered into the back.

"No one else in the car. I have him covered from my side," he yelled to Xavier. Xavier nodded, crept closer, and yanked the driver-side door open with his left hand and stepped back.

"Hands! Show me your hands!" he ordered. Still the driver didn't respond. Xavier took a deep breath and yanked the driver out of the car facedown onto the pavement. His body was heavy and limp. Xavier placed his knee on the back of the terrorist's neck, holstered his weapon, and placed handcuffs on him.

"You got him?" Kamara yelled.

"Yeah, I got him," Xavier responded, turning the driver onto his side, looking into his lifeless blue eyes. He placed a finger on the side of his neck in search of a pulse, then squeezed the button on his radio.

"Officer requesting paramedic units to Prince Street near the Appomattox statue. I have multiple civilian injuries due to a hit-and-run. The assailant is down and in custody with gunshot wounds to the torso and neck."

"Copy that. On their way," the dispatch voice responded. Xavier checked the driver's pockets for weapons and identification as additional officers arrived on the scene.

"They shot him! That coon cop killed our brother!"

Xavier snapped his head around and locked eyes with three white supremacists barreling toward him.

"I got something for you, nigger!" threatened the one with the US-flag bandanna and tactical vest. The supremacist already had his weapon drawn. Xavier reached for his weapon, but he was too late. Xavier was now staring at the dark barrel ready for firing.

Four shots rang out in succession, hitting the supremacist in his vest and spinning his body toward Kamara's firing position.

The distraction allowed Xavier the precious split second he needed to take aim, releasing another two bullets that found their marks where the supremacist wasn't protected by the vest. The supremacist's body recoiled while his two comrades cowered to the ground with their heads down and hands up. Kamara and Xavier traded one more shot each, toppling the racist. Officer Furrman darted onto the scene, gun drawn and barking orders at the two remaining supremacists. His position impeded Xavier's and Kamara's lines of sight.

"We're not armed! Don't shoot! Don't shoot!" the two supremacists yelled with quivering hands raised above their heads.

"On the ground! Hands behind your backs!" Xavier ordered while Furrman checked the fallen supremacist for a pulse, and additional officers came on the scene to handcuff the two surrendering supremacists. It was the first time Xavier had been forced to use his weapon as a cop. Adrenaline coursed through his veins. His legs shook beyond his control. Kamara walked up and placed a hand on his shoulder.

"Breathe, bruh! Breathe," he said as their lieutenant finally arrived on the scene.

"What in the hell, Sergeant?" the lieutenant demanded. Xavier looked over his shoulder at Officer Furrman; Furrman reciprocated a furious stare at Xavier as the rage boiling inside him turned his face a bright red.

"They shot Ritchie! He's fucking dead!" one of the supremacist's comrades yelled from the ground, his arms cuffed behind
his back.

"You just fired the first bullet of the race war!" the other
shouted.

"Get them out of here," the lieutenant ordered. Other officers pulled them from the ground and rushed them away while
the supremacists lobbed more insults and threats at Xavier. The
lieutenant walked toward Xavier and stared him down.

"You have any idea of what you've just done? This isn't our
jurisdiction. We were only here in a support capacity. Alexandria
PD brass is going to be all up my ass for this," he railed. "And
you!" The lieutenant looked at Officer Kamara. "You're not new
here. You should have reined him in. If this shooting doesn't
clear protocol and goes sideways, I'll have both your badges."

Xavier stepped in front of Kamara, absorbing the brunt of
the tirade. The lieutenant stared Xavier up and down. Xavier returned the same glare, disheartened by the lieutenant's response
to the only officers who enforced the law today. He grew angry
as other local and state uniformed officers jogged, some walking,
to the scene after standing idle while these home grown terrorists went unchecked.

"You want my badge? You can have it. As for those *criminals*," Xavier said, pointing at the two dead alt-righters, "they
got exactly what they deserved." He transitioned his gaze from
the lieutenant over to Officer Furrman. "And if it happens again
while I'm on duty, I'll lay them down too . . . sir."

CHAPTER 15

O nce news broke of the Alexandria protest that turned into a terrorist attack by white supremacists, news outlets across the country requested statements and interviews from city and state officials. They wanted explanations of how the sanctioned protest had spun so quickly out of control despite overwhelming law enforcement presence. Meanwhile, back in the Metro DC precinct locker room, Xavier sat on the long wooden bench across from his locker, feverishly rubbing his hands together. The heel of his boot tapped the scuffed concrete floor.

After migrating to the U.S. his family settled down in Camden, New Jersey where he'd been exposed to his share of violence. During his tour of duty in Iraq he'd fired his weapon countless times, but he'd never have guessed his first confirmed kill would happen in suburban Alexandria, Virginia. He stared at the worn, discolored locker with chipping paint.

Weeks after transferring and I kill someone? The news is going to crucify me. The brass? They'll take my stripes for sure. Damnit! I need to call Sandy! She needs to hear what's happened from me before she sees it on the news.

He jumped up from the bench and spun the dial of the

combination lock with trembling hands. Three tries later he finally landed the correct digits. The metal door swung open and crashed against the neighboring locker. He grabbed his phone on the top shelf.

The metal door of the locker room crashed violently against the wall. "Darboe!" a voice yelled. "You in here?" It was the lieutenant. The clicking sound of his cheap dress shoes against the concrete floor was a dead giveaway.

"I'm here, sir," Xavier responded reluctantly.

"Get your ass into my office! *Now!*"

"Yes, s—"

The door slammed more menacingly during the lieutenant's exit. Xavier threw his phone back into his locker and closed it. Sandy would have to wait until he'd survived his lieutenant's wrath. He exited the locker room, pausing as he breached the main floor of the precinct. Almost everyone's eyes were on him after hearing the boisterous summoning. He looked across the room and saw Kamara exiting the lieutenant's office, his gun missing from his holster.

Some officers on the floor pretended to busy themselves with mundane police work, eyes locked on their computer screens, banging away at the keyboard. Others, like Furrman, grimaced. How dare he take the life of someone their complexion? Killing a white man, let alone two, even if they were criminals, meant Xavier's career and possibly his life were now in danger.

I'm definitely losing my stripes.

Xavier peered at Kamara until he looked his way. He placed his hand on his weapon. Kamara responded raising both his hands, fingers typing on an imaginary keyboard in front of him.

Fuck! Administrative duty.

They exchanged nods before Xavier continued his march toward the office. He took a deep breath as he opened the door.

"Sir," Xavier announced entering and taking position in front of his lieutenant's desk.

"At attention and don't you move until I'm done with you!"

Xavier straightened his posture as if back in the academy.

"Our orders were to support Alexandria PD. I ordered you not to break rank, but you did. Then you go all Wild Wild West. I don't know how you guys do things in Texas, but here, in the nation's capital, we don't shoot protestors dead—"

"Terrorists, sir!"

"What the hell did you just say?" the lieutenant demanded.

"The two men I shot, sir. One was a terrorist that used his vehicle as a weapon to plow down American citizens. The second was an armed white supremacist that threatened an officer of the law—"

"Shut the hell up, Darboe!" the lieutenant raged, jumping up from his desk. He walked around his desk and then circled Xavier while he remained at attention. "You're one of *those* officers who thinks he smarter than everyone else. You're one of *those* officers who figures his badge will protect him. Terrorist attack?" the lieutenant scoffed.

"That *terrorist* in the Dodge Charger today mowed down a group of people exactly how the terrorist mowed down French citizens last year. Only difference between the two"—Xavier scoffed at his lieutenant, in contempt—"well, we all know what the difference is . . . sir."

"Looks like we have ourselves an *uppity* officer. Earned yourself some stripes and you think yourself equal to one of us, huh?"

Xavier scowled at the lieutenant and pursed his lips.

"Fix your eyes to the front, Officer! Don't you dare look me in the eyes," the lieutenant growled. Xavier clenched his fists, and his brow tightened. The lieutenant stepped closer into Xavier's space. "Go ahead. Try it. I'll empty my magazine into your African ass without giving it another thought."

Xavier broke posture, unclenching his fists, and stared his lieutenant in the eyes, envisioning beating him until his eyes and ears bled.

"Look at you. You're exactly what's wrong with this country now. You second-generation affirmative action babies thinking you're our equal," the lieutenant said, placing his hand on his weapon. Xavier heard the familiar metallic click of the safety releasing. "You people may have built this country, but don't you ever forget who the foremen were. America, and everything in it, belongs to us! We own it! You! And we'll run it as we see fit," he scoffed. "You and your *people* are nothing more than children honoring their parent's instructions. And like all good parents, when one gets out of line or forgets their place, corrective action is required."

Xavier raged inside, ashamed he'd mistaken his new precinct's commanding officer as a fair man the past couple of months. He stared at the collection of pictures the lieutenant displayed proudly in his office. So many picture frames captured the smiles and handshakes Xavier previously overlooked but now he saw, for the first time, the evidence of his being behind enemy lines. At front and center was the largest of them all. It displayed the lieutenant, one of his arms draped on the shoulder of a senior policy advisor for the current president of the United States. His abnormally large head accentuated by a receding hairline gave Xavier a momentary laugh he used to diffuse his anger.

His blood boiled again as he took notice of the subtle outward sign of their evil inner ideologies. Three parallel, straight fingers crossing the width of their belts were one of the many affiliated signs taught to him while training at the academy. The audacity the lieutenant had to display one of the most well-known hand signs of the Ku Klux Klan in his office only confirmed what Xavier had suspected during the verbal assault. His commanding officer would rather see him lynched than continue to advance his career under his command.

Xavier straightened up and went into survival mode.

"That's right, boy. Correct your posture and know your career lives or dies based upon what I *alone* decide."

Xavier's heart climbed into his throat. Heat flashes ran through his body, and beads of sweat formed on his brow.

"Effective immediately, you and your *brothah* are both on administrative duty," he accentuated in a mocking urban vernacular. "You are to contact your union representative and will have zero communication with the press while a full investigation is conducted into today's shooting. If I catch wind that either you or Kamara have *any* communication with *anyone* outside this department, I will have your badges. Then I'll recommend to the state's attorney that both of you be brought up on charges. Is that understood?"

Xavier's head swirled at the threat of prosecution.

"Answer me when I talk to you, boy!" the lieutenant demanded.

Xavier gritted his teeth, refusing to answer.

"Hand over your gun," the lieutenant ordered.

Xavier complied after a swallowed gulp of pride.

"I'll have those stripes along with your weapon until you learn your proper place when addressing your superiors." The lieutenant stood behind his desk, placing three parallel fingers of his left hand by his belt, and his right hand back on his service weapon.

Xavier looked at the brazen hand signal, then back up at the lieutenant, who'd looked past him and through the glass wall of his office. He turned his head slightly, catching a glimpse of a smiling Officer Furrman saluting his lieutenant.

Xavier reached for his weapon and slowly removed it from his holster, ejected the magazine, and cleared the chamber before stepping forward to place it on the desk.

"You're dismissed," the lieutenant said.

Xavier removed his gaze from the picture and looked directly into his adversary's eyes. "You may *think* my career lives or dies with you, but it does *not*. *I'm* the master of my fate. *I'm* the captain of *my* soul . . . sir," he said before exiting the office, leaving the lieutenant with a perplexed expression on his face.

Outside the office, two men in black suits waited for him. "Officer Darboe?" one questioned.

"Yes, sir."

"We have a few questions that we need answered at our DC field office."

"Field office? If you're Internal Affairs, you can question me right here at the precinct."

The two officers shared a quick glance before they both retrieved their credentials from their jacket pockets.

"We're not Internal Affairs. This is Special Agent Torres, and I'm Special Agent Smothers. We're FBI."

Less than an hour later Xavier was alone and on the side of the interrogation table he was not accustomed to. He could feel his pulse pounding in his temples. He surveyed the small, empty room, anxious.

Then the door opened and the two agents from the precinct walked in. Torres took the seat across from him at the metal table while the larger of the two, Agent Smothers, leaned with his back against the wall a few feet behind Xavier.

Xavier's body temperature rose, and his heart rhythm quickened.

"Okaaay," agent Torres sang. "So we just have a few questions for you, and then you'll be out of here in no time."

"Let's start with why I'm here," Xavier suggested.

Torres ignored him, scribbling on a large notepad. Xavier turned sideways in his chair and looked back at Smothers, who returned the same glare, arms folded across his chest as it rose and fell slowly.

Xavier turned back around to face Torres again as he ripped a page from his notebook. He slowly slid it across the table, staring intently in Xavier's eyes until Xavier leaned in. He silently mouthed the name on Torres's ripped page. Then looked up at the agent across from him.

"Michael Drawoc?" Xavier questioned. The agent's face remained cold and stern. Xavier returned to the list and scanned a few more names.

Brian Fable
Shane Tumaini
Olivia Shelter
Gary White
Barbara Brown
Marcus Pullman
William Light
Robert Carstarphen
David Duran

"What do these names have to do with me being here?"

"That's a good question," Agent Torres replied before sliding the list back to his side of the table. He pulled another pen from his inside jacket pocket. Xavier peered across the table and watched Torres scribble more words to the right of list of names, then pushed the paper back in front of Xavier.

Michael Drawoc (civilian)	10/21/2016 (Texas)
Brian Fable	12/1/2016 (Texas)
Shane Tumaini	2/4/2017 (Louisiana)
Olivia Shelter	2/14/2017 (Oklahoma)
Gary White	7/30/2017 (Washington, DC)
Barbara Brown	7/30/2017 (Washington, DC)
Marcus Pullman	7/30/2017 (Washington, DC)
William Light	7/30/2017 (Washington, DC)
Robert Carstarphen	7/30/2017 (Washington, DC)
David Duran	7/30/2017 (Washington, DC)

Xavier stared at the dates and locations the agents added.

"Okay? Is there a question you want to ask, or are you expecting me to read your mind?"

"Sure," the agent replied, reaching back across the table again to retrieve the sheet. This time he underlined a select few of the names. Xavier sighed impatiently at the tactical dance of his interrogation.

Michael Drawoc (civilian)	10/21/2016 (Texas)
Brian Fable	12/1/2016 (Texas)
Shane Tumaini	2/4/2017 (Louisiana)
Olivia Shelter	2/14/2017 (Oklahoma)
Gary White	7/30/2017 (Washington, DC)
Barbara Brown	7/30/2017 (Washington, DC)
Marcus Pullman	7/30/2017 (Washington, DC)
William Light	7/30/2017 (Washington, DC)
Robert Carstarphen	7/30/2017 (Washington, DC)
David Duran	7/30/2017 (Washington, DC)

The agent pushed the sheet back in front of Xavier.

Xavier shrugged. "Congratulations. You know how to make a straight underline. Is there a point to all this?"

Agent Torres smiled and leaned to the side, looking past Xavier to his partner.

"Listen to the guy," he joked before returning upright, staring Xavier in the eyes.

"This is a list of names the Federal Bureau of Investigation Counter Terrorism Division is looking into in connection to the vigilante manifesto reported on the news recently. Did you happen to catch the reporting of that manifesto?" He monitored Xavier's response with laser focus.

"I did," Xavier responded with another shrug. "Don't see what your investigation has to do with me though."

The agent pursed his lips. "Would you agree that's a pretty long list, Officer Darboe?"

"Yes."

"Glad that we agree," the agent said before continuing.

"Well, the names I've underlined all have one thing in common. Care to guess what that one thing is?" Agent Torres asked.

"No, but I'm all ears if you'd like to stop wasting my time."

"You, Officer Darboe. They all have you in common."

Xavier recoiled in his seat.

"That's right, you were in the same city when several of these murders occurred. Based on your training as a law enforcement officer, wouldn't you think that's a pretty odd *coincidence*?"

"Are you suggesting I'm a suspect?" Xavier questioned.

"Suspect? No. You're just a person of interest . . . for now," Torres corrected.

"Bullshit!" Xavier shot back. "What's my motive? When did I have opportunity to commit these crimes?" Xavier asked, but Agent Torres didn't bother to respond. He just stared at Xavier blankly.

"That's what I thought," Xavier said, rising from the table.

"Not so fast, Officer Darboe," Agent Torres said interrupting Xavier's exit. "Have you ever heard of the group Anonymous?"

"Yes, I've heard of them. Why?" Xavier asked. Agent Torres just scribbled more notes, taking his time before answering.

"Are you a member of the group Anonymous?"

"No!"

"What about your wife? It's Sandy, right? She's here also, in another interview room by the way." Torres explained. "Is she a member of the group Anonymous?"

"No!" Xavier responded. Torres locked eyes with Xavier. He could feel the agent's gaze radiating all over his body as if the agent possessed X-ray vision that somehow could scan him for lies.

"Have you two ever attended a meeting, gathering, or demonstration organized by the group Anonymous?"

"No!" Xavier replied again. The agent's stare continued until he broke it to scribble more notes.

"I need you to start being truthful with me, Officer. We're both on the same team here, and I can't help you if you're not going to be honest with me."

"I've been nothing but honest," Xavier replied.

"Hmph," Torres replied. "So explain to me how did you and your wife just happen to be in three different cities where several of these attacks occurred? As you know, law enforcement officers home addresses, family information, and their locations are not public information. Only other law enforcement officers have access to the information needed to know their locations. So if it wasn't you, then how do you explain the killer or killers knowing where to find them?" Torres concluded before returning an emotionless stare at Xavier.

"I have no idea," Xavier replied.

"Hmph," Agent Torres replied before scribbling more notes.

"Am I a suspect? Am I under arrest?" Xavier demanded.

"No. You're not—"

"Then you can't detain me, and this discussion is over," Xavier declared still standing.

"I sincerely hope you are telling the truth, Officer Darboe. Because we're going to figure out who is responsible for these murders, and that person or *persons* will face multiple charges of conspiracy to commit murder in the first degree, murder in the first degree, and we're going to wrap all these charges into a pretty little bow called terrorism under the PATRIOT Act of 2001. The United States government considers unilateral threats against law enforcement as threats against this country's national security."

Internally, the announcement of these charges shook Xavier to his core, but he refused to respond and instead headed for the door.

"Have it your way," Agent Torres responded. "But before you storm out, you may want to wait for your wife, Sandy," he warned, stopping Xavier in his tracks. "I'm sure your ride home together will be an interesting one. We'll be in touch if we need you, or *your wife*, again. Have a good day, sir," Torres said in a smug and dismissive tone before turning back to update his notes.

CHAPTER 16

Xavier and Sandy sat quietly in the back seat of the Lyft rideshare taking them home. A triangle of exchanged glances bounced between the two of them and their infant child.

"I know you have a lot of questions," Sandy whispered to Xavier while soothing their son.

"Not now," Xavier responded softly, eyeing the driver before placing his hand on her thigh and gently squeezing it a few times. That subtle gesture was one of many endearing and covert expressions the two had developed over the years. Three gentle squeezes, one for each word of "I love you." Sandy smiled and Xavier watched as the initial concern that blanketed her face had receded, even if only for the moment.

He carefully placed his hand on one of hers. Opening it, he then slid his index finger softly across the skin of her palm. A smile broke across her face as he traced the shape of the number eight three times. The number eight, when turned sideways, resembled the symbol for infinity. He looked deep into her eyes, and without sharing a word between them, she knew what he was saying.

I'll love you forever. Sandy reinforced her grip on their son with one arm and grabbed Xavier's right hand, pulling it toward her mouth. She closed her soaked eyes and kissed the back of his large, dark hand. The exchange of reassuring gestures confirmed for them both that, despite being separated and questioned, they were safe, okay, and on the same accord.

When they finally arrived home, Xavier unlocked their apartment door and led them both inside. The ride home had lulled Jason to sleep. Xavier locked the door behind them, and when he turned around, Sandy was leaning into him, lips pursed, delivering an endearing kiss. Xavier returned the sentiment, and they both ended the exchange resting their foreheads gently together.

Jason rustled in between the two, encouraging Sandy to break away from their moment of solace. She disappeared down the hallway to lay the baby down in his nursery. Xavier watched her sashay away from him, her hips swaying side to side. Even in those moments, simply watching her walk away from him flooded his heart with warm reminders of how much he loved her.

He waited until he heard the nursery door shut before he stepped into the kitchen. He opened the pantry door where Sandy kept a makeshift bar of assorted wines and hard liquor. Xavier scanned his options, then grabbed a full bottle of Macallan 18 scotch by its neck. Then, off in a corner, partially blocked by a dusty bottle of red wine, he saw another bottle of Macallan 18. This bottle, in contrast, contained only one or two more servings. He placed the full bottle back on the pantry shelf, opting to finish the already-opened bottle.

He turned toward the dish rack, retrieved two tumblers, and headed over to the couch. He poured the remaining contents of the bottle equally into their glasses. He was preparing for the serious conversation they needed to have. He sank into a spot on the couch, raised his tumbler to his lips, hesitated, and finally deciding to wait for Sandy to join him before enjoying his favorite drink.

Jason's nursery door finally crept open. Sandy slipped through the cracked-open door like a snake maneuvering through grass before softly closing the nursery door behind her. She took a place next to Xavier, resting one foot on their hardwood floor and the other cradled beneath her. She'd already tied her hair up into a sloppy bun and secured it in place with a pen from Jason's nursery.

Xavier turned sideways, mimicking her posture so he could face her. He reached over to the coffee table, picked up her glass, and handed it to her.

"Thank you," Sandy replied, reluctantly accepting the drink. Xavier grabbed his glass, carefully swirled the beverage, and closed his eyes, inhaling its rich aroma. He opened them, and they met Sandy's. Her eyes were bouncing back and forth from his glass to the empty bottle on the coffee table.

"Don't worry, San. I'm just having this one with you, and that's it for the night. I promise," he reassured her. Sandy forced an uneasy smile in response, but she was still anxious. He extended his glass in the air toward her, waiting for her to reciprocate, but Sandy didn't return the sentiment. Her posture was sullen. Her head bowed toward the floor. Xavier raised his glass to his lips to drink.

"Xavier, wait," she interrupted, grabbing his glass with her free hand. A look of concern plastered Sandy's face. Before he could try again, Sandy pulled the glass from his hand.

"What's wrong?" he questioned. Sandy didn't respond. She just shot up from the couch and poured the contents of Xavier's glass into hers. Xavier, now confused, watched as she grabbed the empty bottle from the coffee table and secured it under her arm. Then she turned to the kitchen and headed straight to the sink.

"Sandy?" he questioned. Again, she ignored him. "What are you doing?" Xavier demanded while watching her dump both their drinks into the sink. She grabbed the empty bottle, removed the corked cap, turned it upside down, and shook it feverishly until no more drops fell into the sink. She ran faucet water into the bottle until it was halfway full again. Then she placed the corked cap back on and shook the bottle violently before emptying the water down the drain. Once the bottle emptied again, she stormed out of their apartment with the empty bottle and returned a few moments later without it.

She let the door close behind her and just stood at the entrance. Her gaze met Xavier's before returning to her staring match with the parquet floors.

"Sandy," he asked. "Do we need a lawyer?"

"Yes."

Xavier's heart sank hearing her response. Sandy's hands trembled, projecting defeat and fear.

"There's something I need to tell you, Xavier," she whispered in such a low tone he strained to hear her. Xavier spoke before she could say another word.

"The nights Drawoc and Tumaini were killed, they were the same nights I passed out drunk and woke up with the worst hangovers I've ever had. Did you have something to do with that?" he questioned, voice slightly cracking through his trembling lips.

"Xavier, I'm not going to lie. Not to you," she responded.

Xavier sank deeper into the couch, both hands resting atop his head. His eyes stared up at the ceiling.

"The hangovers? That was you, wasn't it?" he asked in disbelief. Sandy nodded her head.

"Sandy, I missed roll call! I had to go to rehab! The FBI and their list of names? Was that you too?"

Sandy's shame of drugging Xavier washed away the moment he questioned her about the murderers.

"Those *murderers*," Sandy corrected, "on the FBI's list deserved to die!"

Shock overcame Xavier. "You know just as well as I do those thugs in uniforms have been killing people who look like you and I for centuries, Xavier. They're the threats! Always have been! I used to forgive people like them, but not anymore!" Sandy crossed her arms tightly across her chest, backed against the door behind her, and slid to the floor.

"Then they *took* Emmanuel? I won't forgive them again. I can't," she said to herself rocking back and forth in a trance.

"What do you mean you forgave them once?" Xavier questioned. Sandy continued her consoling rock. "Sandy, have you lost your mind?" he yelled.

Sandy shot him a gaze, checking his tone. Just above her tear-washed cheeks, the poignant stare she carried moments ago had been replaced by a blank and empty one. It was the same stare Xavier had witnessed only during his early years as a patrol cop. The "thousand-yard stare", on Sandy's face, he'd first encountered confronting a young soldier. The veteran suffered from PTSD and his wife called 911 because she was in fear for her life.

"Lost my mind?" she scoffed. "I'm as lucid now as I was yesterday and even more so than the day I watched my father's murderers go free."

"Your father? You never talk about him. You told me once he'd passed, but that's it," Xavier said.

"Yeah," she continued from her trancelike state. "I don't speak much about him. It . . ." She paused while resting her arms on top of her knees. "It takes me to a place that's not healthy. Not for me or the people I love."

A cold chill traced Xavier's spine.

"When I was nine"—her voice cracked followed by a deep, cleansing breath—"a mob of men took my father from me. They beat him to death." She paused again. "They beat him to death because he wanted all men and women to have equal rights in this country. For weeks I sat next to my mother, in a courtroom, and witnessed the acquittal of the monsters who murdered my father.

"They walked out of the courtroom, grinning at my mother and I, patting each other and their lawyers on the back. Congratulating one another and celebrating among themselves. I cried myself to sleep for weeks. All that pain and sorrow, it left a blemish on my heart, Xavier. But my mother? My mother never recovered. She became an empty shell of her once outspoken and joyful self. Watching my father's murders go free broke her spirit.

"There is a microscopic part of me that judges her. I wished my mother had been strong like my father. You see, the night they ambushed my father, he fought them back. He fought them till his death. He fought so hard he killed one of his attackers. Yeah." Sandy nodded her head in approval. "He took one of those murderous bastards with him. *That's* who my father was!" she said with pride. "My father was a soldier! He served his country honorably in the Vietnam War before earning his law degree.

"*That* was my father! A civil rights attorney who'd marched with Dr. King, who also subscribed to brother Malcolm and brother Newton's philosophy of self-defense. That day, even in his death, I learned a valuable lesson," she stated before gathering herself off the floor and onto her feet.

"The only way to stop a threat . . . is to *eliminate* that threat."

"Sandy? Please tell me you didn't," Xavier pleaded.

"I won't lie to you, Xavier. Michael Drawoc and Shane Tumaini, I put bullets in both of them. And those Baltimore cops I'm glad they burned. . . they'll never harm another innocent again.

CHAPTER 17

Battle lines had been drawn between Sandy and the District of Columbia. The opposing sides carefully selected their weapons after months of sleepless nights developing strategy, combing through the evidence gathered, and preparing arguments that would forever change lives. The beautifully maintained courtroom of DC's chief judge was the designated battleground. The scent of new carpet and polished wood was intoxicating to all those who packed themselves shoulder to shoulder to witness the beginning of today's proceedings.

News reporters, law enforcement officials, community activists, the Darboes, and the families of the alleged victims all sat anxious but attentive, unsure of what lay in wait for them to witness.

"Oyez, oyez, oyez!" the courtroom deputy bellowed, bringing everyone to their feet. "All persons having business before the Honorable, the District Court of Washington, DC, are admonished to draw near and give their attention, for the court is now in session. God save the United States and this Honorable Court. The Honorable Myer Pisano presiding."

The judge was modest in stature but carried a commanding presence as he exited his chambers and ascended the few stairs to the bench where he would preside over this groundbreaking case. He had earned a reputation of being a strict judge, yet he paired his strictness with fairness.

"You may be seated," the judge ordered, followed by the rumbling of those who arrived early enough to claim a place amongst the hardwood benches lining each side of the courtroom. "Before we begin, I will ask the courtroom deputy to administer the oath to the jurors."

"Would the jurors please rise and raise your right hand? Do you solemnly swear that the answers you shall give to the questions asked by the court, touching upon your qualification to act as jurors in the cause now before the court, shall be the truth, the whole truth, and nothing but the truth?"

"I do," the twelve jurors responded in relative unison before the judge continued.

"Jurors, you may be seated. This a criminal case brought by the United States of America charging the defendant, Dr. Sandy Darboe, with domestic terrorism under section 802 of the USA PATRIOT Act of 2001. The government claims that Dr. Sandy Darboe conspired with premeditation to enact vigilante justice by way of murder to intimidate or coerce a civilian population and influence the policy of a government by intimidation or coercion when she took the lives of Michael Drawoc, Officer—"

"To hell with Michael Drawoc!" someone from the audience belted out. "That racist, wannabe cop!"

"Order! Order!" Judge Pisano fumbled his gavel, affording a few more seconds for the protestor to be heard.

"We're glad he's dead! Finally, justice for the teenager he murdered!"

The judge finally secured his gavel and banged it feverishly.

"Order! Order! Order! Bailiffs remove that person immediately!" Two bailiffs rushed toward the protestor as he continued shouting from the courtroom gallery and igniting another group of protestors to begin chanting.

"Drawoc's in hell and we're dancing on his grave! Black Lives Matter! Drawoc's in hell. Black Lives Matter!"

"Order! Order! Bailiffs remove all persons disrupting these proceedings!" the judge ordered. Sandy turned and saw two rows of protestors removing their coats and pulling hoodies over their heads. The front of the hoodies displayed an artistic drawing of Michael Drawoc hanging in effigy and fire burning beneath him, consuming his feet and legs.

"You can't silence the people, Judge Pisano! We won't stand for it any longer! Black Lives Matter! Black Lives Matter! Black Lives Matter!"

"Order! Order! Order!" the judge continued, his face growing red in frustration. One of the bailiffs spoke a code into his shoulder walkie-talkie. Within moments additional US Marshals poured in the courtroom and assisted with removing the protestors. Those without seats rushed to the now-vacant spaces. Between the bailiffs and Marshals, protestors were shuttled through the heavy, wooden courtroom doors with their balled fists extended to the heavens in defiance.

Their tightly clenched fists, a symbol of rebellion, raised in the air almost emulating the members of the jury who had just taking their oaths. The exiled protestor's oath however promised more than truth. It promised unrelenting allegiance to the revolutionaries that came before them. Their chants reverberated whenever a new protestor was ushered through the doors that led to the courthouse hallway.

Amid the commotion Sandy swung around in her chair and found Xavier sitting next to her mother, who was rocking back and forth comforting Jason with her hands over his ears. Sandy mouthed "I love you" to them both. Xavier and her mother returned the gesture. The entire courtroom buzzed with conversation, cheers, and some tears.

"*I said order!*" the judge, now standing, yelled, banging his gavel repeatedly until the courtroom returned to silence.

"I'm only going to say this once, so it would behoove all of you to take heed." He paused for a moment to ensure no other interruptions lay in waiting. "This courtroom will *not* be turned into a circus. One more outburst and I will clear this entire courtroom whether you caused the disturbance or not. You've all been warned."

As he wrapped up his threat, the few original bailiffs pushed through the courtroom doors and returned to their posts.

"I will now continue to read the charges to the jury." The judge paused once more to scan the courtroom for any hint of additional protestors preparing to interrupt him again. "The government claims that Dr. Sandy Darboe conspired with premeditation to enact terroristic violence by way of murder to take the lives of Michael Drawoc, Shane Tumaini, Gary White, Barbara Brown, Marcus Pullman, William Light, Robert Carstarphen, and David Duran.

"It will be your duty to decide whether or not Dr. Darboe is guilty of the crimes outlined by these charges. It is important that you decide the case based on what the evidence shows. It would be wrong to decide the case because you like or dislike the defendant, prosecutor, lawyers, one or some of the witnesses, etcetera. You must decide what really happened.

"It is my duty as the judge to instruct you on the law in this case. The law states that people are guilty of crime if they, with premeditation, willingly conspired to intimidate or coerce a civilian population and influence the policy of a government by intimidation or coercion. The government's lawyers must convince you that Dr. Darboe is guilty of this intimidation or coercion. If they fail to convince you that she is guilty beyond a reasonable doubt, then Dr. Darboe will go free.

"We will now begin. The attorneys for the government will go first," Judge Pisano concluded. The prosecuting attorney rose from her seat with a yellow legal pad in one hand and a pen in the other. She confidently walked to the podium twenty feet in front of the judge's bench, placed her pad down, and looked off to her right where the jury of seven men and five women of various ethnicities sat alert but silent.

Sandy looked over at them, searching their eyes, style of dress, posture, anything that could hint they would be receptive of the strategy her lawyer planned to execute.

"Your Honor, Counsel, ladies and gentlemen of the jury, my name is Kirsten Bertrand and I am representing the government of the United States of America in this case." She purposely paused, scanning the jurors. "I can't make this point any more direct or blunt. This is a clear case of terrorism, murder, and destruction of public property by way of terroristic vigilantism. Over the course of this trial we will present video evidence and witness testimony that will paint the clearest of pictures proving the defendant"—she motioned her hand toward the defense table—"conspired, executed, and attempted to cover up the murders of not one, not two, but *seven* sworn police officers of the law and one civilian."

The prosecutor paused to let the number sink in and held up both her hands, displaying eight fingers.

Sandy's attorney cleaned his glasses while Sandy sat with a calm, attentive face, perfect posture, and folded hands resting on her lap.

"*Seven* police officers from three different states and one civilian," the prosecutor emphasized. "We will present undeniable facts that will prove, beyond any shred of reasonable doubt, the defendant conspired, stalked, killed, and reveled in the murder of Mr. Drawoc so intently that she decided to commit the same crime again. But this time her crosshairs targeted the sworn men and women of law enforcement on *three* separate occasions."

She paused once more and purposely took a deep breath before continuing. "Four cold-blooded, calculated, planned attacks. One of her chosen methods for murder included tactics used by terrorist organizations like al-Qaida and ISIS. Yes, ladies and gentlemen of the jury. The defendant used an IED, much like the same explosive devices used to kill American soldiers in countries like Iraq and Afghanistan.

"Do not be fooled by her title as a physician or her pristine appearance. I assure you the defendant is a calculated, manipulative killer who needs to be removed from society before she murders again. I know my words may seem harsh, but brutal honesty is what's warranted today, not political correctness. Brutal honesty!" she repeated. "Because the defendant plotted and executed these vicious crimes against law enforcement officers while she herself is married to a sworn officer of the law."

A wave of gasps swept the courtroom. The jurors broke their gaze away from the attorney to take a second look at Sandy.

Sandy ignored the jury's gaze reminding herself the lessons on defendant etiquette she'd practiced repeatedly with her lawyer. Her attorney discreetly tapped his pen at the top corner of his legal pad where he had drawn, in bold, the words "DEEP DISCREET BREATHS & COMPOSURE."

"At the end of this trial, I am confident that you will find the defendant, Sandy Darboe, guilty of terroristic acts as defined by the language our Honorable Judge Pisano first outlined after administering your oath," the attorney concluded before retrieving her materials from the podium and walking back to her desk.

Predictable. My attorney warned me you'd use that "her husband is a cop" angle. Was that your best first pitch of this nine-inning game? If so, ball one, bitch. I'm crowding your plate. What are you going to serve up now that you know I'm not afraid of you? Come on, give me something I can hit.

Beneath the table Sandy's attorney gave her two reassuring taps on her folded hands before he gathered himself. He rose from his seat to take his place at the podium, armed with a legal pad of his own tucked between his biceps and torso. Sandy was locked in and didn't budge. Her attorney removed his glasses, and clasped his hands, slowly looking every juror directly in the eye.

"Your Honor, Counsel, ladies and gentlemen of the jury, my name is Yvon Carlos." He paused for a moment. Sandy quickly stole another glance at the bold words on his notepad, knowing in the next few seconds he would begin a legal defense that no one would expect them to ever use.

"I was up late last night preparing what I would say to you this morning. I'm sure you all can relate to those nights where you know you have a big day ahead of you. In our heart we know we should be asleep because tomorrow is going to be one of those days where you may need a drink afterwards, right?" he said with a smile, prompting a couple of the jurors to nod their heads in agreement before he continued. "Big day!" he repeated. "But still, you're in bed, staring at the ceiling because your mind won't shut off. It *can't* shut off, no matter what you do, right? Because tomorrow may either make or break you. It may even affect how you provide for your family." He paused and looked each juror in the eye once more.

"Yeah, we've all had that moment of anxiousness, right? Luckily for us, though, it's not every night. Some nights we're dreaming as soon as our heads hit the pillow. And then there's the weekend. We can look forward to sleeping in on the weekend. Am I right?"

One of the jurors scoffed before repositioning himself in his chair. He had fat sausage fingers that were cracked and in dire need of moisturizer, and dark residue lined his fingernails, revealing his occupation was one with long days of toil and manual labor.

"Well, some of us can sleep in during the weekends. Others have jobs with no days off, but we don't complain because we make do, make sacrifices, and we persevere. It's what's required to take care of our families and loved ones because it's also our job to make sure they're safe and secure. And my client, Dr. Sandy Darboe, is no different from any one of us.

"She worked hard in school, earned her way to a successful career as a surgeon with no traditional days off. She works twelve-hour-shift weekdays, weekends, overnights, and holidays because there are no days off in health care. We can't control when someone is sick or injured. When her skills are needed, she answers the call. She's also the mother of a beautiful baby boy, who's now a year old, sitting right over there with her husband and her mother. And like you she doesn't complain about providing for her family, making sure they're safe and secure. She just does what's necessary.

"Now, the United States attorney has stated they will present evidence that my client, a surgeon, wife, and mother, is guilty of one of the most heinous of crimes. I'm here to look you all in the eye and tell you that's a lie. However, the prosecution is correct about one thing, though. This is not the time for political correctness. You will receive a healthy serving of brutal honesty from both my side and the prosecution during this trial.

"Honesty," he repeated. "That's the only way to kill a lie, ladies and gentlemen. Now, I, too, must forewarn you this truth is not going to be easy to hear. But as my adversary stated previously and the Honorable Judge Pisano instructed, each of you swore a sacred oath before *God* to hear this truth and then decide if the truth sets Dr. Sandy Darboe free of all responsibility for the charges brought against her.

"So here is the unsettling truth, backed up by facts and overwhelming evidence I'm obligated to share with you. My client, Dr. Sandy Darboe, is not responsible for the untimely deaths she has been charged with. She is *not* responsible. That is because the United States of America's government, its legal system, and the institutions of racism and bigotry they support are *all* responsible for all eight deaths defined in her indictment."

Gasps broke out again within the courtroom.

Sandy kept her eyes fixed on her attorney, just as he'd prepped her to do over the past few weeks. She could hear the whispers and the symphony of shorthand scribbles from reporters making note of her attorney's declaration. A few jurors recoiled deeper into their seats in disbelief while others leaned in, intrigued and woken from their glazed-over stares. However, not one of the twelve were left unengaged by the unorthodox charge.

"Order!" The judge banged his gavel, silencing the rumbling murmurs in the courtroom.

"Let me state my charge *again*," Sandy's attorney continued. "The United States government is responsible for the untimely deaths of those police officers and the civilian. *Not* my client! And that's what I will prove to you by the conclusion of this trial."

CHAPTER 18

The news of Yvon Carlos's opening statement spread like a California wildfire. Before yesterday's bombshell, most news outlets had reported on this story with lukewarm enthusiasm, expecting it to be an open-and-shut case. The usual suspects of chief legal analysts gave their opinions on the usual round of political talk shows and mentally filed this case away.

What they hadn't bargained on was Sandy securing one of DC's top defense attorneys to represent her, let alone his strategy of defense. After Yvon Carlos's opening statement broke, those same legal analysts weighed in declaring the storied litigator's approach as either preposterous or brazenly ingenious. Twenty-four hours later, the front steps of the DC courthouse morphed into the circus Judge Pisano feared it would.

The asphalt was crammed with news vans lining the entire length of the street. Every major news outlet across the country and some international publications joined the horde. The entire world was now an audience to what one news outlet coined as a test of the American promise. US and global citizens alike were set to witness if "the most powerful country in the world" would live up to that promise or relapse into familiar dangerous habits like a drunkard to a bottle.

Overnight coverage created a wave of national outcry from all directions. The law enforcement community demanded an expedited and dire response. Community activists viewed law enforcement's call for "justice" eerily synonymous with the first recorded lynching in US history. That lynching was of a black man named McIntosh who'd killed a deputy sheriff while being taken to jail. Before McIntosh could be legally charged and tried for his alleged crime he was captured by a lynch mob, chained to a tree, and burned to death in front of a crowd of more than a thousand townspeople.

Anarchists created the hashtag #AmeriKarma, claiming Sandy Darboe's acquittal would be the purest sign of the universe self-correcting America's crimes against humanity as poetic justice. Recruitment to far-right and leftist extremist groups soared as they both seized on this opportunity to justify their purpose and mission statements.

"Oyez, oyez, oyez! All persons having business before the Honorable, the District Court of Washington, DC, are admonished to draw near and give their attention, for the court is now in session. God save the United States and this Honorable Court. The Honorable Myer Pisano presiding."

Judge Pisano's courtroom was bursting at the seams due to the flood of new attendees. The wooden benches were jammed so tightly that it was impossible for spectators to breathe without feeling the same rise and fall of their neighbors' diaphragms. The previous day the side aisles along the walls had been empty. Now jostling representatives of the media wedged themselves into whatever spaces remained all hoping to scoop one another.

For the first time in its 242-year history, the United States government was both prosecutor and an accused perpetrator of a crime. The chief judge's reputation for fairness would be tested. The climate of the country would fluctuate with every decision and ruling he made. There would be no winners or losers at the conclusion of this case. Only endless moments of reflection and determinations of how to move forward with the sanctity of America's republic intact.

"You may be seated," Judge Pisano ordered. "Prosecution, are you ready to begin?"

"Yes, Your Honor," Attorney Kirsten Bertrand responded, rising from her chair. "The government calls Detective Paulette Smith to the stand."

One of the bailiffs positioned in the back of the courtroom pushed through the double doors and summoned the middle-aged officer dressed in business casual clothes and a blazer inside. A small murmur buzzed through the gallery as she entered. She walked through the sea of onlooking eyes with a purposeful stride until she reached the stand.

The bailiff approached her with a Bible. "Place your right hand in the air and your left on the Bible, please."

The detective did as instructed.

"Do you swear to tell the truth, the whole truth, and nothing but the truth, so help you God?"

"I do," the detective responded.

"You may be seated," the bailiff concluded and handed the witness over to the prosecutor.

"Good morning, Detective."

"Good morning, ma'am."

"Would you please state your name for the record?"

"My name is Detective Paulette Smith of the Fort Worth, Texas, Police Department."

"Detective Smith, you were the lead investigator for the Drawoc murder, correct?"

"Yes, ma'am. That's correct."

"What was the official cause of death?"

"The deceased, Mr. Drawoc, sustained a single gunshot wound to the head. The bullet penetrated the left side of his skull close to the temple, entered and destroyed thirty percent of his brain, and lodged itself halfway through the right side of his skull. The resulting damage killed him instantly."

"What type of weapon was used to murder Mr. Drawoc?"

"The bullet caliber was a .244 Remington that belongs to the Remington Model 700 hunting rifle."

"Does this choice of weapon suggest anything specific about the shooter?"

"When interviewing witnesses, there were no reports of a gunshot, which suggests the shooter was at a far distance or used a silencer. Our best guess would be silencer since the bullet did not have enough velocity to exit the victim's skull."

"Were there any security video cameras used by the apartment complex or nearby that captured the murder?"

"Yes, ma'am. The apartment complex has several three-hundred-and-sixty-degree cameras on its property, and one of the cameras captured the actual shot that killed the victim."

"Were you able to also capture audio?"

"No, ma'am."

"The apartment security video, officer? Were you able to identify where the fatal shot originated from or the person responsible for firing the shot?"

"Based on where the victim was standing and how his body fell, we were able to determine the location but not the perpetrator. When we canvassed the area where the shot most likely came from, we did not discover any evidence like shell casings or footprints that would have helped determine the identity of the shooter. The perpetrator must have collected the shell after firing the shot."

"Did any of the surveillance video you reviewed capture any interaction or exchange with Mr. Drawoc and the defendant?"

"Yes."

"And what time did the exchange begin?"

"The exchange started at approximately nine ten p.m. In the video, Mr. Drawoc, appeared to be helping the defendant with changing her tire."

"What time did the exchange end?

"Approximately fifteen to twenty minutes later, once the tire was fixed the surveillance camera's time stamp said nine thirty-one p.m."

"What was the official time of death?"

"Police arrived on the scene approximately nine forty p.m."

"So the official timeline says Drawoc was shot in the span of ten minutes after he helped the defendant, Sandy Darboe, change her tire?

"That is correct, ma'am."

"No more questions for this witness, Your Honor."

"Defense Counsel, you may cross-examine the witness."

"Thank you, Your Honor." Sandy's defense attorney rose from his desk and approached the podium.

"Detective, how long have you been a detective for the Fort Worth Police Department?"

"Eight years, sir."

"And during those eight years, were they all homicide investigations?"

"Yes, sir."

"Fort Worth, where the deceased was found shot, is it a high-crime area?"

"No."

"So is it safe to say this wasn't some random act of violence, like a gang initiation?"

"Correct."

"And when you start your investigations, has it been your experience that random strangers kill someone who's just helped them change their tire?"

"Typically, no. Usually in instances of gun violence there is a motive. There are also rare instances where someone dies due to random accidents, for example, a stray bullet during a hunting accident. But nine times out of ten there is a motive and the victim either knows the person or there was some type of dispute prior to the murder."

Sandy's attorney walked back to his desk and opened his laptop. He inserted a USB cord that connected his laptop to the courtroom's display screens.

"Your Honor, if the court would allow, I'd like to perform two live Google searches," Yvon requested.

The judge looked at the prosecutor's table.

"Any objections?"

"None, Your Honor," the prosecution responded.

"My first search will be 'Michael Drawoc death threats.'" He typed the short phrase, and everyone watched their respective screens as the words appeared in real time before their eyes. Yvon hit the enter key. He took his mouse and highlighted the total number of search results. He looked at the jury.

"One million fifty thousand results returned when you search 'Michael Drawoc death threats.' Let's focus on the top few search results before I perform my second and final search. Looks like Mr. Drawoc issued online threats to a couple celebrities. We also find Mr. Drawoc's parents have had to go into hiding because they've received death threats because of statements Mr. Drawoc made during an interview about the teenager he killed before relocating to Texas for his own safety. If you were to ask me or any other reasonable person, it looks like a lot of people wanted to harm Mr. Drawoc *and* his family."

Yvon scrolled down the screen to show more results. "Would you look at that? A few articles of Mr. Drawoc's run-ins with the law. November 2013 he's charged with felony aggravated assault after pointing a shotgun at his girlfriend. Then charged with domestic violence of the same girlfriend. January 2015, another arrest associated with domestic violence. May 2015, someone shoots at Drawoc in a Florida road rage incident. I could continue scrolling, but we'd be here all day and I think you get the point I'm making here." Yvon began typing his second and final search.

"Now let's search my client's name and see what we come up with," he said typing and then punching the enter key. Just like with the previous search, he highlighted the number of returned search results. "Nine thousand nine hundred and twenty results in comparison to over a million results for Mr. Drawoc. And will you look at that? Not *one* of them about my client. Not one online death threat against her or her family's life. Google even asked if I spelled her name correctly because it doesn't know who she is, and Google knows everything.

"Mr. Drawoc, on the other hand, over one million results, and at the very top were the threats he'd made to some very influential and powerful people. That's a lot of motive for a lot of people *other* than my client." Yvon closed his laptop and the courtroom video displays went back to black.

"I have no more questions for this witness, Your Honor."

CHAPTER 19

After Yvon's Google-search defense, Judge Pisano broke the court for lunch. After an hour filled with eating sandwiches, news updates, and courtroom chatter, the courtroom was back in session for the next round of sparring.

"Prosecution, please present your next witness," Judge Pisano instructed.

"Yes, Your Honor," Attorney Kirsten Bertrand responded, rising from her chair. "The government calls Devonte Armstrong to the stand."

One of the bailiffs pushed through the double doors and summoned a teenager into the courtroom. A small murmur buzzed through the room as the young man entered. He wore khaki pants, a pressed white button-up shirt, and black shoes with rubber soles. He walked through the sea of onlooking eyes, timid until he found his mother's gaze guiding him to the stand.

His pace quickened as his mother placed a finger under her chin to slightly raise her own head. The young man smiled and responded to the signal, straightening his posture, throwing his shoulders back, and taking his place at the front of the court-room. He was tall for his age and a chubby youngster. The bailiff approached with a Bible set to administer his oath. Devonte saw Sandy seated at her table and smiled once more.

"Do you swear to tell the truth, the whole truth, and nothing but the truth, so help you God?"

"I do," Devonte responded.

"You may be seated," the judge said to the young man.

"Will you state your name for the record, please," the prosecutor instructed.

"My name is Devonte Armstrong."

"Mr. Armstrong, I'm going to ask you a few questions, and all I need you to do is answer them the best you can, okay?"

"Yes."

"Where do you live and how long have you lived there?"

"At 2012 Sandford Avenue, Fort Worth, Texas. I've lived there my whole life."

"Did you know a man by the name Michael Drawoc?"

Devonte grimaced and his face fell sullen hearing Drawoc's name. "Yes," he responded.

"How did you know Mr. Drawoc?"

"I didn't know him personally. I just know he killed a kid in Florida a few years before he moved to my apartment building."

"So he was your neighbor?"

"Not like a next-door neighbor, but he lived in the same building."

"Do you recognize the defendant, Mrs. Darboe?" Attorney Bertrand asked, gesturing at Sandy.

Devonte smiled. "Yes."

"Is Mrs. Darboe a resident of your building?"

"No, I don't think so."

"So the night in question, January 21, 2016, was the first time you had ever seen the defendant, Mrs. Darboe?"

"Yes."

"That same night, did you see Mr. Drawoc?"

"Yeah, I saw him."

From the parlor of the courtroom Davonte's mother perched her neck and snapped her fingers at him.

He sat up in his seat and corrected himself. "I mean yes, not yeah. Sorry, Momma."

His mother nodded in approval and settled back into her seat while the courtroom chuckled in amusement.

"Order!" Judge Pisano banged his gavel respectfully. "May I remind the attendees in the gallery to refrain from signaling or leading the witnesses while they're testifying. Even if it's with good intentions." Then he graciously nodded in Devonte's mother's direction.

She smiled and silently mouthed "sorry" at the judge as the courtroom giggled once more. Judge Pisano returned a smile in acknowledgment.

"So, Devonte," the prosecuting attorney continued, "did you also see the defendant, Mrs. Darboe, with Mr. Drawoc that same night?"

"Yes."

"What time did you see Mrs. Darboe and Mr. Drawoc together?"

"About nine ten, nine fifteen."

"At night, correct?"

"Yes."

"What were they doing?"

"He was helping her change her tire."

"How did you see all this happening?"

"There's a basketball court outside my building. Me and my friends usually hang out there. I would have helped, but Mrs. Darboe said to stay away."

"Really? Mrs. Darboe told you to stay away? Those were her exact words?"

"Yes, because Mr. Drawoc—"

"Wait a second, Devonte," she interrupted, holding her hand up to silence him. "You have to be careful and just answer the questions I'm asking you, okay?"

He looked at the judge and then his mother before conceding to her instructions. "Yes, that's what she said."

"Good. About what time was it when the defendant instructed you to stay away and keep your distance?"

"About nine twenty-five."

"Was that the last time you saw Mr. Drawoc that day?"

"Yes. Well, that's the last time I saw him alive," he corrected.

The prosecutor tilted her head in curiosity.

"What do you mean by that?"

"I saw him again after the police came and taped off the area."

"You mean the next time you saw Mr. Drawoc, after he helped Mrs. Darboe, he was dead?"

"Yes. Next time I saw him he was dead."

"And what time was that?"

"About nine forty."

"Thank you. No further questions, Your Honor," she said, walking away from the podium to take her seat.

The judge motioned toward Sandy's attorney.

"Defense Counsel, would you like to cross-examine this witness?"

"Yes, Your Honor." Sandy's attorney rose from the desk and approached the podium. "Hey, Devonte," he said with a smile. "I just have a few more questions for you and we'll be done, okay?"

Devonte nodded and returned the smile.

"Okay, so you said before that you have lived in your apartment building your entire life. Is that correct?" Yvon asked.

"Yes."

"And who do you live with?"

"My mother and father."

"You also stated that you recall when Mr. Drawoc left Florida after killing a teenager not that much older than you, is that right?"

"Yes."

"How did that make you and your parents feel?"

"Objection! He can't testify to the feelings of his parents, Your Honor," the government's attorney interrupted.

"Sustained."

"I'll rephrase my question. How did it make you feel, Devonte, knowing that Mr. Drawoc would be living in the same building as you and your parents?"

"At first, a little nervous. I didn't want the same thing to happen to me or my friends."

"And did your parents ever say anything to you about their thoughts on Mr. Drawoc moving to the same building?"

"Objection, Your Honor. A question to relevance? Mr. Drawoc isn't on trial here," the defense counsel said.

"Your Honor, if you would allow a little leeway, my reason for referencing Mr. Drawoc will become clear," the defense assured.

"Overruled. I'll allow it, but make your point quickly, Counsel," the judge advised, leaving Devonte slightly confused.

"Of course, Your Honor. It's okay, Devonte. You can answer the question."

"Yes. My dad said if I see him, walk in the opposite direction. Don't run, just calmly walk. Don't speak to him or get into any conversation with him even if he starts it. My dad said if he ever tries to follow me, walk straight home and tell him."

"So is it safe to say that between you and your parents, you wanted nothing to do with Mr. Drawoc and planned on avoiding him no matter what?"

"Yes."

"So after that talk, had you ever had an instance where you encountered Mr. Drawoc?"

"No. Well, occasionally we would see him leaving or going into his apartment when me and my friends were at the basketball courts. We play basketball a lot." He smiled.

"Okay, so you saw him in passing but always at a distance. You and your friends never spoke with Mr. Drawoc?"

"Not really. We all kept away from him."

"You said not really. Are you sure you've never had an encounter with Mr. Drawoc? Remember, you're under oath and you have to tell the truth, Devonte?"

Devonte paused for a second, looked at his mother, and put his head down before he responded. "Mom, don't be mad," he cautioned before reluctantly responding. "There was this one time when we were at the basketball court. It was the first time we'd seen Mr. Drawoc after he moved to our building." He looked at his mother. "I'm sorry I didn't say anything, Mom, but I didn't lie to you and Dad. It happened before you guys told me to stay away from him."

"It's okay, Devonte. I'm sure you mother understands. Just tell us what happened," the defense attorney prodded.

"Mr. Drawoc pulled up to our building across from the basketball court. He had gone grocery shopping or something because he was unloading a bunch of plastic bags from the trunk of his truck." Devonte paused again. "I'm not a snitch, so I'm not going to say who said it. But one of my friends yelled, 'You shoot anyone today, Drawoc?'" Devonte stole a peek at his mother's stern face.

"Then what happened, Devonte?"

"Drawoc looked over at us and put the bag he was carrying down on the ground. Then he walked towards the basketball court. He came up to the gate surrounding the court and pulled his shirt up so all of us could see the gun on his hip." A slight gasp swept over the courtroom.

"Anything else happen after he flashed his gun at you and your friends?"

"He said, 'If any of you thugs have a problem, you know where to find me,' and he pointed up the stairs to his apartment."

Devonte's mother's jaw dropped; reporters feverishly scribbled on their notepads and punched at the keys of their smartphones. The noise in the courtroom escalated.

"Order! Order in this courtroom," the judge commanded, banging his gavel.

Sandy's attorney pounced. "So Mr. Drawoc flashed a firearm and threatened you and your friends?"

"Yes."

"Anything happen after that?"

"No, we all ran away after he said that."

"Okay, now, Devonte, I'm sorry I have to ask this, but it's my job to get to the truth, okay?"

"Okay."

"I know you're only a teenager, but you're a pretty decent-size guy, and I would assume your friends are all the same age, probably around the same size. *And* there were more of you than him. Why did you guys feel like you had to run away?"

"Man, we aren't bulletproof," Devonte responded before realizing that he'd been too casual responding. He looked at his mother and mouthed "sorry." "I mean, we all knew what he'd done to that other kid he didn't like. If he already got away with killing him, what's to stop him from killing one of us? So we ran."

"I can see your point there, but why didn't you guys tell your parents?

"That happened before my parents told me not to say anything to him. But after that I did exactly what my parents told me."

"What about the police? This day and age, all you kids have smartphones. Why didn't one of you dial 911? Afterall he did flash a firearm and threatened all of you with it."

Yvon's last question made Devonte shake his head and forget for a moment he was speaking in a court of law and not to one of his friends. "Come on, man. Are you serious? No one I know dials 911 unless someone's house is on fire. The police will take one look at Mr. Drawoc and then at us and, somehow, we'll be the ones in handcuffs. Nah, man. We don't trust the police."

Sandy's attorney turned at the podium to face the jury to reiterate what the young man professed. "No one he knows dials 911 unless someone's house is on fire . . . we . . . don't . . . trust . . . the police."

Sandy's defense attorney turned back to look at Devonte. "Young man, thank you for your testimony, but before I take my seat, I hope you do know that the way *some* police conduct themselves isn't the way it *should* be. That's why we're here trying to fix that."

Devonte nodded his head to acknowledge he understood Yvon's point, but Sandy could see something else was weighing on the young man before he finally spoke.

"The way it *should* be and the way it *is* are like night and day in my world, Mr. Carlos. If you can fix it, great. Until then I have to focus on surviving how it is *right now*."

Yvon nodded in agreement.

"No more questions for this witness, Your Honor."

CHAPTER 20

After Yvon concluded his cross-examination of Devonte, Judge Pisano adjourned for the day. The instant his gavel rapped against wood, reporters shot out of their seats like sprinters from a starting block. The courtroom lobby was transformed into a hundred-meter-dash final where competitors feverishly punched at the keys of their smartphones and tablets. Their profession afforded a modest allowance of only a few minutes to summarize the day's events and beat competing news outlets.

Moments into the court's closure of day's proceedings, the information gathered by reporters was already in transit. Hundreds of words relayed through wireless networks to the feeding frenzy of polished television newscasters outside. With only a few feet separating reporters, they told their version of the last moments leading up to Michael Drawoc's violent demise.

Online trending news and hashtags went viral shortly after. The masses of social media communities spread posts and memes depicting their version of the news. For news connoisseurs, not privy to witness the live court proceedings, the version of truth they receive would be a crap shoot. Depending on where citizens received their news or worse whichever side of the pendulum their political views fell meant the same news story could be screwed to either celebrate or condemn Sandy.

●

Just as quickly as day two of Sandy's trial ended, day three convened. Reporters arrived even earlier than the previous day, knowing that would be the only way to retain or improve their position in the courtroom. With the judge absent, the noise level in the courtroom resembled a high school cafeteria more than a place of law. When the bailiffs entered and resumed their positions, the noise levels receded knowing the judge would soon follow.

"Government's Counsel, call your next witness."

"The government calls Sarah Ecosta to the stand." As he had done before, the bailiff disappeared into the hallway and returned with the government's newest witness. After the bailiff administered the oath, Ms. Ecosta sat on the stand and glared at Sandy.

"Will you state your name for the record, please?"

"My name is Sarah Ecosta."

"And, Ms. Ecosta, where do you live?"

"Baton Rouge, Louisiana."

"Where are you employed?'

"The Radio Bar on Government Street in Baton Rouge."

"And what was your job at the Radio Bar?"

"I'm a bouncer for female patrons."

"During your time as a bouncer, did you ever work with another bouncer by the name of Shane Tumaini?" Sandy could see Sarah's posture stiffen hearing his name.

"Yes. We worked together for three to four months before . . ." She paused before completing her thought.

"Before what, Ms. Ecosta?"

"Before he passed away."

"Passed away?" the attorney questioned. "Shane Tumaini's death has been ruled a homicide. *Murdered* would be a more appropriate term, wouldn't it, Ms. Ecosta?"

"Objection, Your Honor," Sandy's defense announced. "Leading the witness."

"Sustained," Judge Pisano concurred. The prosecution shot a glance over at her adversary.

"Ms. Ecosta, would you agree Mr. Tumaini's passing away, as you've described it, was the result of the multiple bullets shot into his chest and the one bullet shot into one of his eyes?"

"Yes."

"Thank you. Now, back to the night of May 4, 2016. Were the two of you working as bouncers that night?"

"Yes."

"Do you recall also seeing the defendant that night at the Radio Bar as well?"

"Yes."

"Did you witness Mrs. Darboe interacting with Mr. Tumaini?"

"Yes."

"Can you describe their interaction at the bar that night?"

Ms. Ecosta paused and looked at Sandy again before answering.

"Yes, Mrs. Darboe came to the bar that night alone, and as you can see, she's a pretty lady, so she caught Shane's eye. He was a hound like that most nights."

"Your Honor, I move to strike that last comment about Mr.

Tumaini being referred to as a hound from the record," the prosecutor demanded.

"You asked *your* witness a question and object at the answer?" the judge scoffed. "Overruled."

"Ms. Ecosta," the prosecutor continued, "please describe the interactions between the defendant and Mr. Tumaini that night."

"About an hour after we admitted Mrs. Darboe into the bar, Shane took a break and went inside. When he didn't come back on time, I looked back into the bar and I saw Shane and Mrs. Darboe having a conversation. A few minutes later I caught his attention and waved him back outside, so I could go on my break."

"Any other interactions between the two of them after that?" the prosecutor asked.

"Yes. When the bartenders made the last-call announcement, Shane went back inside and they started talking at the bar again."

"And after that, Ms. Ecosta?"

"When the bar closed, Shane and Mrs. Darboe left together."

Small pocket conversations broke out in the courtroom.

Sandy could feel eyes on her as she struggled to look calm all the while; her body temperature rose. Then worry struck her. She could only imagine what thoughts were racing through Xavier's head. Turning around to look or mouthing something to him would not go over well with her attorney or in the eyes of onlookers. So she pulled all of her curly hair over her right shoulder, exposing the back of her neck, and subtly traced the infinity sign just below her hairline three times.

Xavier caught the signal, looked down at their resting son,

and kissed him on the forehead as he rocked back and forth soothing him.

"So the two of them left together after she'd spent most of that evening drinking and having extended conversations with him through the night, is that correct?"

"Yes."

"Is that that last time you saw Tumaini alive?"

"Yes."

"I have no further questions for this witness, your Honor."

"Defense Counsel, you may cross-examine," the judge said.

"Thank you, Your Honor. Ms. Ecosta, could you elaborate on what you meant when you described Mr. Tumaini as a hound?"

"I'm sorry, Your Honor," she said, turning to Judge Pisano, "I wasn't trying to be smart when I said that. I'm just being honest."

"It's fine, Ms. Ecosta. Please just answer the question."

"Right. Well, part of our job is to check patrons for weapons for obvious safety reasons. Shane's and other male bouncers' jobs are to check the guys, and I check the girls. I called Shane a hound because the night when Mrs. Darboe showed up, Shane did what Shane usually does when a pretty girl tries to come into the bar. While I was checking another girl, Shane waved Mrs. Darboe forward to be checked by him instead of making her wait until I was ready to check her.

"Most nights I can finish checking a female patron and get to the next one before he tries to get handsy, but some nights there's just too many of them and I can't always pay attention to what he's doing and do my job thoroughly. And I can't take it easy on checking the girls because most times guys will use girls to sneak weapons or drugs into the bar. Plus, I need my job, so I can't piss off the other bouncers either by calling one of them out.

"We rely on each other to watch each other's backs. We can't just go around making another bouncer look bad in front of patrons even if the bouncer is being a creep. It sends the wrong message, and the last thing you want is to get into a scuffle with a drunk patron and your coworker is leaving you out to dry."

"So what are you saying about Mr. Tumaini's behavior that night or any other night a young, pretty patron shows up at the bar?"

"If Shane checks a pretty girl, nine times out of ten he's going to get handsy," she said.

"Handsy? Ms. Ecosta, I don't want to put words in your mouth, so can you be as plain as possible and elaborate on what you mean by *handsy*?"

"When Shane pats pretty women down, he takes his time, he grabs their butts and lingers around certain parts of their bodies, like their breasts, longer than he has to."

"So he sexually assaults women while performing his job as a bouncer—"

"Objection!" the prosecution demanded. "Your Honor, Shane Tumaini is not on trial here, and I have to question the relevance of smearing the name of a police officer who lost his life."

"Your Honor," Yvon interjected, "the summarization of these minor details, when combined, tell the full story of what ultimately happened the night in question."

"Objection overruled." Judge Pisano announced.

"Thank you, Your Honor," Yvon said. "Please continue, Ms. Ecosta."

"Look, it's not my place to say if it's sexual assault. I mean, he's not sticking his hand down their pants or their shirts. But there were a few times when I could tell some of the women were uncomfortable. When that happens, the sober ones just endure the few seconds of it. Others, who are already drunk, mostly laugh it off and just go into the bar."

"I see. Have you witnessed any women ever complain about his behavior?"

"Yes. At least two women have complained to the bar manager that I'm aware of."

"And what happened after they complained?

"Well, he wasn't fired. The two times I'm aware of, the bar owner suspended him for a week, but after that he was back on the door with me."

"Do you think he should have been fired?"

"Yes."

"Would you have felt comfortable being checked for weapons or drugs by Mr. Tumaini like those other women?"

"Absolutely not."

"Did those women who you witnessed being touched by Mr. Tumaini give him permission to touch their buttocks, breasts, etcetera?"

"No."

"Did he ask for permission to touch them before he patted them down?"

"No."

Sandy's defense attorney turned toward the jury with his arms extended in the air. "Sounds like sexual assault to me," he announced.

"*Objection, Your Honor!*" the prosecutor demanded.

"My apologies, Your Honor and members of the jury. Sexual assault is a very serious *crime* and should not be made light of."

"Mr. Yvon! Approach my bench now!" Judge Pisano ordered. Sandy's attorney headed toward the bench, and the prosecuting attorney joined them. The judge turned off the microphone, but everyone could see the scolding Sandy's defense attorney was receiving. Yvon nodded his head obediently while mouthing multiple "My apologies, Your Honor." Once the judge was satisfied with verbally flogging the defense, he shooed him away.

Sandy watched helpless as her pulsed raced, wondering if his antics had drawn disfavor from the jury and judge simultaneously. As Yvon headed back to the podium, Sandy locked eyes with him and he returned a quick smirk and a wink that the judge and jury could not see. She was elated and had to hold back a budding smirk of her own.

"Ms. Ecosta, please continue telling us what else happened that night."

"When Shane and Mrs. Darboe left the bar together, Shane tried putting his arm around her waist, but she moved away and swatted his hand. Then after a few more steps he tried again, but this time he grabbed her butt and she got angry. She stopped in her tracks, shoved him away from her, and then pointed her finger in his face, yelling at him. I couldn't make out exactly what she was saying, but you could tell she wasn't happy. Shane said a few things in return, and whatever it was must have calmed her down because they continued walking around the corner."

"Were you the only person who saw this encounter?"

"No, another bouncer joined me at the door when Shane

left, and we joked about him getting yelled at." Ms. Ecosta paused for a moment before continuing. "Then it happened."

"What happened?" Sandy's attorney questioned.

"We heard a scream from around the corner where they had just turned. Me and the other bouncer headed up the street toward the scream, and then we heard the gunshots. I made out five or six shots. Me and the other bouncer stopped in our tracks because we're not armed security, so we called it in that we heard gunshots over our walkie-talkies.

"The bar manager said he was calling the police, and after that, me and the bouncer slowly walked around the corner. When we turned the corner, we saw Shane's legs sticking out from an alley. When we got to the alley, we saw Shane on his back with a gunshot wound to the face and a few more to his chest."

"Then what did you do?"

"We radioed that Shane had been shot and to call 911 again for paramedics. Then we waited for police and the ambulance to show up. The cops showed up first and confirmed what we already suspected. Shane was dead."

"And what about Dr. Darboe? Any sign of her?" Yvon asked.

"No."

"So you didn't physically see Dr. Darboe shoot Tumaini?"

"No."

"So you don't know for sure who shot Tumaini?"

"No."

"Is it possible someone who's familiar with the bar's closing time, familiar with the amount of drunk and impaired patrons spilling out, waited in the alley for the perfect opportunity to rob someone? That would explain the scream. Then, while being robbed, perhaps there's a struggle over the gun and Dr. Darboe runs away, and unfortunately for Mr. Tumaini, he's shot and killed by the robber?"

"Yes, I guess that's possible," Ms. Ecosta answered.

"Your Honor, I have no further questions."

CHAPTER 21

Three days into Sandy's trial and the flair of her high-priced lawyer and his parlor-trick strategy to win over the jury and raise reasonable doubt was losing steam. The prosecutor stayed the course of presenting evidence and timelines that placed Sandy at the scene of each of the first two murders. Sandy's defense attorney countered the evidence as being circumstantial, but even the most talented of lawyers would have a difficult time convincing twelve strangers their client just happened to stumble upon multiple murder scenes in the span of five months.

"Oyez, oyez, oyez! All persons having business before the Honorable, the District Court of Washington, DC, are admonished to draw near and give their attention, for the court is now in session. God save the United States and this Honorable Court. The Honorable Myer Pisano, presiding."

"You may be seated. Government's Counsel, you may present your next witness."

"Your Honor, the government calls Special Agent Danilo Torres to the stand." An FBI agent with thinning hair and a clean-shaven face, dressed in a modest blue suit, strode down the middle aisle of the courtroom. He took his place at the witness stand, straightened his tie, and raised his hand to take his oath. When done he provided his name for the record.

"My name is Danilo Torres."

"And what is your occupation, Mr. Torres?"

"I'm a special agent for the FBI Counter Terrorism Division, DC field office, ma'am."

"Aren't you actually the lead investigator in the case of the six Baltimore police officers who were assassinated not very long ago?"

"We've classified their deaths as a homicide, not assassination, ma'am. But to answer your question, yes, I am the lead investigator, ma'am."

"I stand corrected. Will you please tell the court what your investigation has determined as the cause of death of the six Baltimore police officers?"

"Yes, ma'am. We were able to gather sufficient evidence from the crime scene and from witnesses that the six Baltimore police officers were indeed the victims of a premeditated attack."

"Can you elaborate on what brought you to this conclusion?"

"Yes, ma'am. First there are surveillance videotapes we were able to recover from nearby retail stores," the agent advised before the prosecutor stood holding a DVD in a clear, thin case.

"Your Honor, may I approach?" the prosecutor requested.

"You may approach."

"Your Honor, the government would like to enter the government's exhibit A into evidence," the prosecutor stated before placing the disc in the DVD player positioned inside the rectangular console in front of the judge's bench.

"Special Agent Torres, I'm going to press play and I'd like for you to narrate what we are seeing in the video footage."

After a few seconds the grainy video could be seen on the monitors positioned throughout the courtroom. Sandy glanced away from the monitor at her table. She was more interested in the reactions of the jury as they watched monitors positioned across the ledge of the front row of the jury box. Jurors in the second row slid forward in their seats to get a better view of the black party bus that was cruising toward an intersection.

"As you can see in the video there is a party bus where all six of the deceased Baltimore police officers had entered after leaving Kelly's Irish Times located in Northwest, DC. After driving a few minutes to a secluded neighborhood, the party bus comes to a stop at the red light. A few seconds after stopping, you can see someone exiting the bus. From the clothes the person leaving the vehicle wore, and after examining the remains of the victims on the bus, we were able to determine the person exiting the bus was the driver. After the driver exited the vehicle, you can see them push a button on the exterior of the bus to close the mechanical door behind him- or herself—"

"Excuse me for a moment, Special Agent Torres." The prosecutor paused the DVD player. "You said him- *or* herself?"

"Yes. Due to the quality of the video and the distance of the cameras in relation to the vehicle, we were unable to determine for sure if the person was male or female."

"So the FBI has not ruled out a *female* being a culprit of this crime?"

"That is correct, ma'am."

"Understood. Please continue." The prosecutor continued playing the DVD.

"After the door closes, the driver then walks away from the

vehicle towards the nearby sidewalk and then further down the block out of the camera's view. Then the vehicle explodes."

The courtroom went quiet as all craned their necks to watch the nearest video display. Flames and smoke shot out of the windows until a secondary explosion engulfed the entire vehicle. The courtroom gasped seeing the footage.

Sandy caught a few jurors stealing glances at her. She wondered if they were questioning if she could do such a thing or instantly condemning her.

"What else did your investigation determine, Special Agent Torres?" the prosecutor questioned after pausing the video, leaving the frozen frame of the burning bus on the screen.

"Based on the autopsies of what remains we were able to recover from the explosion, it is our belief the six officers did not suffer and perished instantly from the explosion."

"Were you able to determine what caused the explosion?"

"Yes, ma'am. The bureau's bomb unit was able to determine the explosion was caused by an IED. Otherwise known as an improvised explosive device."

"An IED? Those are the same explosive devices used by terrorists against our soldiers in wars overseas, correct?"

"Yes. That is one place where they are commonly used."

"Is there anything else you can tell us about this IED that can help us determine who the bomb maker was?"

"Yes, ma'am. Based on the materials used and the sophistication of the trigger device, we have determined the IED was more than likely constructed by someone with a military background."

"Military background?" the prosecutor repeated.

"That is correct, ma'am."

"Your Honor, may I approach?" the prosecutor asked.

"You may." Judge Pisano waved the two attorneys forward as he turned off his microphone. The prosecutor carried a gray file with her. Sandy's attorney brought a stack of documents and folders with him. After a quick conversation, Sandy saw her attorney mouth a lengthy statement, pull two folders from his stack, and gesture adamantly with his hands. The prosecutor's body language changed. The three exchanged additional words before the judge leaned back into his chair, signaling the discussion was over. The attorneys retreated from the bench.

"Is everything okay?" Sandy whispered to Yvon.

"Don't worry," he reassured her.

"I'd like to admit the contents of this file as government's exhibit B," the prosecutor said, holding up the gray folder for the judge and jury to see. "May I approach the witness, Your Honor?"

"You may." The prosecutor walked over and handed the agent a gray-jacket military file.

"Special Agent Torres, would you please open the folder to the first page and read the identifying information for the military personnel folder in front of you, please?" The agent removed the string that kept the folder securely closed, opened it, and did as instructed. "Private First Class Sandy Dorsey, age twenty-two, race black or African American."

"Will you turn to the back pages I have marked off with colored tabs and read the contents of those pages?"

"'Private First Class Sandy Dorsey has attained the title of Marksman with the weapon M4 carbine.'"

"Thank you, Special Agent Torres. From your experience with firearms, is it conceivable that the defendant has enough training to fire a Remington Model 700 from a distance that could have killed Michael Drawoc without her being detected?

"Yes."

"I have no further questions, Your Honor," Bertrand said.

"Defense may now cross-examine," the judge advised.

"Thank you, Your Honor." Sandy's defense attorney stood from behind his desk and retrieved two similar folders, raising them in the air to mock the prosecutor.

"Your Honor, may I approach?"

"You may," the judge responded.

"Special Agent Torres, how long have you been a special agent for the FBI?"

"Fourteen years, sir."

"And of those fourteen years, how many of them have been with the Counter Terrorism Division?"

"All of them, sir" the agent responded, prompting an exaggerated look of surprise from Sandy's defense attorney.

"Fourteen years. That's *a lot* of experience," he said, eyeing the jury.

"Now, you've testified that you're from the Federal Bureau of Investigation, the premier investigative arm of this country. With all its technological advantages to enhance video quality, you testified that you were unable to determine if the driver of the vehicle was a male or female. Is that correct?"

"Yes. That is correct, sir."

"Could you determine the driver's ethnicity?"

"No, sir. The driver wore a brimmed hat to help in disguising their face."

"I see," the attorney said. "Well, what about the suspect's

hair? Were you able to determine the type of hair the suspect had? Was it short or long?" Sandy's attorney asked.

"We were not able to determine length of hair based on the video."

"I see," Sandy's attorney repeated. "Well, as you can see, my client has a head of thick, long, and curly hair. So much hair, in fact, that I doubt she'd be able to fit even half of it under a brimmed cap. Don't you think, Agent Torres?"

"I can't say with certainty it's impossible. For example, if the defendant wet her hair, then wrapped it, and placed a baseball cap over it, that could possibly all fit underneath the cap and conceal the true length of her hair."

"But like you said, the quality of the video and the distance of the suspect from the camera made it impossible to determine if that's the case, right? But I digress," Sandy's attorney said presenting the folder he'd brought over from his desk. "Your Honor, I'd like to admit defense exhibits A and B into evidence." The judge nodded in acknowledgment.

"Special Agent Torres, would you be so kind to read the identifying information of this military folder, please?"

The agent unwound the string that bound it. Flipping the folder over to the first page, he then looked at it and back at the lawyer and shook his head in disappointment.

"Your Honor, will you please direct the witness to read the contents of the folder as instructed?"

"'Private First Class Yvon Carlos, age nineteen, race Hispanic nonblack.'"

Yvon looked at the jury. "That's my military personnel file, isn't it, Special Agent Torres?"

"Yes, sir. It appears so."

"Will you turn to the same back-page section the prosecutor had you read previously and read the contents of that page?"

"'Private First Class Yvon Carlos has attained the title of Marksman with the weapon M4 carbine and M9 service pistol.'"

"Now, Special Agent Torres, open the second folder and do the same as the previous two folders, please."

The agent flipped open the second folder, and a scowl instantly formed on his brow. He shot a look at Yvon and proceeded to read. "'Private First Class Danilo Torres, age eighteen, race Hispanic nonblack.'"

"Please continue to the back pages."

"'Private First Class Danilo Torres has attained the title of Markman with the weapon M4 carbine and M9 service pistol.'"

Sandy's attorney extended his hand to take back the folders, and the agent placed them firmly in his open palm.

"You don't know if the driver was male or female. You don't know the driver's ethnicity? In fact, we don't even know *for sure* that whoever committed this crime of planting an IED was in fact military, do we, Agent Torres?" Sandy's attorney didn't even wait for his response before walking back to his table to retrieve a legal notepad.

"That's absurd," the agent responded.

Sandy's attorney turned around with a look of shock on his face. "Absurd?" he shot back. "I made note of your testimony, Agent Torres. We also have it on record to read back to you from the court stenographer if we must." The attorney flipped the page of his legal pad in a dramatic fashion before regurgitating the prosecutor's and the agent's exchange.

"When asked by the prosecuting attorney, *Is there anything else you can tell us about this IED that can help us determine who the bomb maker was?'* your response was—and correct me if you believe I'm quoting you incorrectly—*'Yes, ma'am. Based on the materials used and the sophistication of the trigger device, we have determined the IED was more than likely constructed by someone with a military background.'* You said *more than likely*, not one hundred percent?"

The agent paused, visibly upset. "If you're asking me for one hundred percent certainty if we know that the bomb maker was military, the answer is no. But like *you* stated previously, Mr. Yvon, as an FBI agent with all its technological resources at my disposal in addition to my fourteen years of investigative experience, it is my expert opinion that the bomb maker was most likely military trained. As I stated previously," the agent contested.

"Sounds like a no to me. My client having a military record is coincidental and circumstantial at best," Sandy's attorney said. "She should be celebrated for serving her country, not prosecuted for it. You and I are both military trained *just* like my client. Does that mean you and I are as likely a suspect as well? What about anyone else in this courtroom who just happens to have served? Should we have all the veterans in this courtroom raise their hands so we may indict them as well?"

"Objection, Your Honor. Counsel is badgering the witness," the prosecutor said.

"Sustained."

"I have no further ques—"

A sudden, distinct, unbroken siren filled the courtroom's audio system, breaking everyone's attention away from Sandy's attorney. The still frame of the enflamed party bus on the courtroom video displays disappeared, and they now streamed a prism of vertical colored bars with the words EMERGENCY BROADCAST in the center. Then the siren suddenly stopped; the parallel colored bars slowly broke into a synchronized wave. The courtroom bustled into a sudden state of anxiety.

Sandy looked around finding Xavier, her mother, and Jason in their usual spot behind her. A general look of concern overtook the courtroom while reporters feverishly took note of the mood of the room. Then the screens filled with white snow as if they no longer had a signal. Finally, the snow broke and a 3-D animation of the Guy Fawkes mask displayed on the screen. The eerie masked symbol synonymous with the organization known as Anonymous slowly scanned from left to right.

"What the hell is going on?" a spectator yelled out.

"Order!" The judge banged his gavel. "Order in this court—"

The loud, unbroken siren filled the courtroom's audio system again.

Xavier placed his palms over Jason's ears and suffered through the discomfort while others, including Judge Pisano, winced and plugged their ears with their fingers.

"Judge Pisano, do not interrupt again," a calm voice warned as soon as the piercing siren broke. "This is Anonymous. We have been monitoring these proceedings with an equal amount of amusement and disgust. Amusement because it tickles us to witness the Department of Justice scramble to scapegoat an innocent US citizen for a crime she did not commit. Disgust because it's sickening to witness our country devolve into the political cesspool it's become. How did we arrive at an existence where US citizens can no longer depend on their government and elected officials to protect them from those who wish to do them harm?"

"ORDER!" The judge banged his gavel. "ORD—"

The siren returned. Louder than before, until one of the speakers blew.

Sandy plugged her ears and looked back at Xavier.

"Get Jason out of here," she called out.

Xavier rose from his place and shuffled past the sea of people packed into the courtroom. Screaming child in tow, one hand over Jason's left ear, pressing his small head against his chest to protect him from the audio assault.

As the siren continued, the lights in the courtroom began to flicker violently before smoke rose from behind the judge's bench. Sandy saw Judge Pisano look down before pushing himself back away so quickly his chair crashed into the wall behind him, knocking over the American flag flanking him to the right. A small, contained explosion sounded from underneath his desk as he scrambled down the side toward a bailiff. The bailiff grabbed a fire extinguisher to spray the small fire that had enveloped the judge's desktop computer beneath his desk. Finally, the siren over the audio system subsided.

"You were warned, Judge Pisano, yet you remain defiant," Anonymous's computerized voice chastised before the screen display split into two. In the top half remained the masked face of Anonymous, and the lower half displayed live closed-circuit television footage of an affluent-looking middle-aged woman with her teenage daughter and son shopping.

"That's my family!" the judge yelled. "Bailiff, notify the Marshals!"

"Yes, it is," Anonymous responded as the judge frantically pulled at the length of his robe until he could retrieve his phone from the pocket of his suit pants. "You're wasting time, Judge Pisano. All telephonic communications are currently being disrupted. Sit down and do as instructed, and this will all be over in a matter of minutes."

Sandy watched as the judge disregarded the warnings and checked his phone. He held it up in the air, trying to get a signal.

The screen monitor changed again. A sniper's crosshair appeared on the lower screen where the judge's family shopped unaware of the threat.

"Put your phone away, sit down, and be silent before your stubbornness affects your family's well-being," Anonymous warned.

The judge, helpless and defeated, finally succumbed to the demands.

"Very good," Anonymous said as the screen with the judge's family disappeared. "The defendant, Dr. Sandy Darboe, is not responsible for the crimes she's been accused of. Anonymous is responsible for carrying out the justice the American government has failed to perform. The driver of the party bus was one of our own. Anonymous is responsible for the execution of the officers complicit in the death of the young west Baltimore citizen."

The courtroom's mood was gradually rising to a panic.

The screen split again with the lower half now showing footage of two people in an enclosed garage, dressed in identical one-piece mechanic overalls and ski masks to hide their identities. The party bus was in the center of the garage, being outfitted with what appeared to be an IED. Then the display split into seven screens, the Anonymous mask at the top, and six smaller screens below displaying police personal file photos of six different police officers.

"The six split screens you see below are all police officers who have murdered unarmed, innocent US citizens the past few years. Anonymous has obtained all digital records and police personnel files and conducted our own independent investigation by law enforcement officials who are also members of Anonymous. Our investigations indicate before these officers committed their respective murders, numerous complaints of racial profiling, brutality, and violation of civil rights had been filed against them.

"Despite overwhelming evidence of misdeeds, these officers were never arrested, charged, or tried for their crimes. In addition, we found documented evidence of eyewitness accounts and video that each officer had a history of discriminatory behavior, bigotry, and/or racial bias against the members of the communities they were responsible for policing."

The split screen then switched to display the same six officers Anonymous previously mentioned in real time. The majority of the officers were on patrol, one was in the grocery store, and another in his home, napping on a Barcalounger.

"The commanding officers, Departments of Internal Affairs, and their colleagues on the police force have proven themselves incapable of protecting citizens from these predators."

The six screens cut to dashcam, body camera, and street surveillance video footage of the six accused officers physically brutalizing citizens. Then the display screens showed a private chat room where police officers were communicating. The chats referred to people of color in a barrage of racial slurs, demanding they go back to the countries they came from.

The screen scrolled through an infinity of comments made by police officers describing their most violent and carnal desires toward people of color. Some said they'd castrate the men. Others suggested systematic rape of the women. While the most violent of commenting police simply wanted to kill people of color and immigrants arbitrarily. The single video screen of the private law enforcement chat group disappeared before splitting into seven screens again. This time the video displayed footage of each accused officer shooting an unarmed citizen while on duty.

The courtroom was quieted by tears, disgust, and horror.

Anonymous continued. "As a result of both local and federal government's indifference to its minority citizens' right to live peacefully in this country, Judge Pisano, you now have fifty minutes to take the first step towards fixing the broken justice system you're a part of. Anonymous, on the behalf of all US citizens, demands you, Judge Pisano, enter a summary judgment of not guilty, end these proceedings, and immediately release Dr. Sandy Darboe from your custody.

"Additionally, you will enter bench warrants for the arrest of the six police officers accused of murdering unarmed citizens previously shown in the split screens. We've just sent you an email with all information needed for the warrants."

Sandy watched as the judge reached into his pocket to retrieve his phone. The shock on his face signified he'd received the new email from Anonymous.

"Judge Pisano, you are now on the clock. You have until five p.m., eastern standard time, today to comply."

Sandy looked at her watch as Anonymous continued. "You

have exactly forty-seven minutes and thirty-five seconds to meet our demands. If you fail to issue the bench warrants for the six police officers, six other unnamed police officers whom we have also investigated for the same crimes will be executed in their stead via livestream on the internet."

A graphic of a crosshair overlaying the six murderous police officers displayed on the lower half of the screens. A live digital clock counting down what remained of the final forty-five minutes replaced the Anonymous mask.

"This is Anonymous. Comply or die."

CHAPTER 22

I t was a somber evening across the entire country. Sandy joined the millions of US citizens and countless international viewers waiting in front of their televisions, anticipating the president's nine p.m. EST press conference.

Judge Pisano, at the direction of the White House, had not issued the federal bench warrants for the six police officers Anonymous demanded be brought to justice. At 5:01 p.m. EST, one minute past the deadline, a social media post chauffeured everyone with internet access to a new website, www. NoJusticeNoPeaceinAmerica.com ← (Live site you can visit).

All who dared to visit the untraceable site watched Anonymous follow through with its threat. With less than an hour to react, combined with the hacker group's disruption of key telecommunications systems, six unnamed officers were executed. In the span of thirteen minutes, despite the scrambling of law enforcement's best efforts to intercept the threats, all six officers were executed. Some were targeted from a distance by high-power rifles. Others at point-blank range with handguns by an unassuming passersby. The worst of all the executions was a brute force home invasion. Two men kicked in the door of the unsuspecting officer and shot him at his dinner table in front of his wife and children.

As news spread about the Anonymous organization court-room hacking, so did national panic once Anonymous claimed responsibility for the IED explosion that executed the Western District Baltimore police officers. The moment Anonymous demanded the release of Sandy Darboe in exchange for a stay in the execution of law enforcement officers, the FBI placed Anonymous at the top of the FBI's most wanted list. Sandy was ordered to remain in solitary confinement until her trial was over.

She sat in her new, smaller cell, pressing her body against the bars, straining her eyes and ears to watch and listen to a small wall-mounted TV outside her cell. The president had been briefed on Anonymous's threat and now was the time for him to address the nation and hopefully deliver peace of mind to its citizens. Subtle trumpets sounded to the backdrop of a BREAK-ING NEWS graphic on everyone's television screen announcing the beginning of the presidential press conference.

"We interrupt this regularly scheduled program to bring you the president of the United States of America," the network news anchor announced as the screen showed the president sitting in his pristine office at an empty desk, a single black phone to his left, and tall gold-colored drapes behind him. The thin-lipped, stubby handed man appeared before the camera; his skin was flushed red, visible even beneath a fresh tan. He leaned forward, chomping at the bit to hear his own voice.

"Tonight, is a sad, sad day for America," he began. "Just a few hours ago, six police officers were murdered at the orders of a terrorist group called Anonymous. In response, I've directed the Department of Justice to use any and all means necessary to bring these really bad people to justice because they are some really bad people. The United States of America has not and will not negotiate with terrorists, that I can tell you. These people will be found, arrested, and brought in to face the highest penalty of the law, even death. That's right folks, the death penalty is on the table.

"Me and my administration support law and order. This is a law-and-order country. And we will continue to support the men and women in law enforcement. And when we catch whoever these people are, we're not going to be nice to them. We're going to prosecute them and send them to the worst prisons we have. I want the families of Raymond Tensing, Brentley Vinson, Anthony Coughlin Jr., Jose Velasquez , Brad Miller, and Daniel Pantaleo to know our thoughts and prayers go out to you.

"When I ran for president, I campaigned on being tough on crime and supporting law and order and our people in uniform. That's what I've done, and because of that, people have told me we've seen record lows of crime across the country. Probably the lowest crime we've seen in the history of the United States. At least that's what they're telling me. And by the time I run for reelection, we'll be doing such a good job on crime the world will want to know what we're doing and probably try and copy what we're doing. I'm telling you, they'll probably ask me 'Hey, how did you get crime to be so low?' And these guys like me and I like them so I'll probably share with them what I did because they'll probably want to copy it. I'm telling you, we may see crime go down across the whole world.

"I'm going to have the Department of Justice go after these people, and they're going to get the job done, because if they don't, they know what'll happen." The president looked feruously into the camera and pointed his stubby finger. "You're fired! America, this is a time to show strength, and that's what me and my administration will be doing. Showing a lot of strength, big league. God bless you and God bless the United States of America."

With that salutation, the transmission was over. The sound of a correctional officer's boots marching down the concrete floors stole Sandy's attention. She peered down the hallway, anxious to make eye contact with whatever officer came in sight. With her cheek pressed against the cold metal bars, her lips dry, and stomach growling, she called out.

"Guard! Guard, they didn't bring me dinner tonight and I'm starting to get dizzy. May I have some—"

"Off the bars!" a male correctional officer ordered.

"Please? I'm getting light-head—"

The correctional officer hit one of Sandy's hands that was wrapped around the bars with his baton.

"FUUUCK! *My haand!*" Sandy jumped back from the bars and stumbled backward onto the bare concrete slab that served as her bed in solitary.

"Why the fuck did you do that?" she demanded, hunched over and rubbing her swelling knuckles.

"You're having sleep for dinner tonight," the officer growled through the bars as another correctional officer with sergeant stripes arrived.

"What the hell is going on down here?" the female sergeant asked.

"Sergeant, I want to file a complaint against this correctional officer. I haven't been given dinner tonight, and when I asked for it, he hit me in the hand with his baton. I need to go to the infirmary. I think my hand is broken."

Sandy winced in pain as she watched the sergeant eye her subordinate.

"Come here. Let me see it," the sergeant requested.

Sandy, seated painfully on the concrete slab only a few inches off the ground, rocked forward to her feet, she walked to the entrance of her cell, and carefully slipped her swelling hand through the bars for inspection. The sergeant stepped closer and gently grabbed Sandy's wrist with one hand evaluating her injury.

"Hmmm. It's definitely looks bad," the sergeant said, looking over her shoulder again at her subordinate. "But I don't think it's broken." She slowly stepped to the side. "Wait, on second thought." In one lightning-fast motion, the officer whipped out her baton with both hands and violently smacked Sandy's dangling hand once herself.

"AAAAHHHH!" Sandy yelled out in agony.

"*Now* it's broken!" the sergeant taunted.

The other correctional officer hunched over in laughter.

"What about dinner, Sarge? Should I get her some food now?" he asked.

"Hell no. This cop-killing bitch is on [1]'Ramadan!' As-salamu alaykum, you cunt!"

●

The following morning Xavier sat alone on the cherrywood

---

1 'Ramadan: A common prison code word used by Correctional Officers to instruct other Correctional Officers to illegally deny an inmate food as punishment.

bench directly behind Sandy's defense attorney's table. He checked his watch, seeing she was already two hours later than she usually arrived for the proceedings. Her lawyer was in the back of the courtroom on the phone with the Department of Corrections, getting an update on her arrival. Xavier watched as the lawyer quietly barked into the phone, trying to preserve the sanctity of the now-empty courtroom.

After yesterday's events the judge had ordered only immediate family and counsel be allowed to witness the proceedings, citing security concerns.

Moments later, Sandy's attorney marched down the center aisle, visibly angry. Xavier met him just before he reached the front of the courtroom.

"What's going on? Is everything okay?"

"Um, yeah. She just arrived, and they are escorting her to the courtroom now. But you should know there was an incident last night while she was in solitary."

"The hell you mean an incident?"

"No need to worry, much. She's fine, now. But—"

"Oyez, oyez, oyez!" the courtroom deputy bellowed, interrupting their conversation. Yvon rushed to his table, and Xavier took his place at the bench behind him. The bailiff finished his usual announcement; the judge ascended the bench just as an IT support person rushed down the other side of the bench now that he'd finished replacing the sabotaged desktop computer from yesterday. Xavier noticed the judge's upper body was stouter than yesterday. He surmised the extra bulk to be from a bulletproof vest he now wore beneath his robe.

Seconds later, Sandy appeared from the usual side door,

except this time she was escorted into the courtroom wearing wrist and ankle shackles, an orange jumpsuit, and a cast on her right hand.

Xavier was livid and leaned forward, firmly tapping her lawyer multiple times. "What . . . the . . . *fuck?*" he demanded.

Sandy anticipated his reaction, stared him down, and tilted her head. He knew that look. Still angry, he slid back in his seat and sat patiently with the heel of his foot bouncing rapidly on the courtroom carpet and his arms folded across his chest.

Sandy's lawyer slowly turned his head to lock eyes with Xavier and whispered, "I know, and I'll take care of it."

Xavier peered back, burning an imaginary hole through the lawyer.

The moment Sandy took her seat, her lawyer stood. "Your Honor?" he announced.

The judge broke his attention away from his computer keyboard.

"Yes, Counsel?" the judge responded.

Yvon scoffed before he could begin his tirade. "Judge? Where do I begin?"

"Try the beginning, Counsel," the judge responded before turning his attention back to his keyboard and punching away at the keys of his new computer.

"Your Honor? My client?" Yvon exclaimed, gesturing toward Sandy with both palms open.

"It's obvious she's been mistreated as a result of yesterday's event *despite* it having absolutely *nothing* to do with her. First, where are her clothes? This orange jumpsuit makes her look like a criminal, an obvious ploy to make her look guilty in front of the jury and stain her presumption of innocence.

"Second, why is she shackled? My client is an accomplished physician and mother, with no previous criminal record and no history of outbursts or misbehaving in this courtroom. So why the restraints? Again, another ploy to plant a perception of violence and needing to be controlled to influence the jury. Third, I want charges brought against whoever broke my client's hand. She has obviously been brutalized while also having her livelihood as a surgeon threatened," he concluded.

The judge pondered the claims.

"I, too, have my concerns about her appearance. I was informed this morning ahead of these proceedings that her usual attire was misplaced. Thus, she was provided the jumpsuit. Also, you were present during yesterday's unprecedented 'event,' as you describe it, so you are also aware my family was threatened, six police officers murdered, the courtroom's technology hacked, and the culprits' only demand was that the defendant be released.

"These being unusual circumstances, I have taken it upon myself, as a precaution and within the boundaries of the law bestowed up me as chief justice of this court, to enforce additional measures of security to ensure the safety and sanctity of this courtroom are not further infringed upon while we try this case. As to your client's injuries . . ." Judge Pisano paused, leaned forward on his bench, and peered over at the correctional officer who brought Sandy in.

"I do acknowledge your complaint, Counsel, and a full inquiry into the cause of her injuries will happen. At the completion of said inquiry, if any wrongdoing is discovered, I assure you and this court I will personally hear those complaints. Further, if it is revealed a crime was committed that caused the defendant's injuries, that perpetrator will be fully prosecuted and punished by the law. I have never and will never stand for the violation of anyone's right to due process and protection under the laws of this great nation."

The correctional officer's complexion went pale as Judge Pisano returned his gaze to Sandy's attorney.

"Now, if you don't mind, I'd like to call in the jury and continue with the proceedings."

"Absolutely, Your Honor. Thank you, Your Honor," Sandy's attorney acknowledged while sitting down with haste.

"Good. Now, before I call in the jury, I have a couple of announcements. I have been working with the Department of Justice since yesterday's *event*. They were able to obtain a copy of the video and audio displayed after the hacking of our technology systems. Upon evaluation, it was determined that videos were authentic, and thus the charges against Mrs. Darboe in relation to the homicide of the six Baltimore city police officers will be dismissed. The pursuit of the offenders, Anonymous, is underway, and when apprehended, they will be brought to justice.

"That, however, does *not* relieve the defendant, Mrs. Darboe, of the remaining accused crimes in relation to the homicides of Michael Drawoc and Shane Tumaini, so the trial will continue under those parameters. Are there any questions?" The judge looked at both attorneys, anticipating their objections.

Sandy's attorney whispered in her ear before shaking his head at the judge, signifying no objection.

The judge turned his attention to the government's attorney.

She was in deep conversation with her team, and after a lightly excited discussion, she stood to speak. "The government's remaining witnesses to call were predicated on the further prosecution of the defendant for the homicides of the six Baltimore police officers. Given the new circumstances, we do not object to the court's decision, and the prosecution rests its case."

CHAPTER 23

The next day marked the beginning of Sandy's defense. She sat comfortably in her chair for a half hour before all the usual spectators arrived in the courtroom. After the previous day's tardiness was blamed on missing clothes and Sandy's trip to the infirmary, Judge Pisano left a strong message with the Department of Corrections to ensure his courtroom would not be inconvenienced again.

As a result, the orange jumpsuit was gone after her regular clothes had miraculously reappeared after being dry cleaned and beautifully pressed. Although she remained shackled, she was seated before the jury entered, so she wouldn't have to shuffle past them under lock and key and sour their perception of her. Then Judge Pisano summoned Sandy's lawyer and the prosecution's lead counsel to his chambers for a discussion.

Sandy optimized this rare moment of solace, whispering back and forth with Xavier, who was seated in his usual spot directly behind her while the bailiffs kept close watch. The discussion in Judge Pisano's chambers, spawned by Sandy's lawyer, would be the first hurdle they needed to clear in order to mount her defense. Sandy and Xavier were both nervous and kept an eye on the wooden door leading to the judge's chambers, waiting for it to open. Both figured they'd be able to distinguish the outcome of the discussion by the expression on both lawyers' faces.

"Speak of the devil," Sandy whispered to Xavier the moment the prosecuting attorney burst through the chamber doors along with Sandy's attorney. The prosecutor, Bertrand, was visibly angry while Yvon's nose and brow uncharacteristically glistened with perspiration. A lone bailiff trailed behind both before he split off toward the aisle along the side, headed to his post at the back of the courtroom, securing the main entrance double doors in the back.

Sandy's attorney, Yvon, locked eyes with her and smiled before taking his seat. He grabbed a glass and the pitcher of water.

Sandy eyed him, gauging his confidence. "Are we good to go?" she asked.

Xavier leaned forward to hear his response.

Yvon returned another smile and a rapid nod of the head as assurances while devouring the room-temperature water. "Judge Pisano agreed, but reluctantly. I'm on a tight leash, but, yes, we're in a good place."

She watched as he placed his briefcase on the table, flipped to the correct combination, and retrieved a small, white paper bag with the symbol Rx on the face. He carefully retrieved a new syringe, still in its plastic packaging, a medical vial containing a dark-colored liquid, and a manila envelope. He placed them all on the table.

The bailiff called the court to order. Sandy shared one last, endearing glance with Xavier before the jury and judge filed in.

"Defense, you may call your first witness," Judge Pisano announced.

"Your Honor, I'd like to call Officer Karl Yelverton to the stand." The bailiff posted near the locked double doors unlocked and exited the courtroom to retrieve and escort the new witness to the stand to receive his oath. The young, unassuming officer marched down the center aisle with the posture and attitude of being fresh out of the police academy. After the bailiff administered the oath, Sandy's defense attorney began.

"Would you please state your name for the record?" Sandy's defense attorney requested.

"My name is Karl Yelverton, sir."

"And what is your occupation, Mr. Yelverton?"

"I'm a police officer for the DC Metro Police Department."

"And how long have you been with DC Metro?"

"Barely over a year, sir."

"Did you attend college before applying to the police academy?"

"Yes, sir. I earned a bachelor's degree in criminal justice, with honors, sir," the baby face officer declared proudly.

"Congratulations."

"Thank you, sir."

"Officer Yelverton, do you know why you were subpoenaed to appear in court today?"

"No, sir."

"You were brought here today to give us your opinion about law enforcement policy and procedures. We needed the opinion of someone young and open-minded, so we randomly selected you from a pool of fresh academy graduates," Yvon advised before continuing. "Now, Officer Yelverton, how would you describe your precinct? Would you call it a normal, everyday police department?"

"Yes, sir. From what I can tell."

"I also looked at your file and saw you participate in cross-department competitions. Can you tell us about that?"

"Yes, sir. They are mostly fitness and marksmanship competitions so officers from different precincts across different cities and states meet and compete against each other."

"I see. How would you describe these other officers from all over the country?"

"I'm not sure what you mean by that, sir. Can you ask the question another way?"

"What I mean is, although you guys are from different precincts, cities, and even backgrounds, I would assume you all have some commonality in your belief in upholding the law. That you all share a foundation of being good guys, wanting to help people, and do the right thing."

"Oh, I see. Yes, sir. We're all different in some way or another, of course, but like you said, we have a relatively common belief in law and order. Most of which we internalized in the academy. The academy is designed to remove the individualist tendencies of being a civilian. Who we were before we walked through the academy doors is not the same person who walks out. It's designed to break you down and build you back up with the right body and mind-set to properly perform the duties of our profession."

"Okay, that makes sense. Now, tell me, are you familiar with the stand-your-ground law?"

"Yes, sir," the officer said decisively.

"Okay, and you're aware the stand-your-ground law is legal in about half the states in our country, correct?"

"Twenty-five states to be exact, sir."

"What are your feelings on that? Do you think stand your ground should be legal in every state, or a federal law?"

"Yes, sir."

"So, as a law enforcement officer, is it fair to say you believe that every human being in this country should be able to exercise their legal right to live? Meaning, if someone feels their life is threatened or under attack, they possess the most basic human right to preserve their life, even if it means possibly taking the life of the person trying to harm them?"

"Yes, sir! I do!"

"What if that person trying to harm you is a loved one like a family member?" Yvon asked.

"I would hate to think a family member or someone I love would try and hurt me, but if that was the case and I found myself in that position where they were actively threatening my life, I would defend myself."

"*Even* if stopping them from harming you required that you'd have to kill them?"

The young man paused only briefly before responding. "Unfortunately, yes, sir. Even if it meant killing them."

"Officer Yelverton, are you a racist?"

A few jurors gasped while others leaned in awaiting his response.

"Excuse me?" the officer asked.

"You heard me correctly. Are . . . you . . . a racist? A bigot? Do you harbor any cultural bias against people of other races, skin color, faiths, or nationalities other than your own? And remember, you're under oath."

"No! I am not any of those things. I don't see color, sir."

"Have you ever had any disciplinary issues since becoming a cop?"

"No, sir."

"Have you ever had a complaint filed against you for police brutality or violation of a citizen's civil rights?"

"No, sir."

"So you would consider yourself a fair and decent person?"

"Absolutely, one hundred percent, sir."

"I can't tell you how glad I am to hear your say that. Especially now where there's such a climate of too many bad cops giving good police officers like you such a bad name. I have something especially for you, Officer." Yvon paused and took a drink of water before walking back to his table to retrieve the manila folder he placed there earlier.

"Your Honor, may I approach the witness?" Yvon asked.

"You may." Judge Pisano waved the defense attorney forward. Yvon stood in front of the witness and spread the manila folder open in front of him on the ledge of the witness stand.

Sandy watched from her seat as Officer Yelverton's eyes lit up. Yvon continued. "Officer Yelverton, what you see before you is a contract drawn up specifically for you. The contract states, once signed, you can retire from the police force *immediately.* Your retirement will entitle you to a *tax-free*, lump-sum compensation of ten million dollars. In front of you is a certified check made out to cash for that ten-million-dollar amount." Several jury members gasped. Yvon reached into his suit jacket pocket, retrieved a pen, and handed it over to the officer to sign.

Officer Yelverton grabbed the pen from the attorney's hand

and skimmed the three-page document. His hands shook as he scribbled his name on the signature page at the end and handed it back to Yvon. His smile was as wide as the jury box.

"This is like winning the lottery," the officer rejoiced. "Is that it?"

"Almost, just need to make sure your signature and initials are all there." Yvon ran his finger methodically down each line of the pages. "Yup, everything looks in order. Here's your check," Sandy's attorney said, handing the check over to the officer. "Your Honor, I'd like to submit this legally binding document into evidence as defense exhibit C."

"Acknowledged," the judge responded. Yvon turned to walk back to his table once again. He then waved his hand at the bailiff guarding the door.

"Bailiff, can you bring Dr. Irving in from the hallway, please? Thank you." Yvon turned to face Officer Yelverton again. "Before you go, Officer, we just need to review the contract verbally so the court stenographer can document the agreement for the court's record."

"Whatever you need! I can't wait to tell my family," the officer said, excited.

"Don't worry, I'll make it quick as possible," Yvon said, picking up the syringe and vial and walking back toward the officer. When he reached the witness stand, he placed the syringe and vial on the ledge in front of him.

"What are those for?" the officer asked.

"We'll get to that in a second," Yvon assured him. Then one of the double doors of the courtroom swung opened. In walked a physician in a pantsuit, with a short bob haircut and glasses pushed down to the tip of her nose.

"Okay, let's get you out of here," Yvon said. "As agreed, you, Officer Yelverton, have accepted a onetime, tax-free lump sum of ten million dollars as outlined in the contract you've signed. Per the contract, this money will be released to you under only two stipulations. The first stipulation, you must maintain residence in the precinct you are currently policing. We want this money to stay in the community, you see."

"Not a problem. I've lived here my whole life and didn't have plans on leaving anyway."

"Excellent! By the way, you're not afraid of needles, right?"

"N . . . no, sir?" the officer answered, confused.

"Great! Now, the second stipulation is that you agree to receive the FDA-approved medication in front of you."

"Wait! What? What is it? I've never seen medicine that dark before."

"Don't worry, it's totally harmless. The medication is *not* like the ones you see on television with that endless list of side effects. You won't even notice any change. You will have the same blood type, bone structure, muscle mass, height, etcetera. All this medication does is increase the melanin levels in your skin. That's all."

"Wait, you said melanin?"

"Yes, Officer. Melanin. It'll simply darken your skin tone."

"Like a tan?"

"I'd say a little bit darker than your average tan. Twenty-four hours after injection, your skin tone will darken and match the same color level of brown as say, Denzel Washington."

The officer's eyes lit up again, and he scoffed. "You just said a second ago I wouldn't notice any change! I think I would notice being black." Officer Yelverton nervously laughed.

Yvon titled his head as if confused.

"But Officer Yelverton, a few minutes ago you testified, under oath, that you didn't see color."

"I don't . . . but that's not what I meant."

"What exactly did you mean then, Officer?"

"I don't mean it literally. No one means it literally. It's just a saying, you know?"

"No, I don't. I live in DC, one of the most diverse cities in the country. I see a range of color every day. I do think I understand what you're saying, though. You're saying being part of a community where people are various shades of color and exposed to a variety of languages doesn't affect how you judge people without knowing them first. Would that be a fair statement?"

"Yes! That's what I meant."

"Understood. Glad we cleared that up. Are we ready to proceed, Officer Yelverton? We still need you to verbally respond that you agree to receiving the injection, so the court stenographer has it documented for the court's official records."

The officer looked at the judge, who remained expressionless.

"Wait . . . you're serious?" the officer questioned. "The only way I can have this money is if I agree to be black?"

"Ha ha, no, Officer Yelverton. No medication can change your ethnicity, Officer." Yvon turned to the physician who walked in earlier. "I'll let the doctor explain it to you. Doctor, would you please?"

The doctor rose from her seat and approached the podium to speak into the microphone. "What would you like for me to explain to you, Officer?"

"The medication in front of me. It's going to make my skin darker?"

"Yes, that's correct," the doctor responded.

"So it *will* make me black!" he exclaimed.

Sandy glanced over at the jury. Some of them wore the same confused expressions while a few others covered their mouths in shock. An older African American gentleman chuckled silently in obvious amusement while the doctor answered the officer's question.

"Human skin color ranges in variety from the darkest of browns to the lightest of hues. An individual's skin pigmentation is the result of two main factors. One, the individual's biological parents' genetic makeup and, two, exposure to sun. In human evolution, our skin pigmentation evolved by a process of natural selection primarily to regulate the amount of ultraviolet radiation penetrating our skin. Basically, if you lived in a very hot climate, nature made sure your skin became darker over time to protect you from the sun. And if you lived in a climate that was colder with less sunlight, you did not need as much protection, thus resulting in lighter skin.

"Our skin color can be affected by many substances, although the single, most important substance is the pigment melanin. The more melanin you naturally have, the darker your skin. The less you have, the lighter your skin. The medication in front of you will merely increase your melanin levels so your skin will become darker, but nothing else about your body will change," the doctor concluded.

"So I won't be black. I'll just look black?" the officer questioned.

The doctor tilted her head and looked over the top of her

glasses and sighed. "Young man. The whole idea of a black and a white 'race,'" she said, fashioning air quotes with her fingers, "is a social construct created by us human beings to compartmentalize ourselves into subgroups. The same way we separate ourselves by nationalities since we live in different countries. If you're from here, you're an American, if you cross an imaginary line to far north, you're Canadian, another imaginary line to far south, you're Mexican, and so on and so on.

"Some human beings are men while others women, some taller than others, some shorter, some thinner while others are bulkier, and in this case, some of us are darker while others are lighter. But at the very root of it all, we are all human beings, nothing more, nothing less.

"So to answer your question. No, the medication won't make you black, nor will you *look* black, whatever that means. You will have the same hands, feet, hair, and facial features as you walked in here with. The only difference is your skin tone will become significantly darker. Understand?"

"Yes, I . . . I understand," the officer responded.

"Do you have any other questions before I administer the medication?"

"Uh, no, ma'am. Thank you, ma'am," the officer responded, processing everything that was just said.

"Your Honor, may the doctor approach the witness to administer the medication?"

"She may."

"Wait a second," the officer interrupted, "but my skin will look black!" the officer said.

"Does that matter?" Yvon questioned. "Earlier, you testified you're a good person. One of the good guys. That's why we're awarding you this early retirement. Who you are as a person won't change, and that's all that matters." The doctor removed sterile gloves from her inside pocket and placed them on her hands.

"We still need you to verbally say you accept the terms for the court record before the doctor can give you the injection. Then you get to go home and tell your family that you're rich."

The officer's face turned red hearing that.

"When people see me, they will think I'm black," the officer said.

"It's possible, but so what if they do? You'll look like Denzel, and who doesn't love Denzel, right?"

The officer's head snapped up, and he looked the lawyer and the doctor in the eye.

"Denzel? People will *definitely* think I'm black!"

"But you're a good guy. That's all that matters, right?"

"What about strangers? They won't know if I'm a good guy or not just looking at me. All they'll see is some black guy. And the guys on the force, I don't want to be treated like them!"

The jury gasped.

Yvon looked at the prosecuting attorney and then at the judge.

"Thank you, Officer Yelverton, for your candor. It has been very enlightening." Yvon extended his hand toward the officer. "The check please, Officer?" Yvon waited as the officer handed the fortune back over to the lawyer with his head hanging low.

"Your Honor, let the court record reflect that after such initial enthusiasm, Office Karl Yelverton has forfeited his claim to the ten million dollars because he doesn't wish to be treated as if he were a black man. Thank you, Doctor, for your time. You may return to your seat now."

The doctor removed her gloves and headed back to the courtroom gallery.

"Government's Counsel, do you wish to cross-examine?" Judge Pisano asked as Yvon returned to his table and stole a glance at a visibly shaken jury.

"No questions for this witness, Your Honor."

"Officer Yelverton, you may step down. Defense, you may call your next witness." The officer slowly rose from his seat, sullen and defeated.

CHAPTER 24

J udge Pisano broke the courtroom for an early lunch after Sandy's defense attorney finished questioning his first witness. Sandy and her attorney watched as the prosecution's team of young lawyers scrambled out of the courtroom.

A slight hint of confidence spread over Sandy's body like a chill. It was the first time in months she had a good feeling about her legal troubles.

"Nice job," she said to her lawyer.

Yvon patted her folded hands once more.

"Don't roll in the champagne just yet, Dr. Darboe. I'm not a betting man, but if I were, I'd wager the entirety of my son's college fund the prosecution's team is brainstorming ways to counter our strategy now that they've gotten a taste of it."

"Did you not see the jury after he turned down the money? You exposed him. They didn't even ask *one* question," she said, protruding one of her index fingers out of her shackled hands. "You had to see some of the jurors were moved."

"I saw it," he assured her. "But I also saw her team shoot out of this courtroom like bloodhounds searching for that one piece of evidence they're hoping will eliminate all the progress we made with that witness. The next time it's their turn to cross-examine, believe me, they'll be ready."

⬤

"Defense, you may call your next witness," Judge Pisano announced after the courtroom reassembled from the lunch break.

"Your Honor, defense calls Mrs. Patricia Thompson to the stand." The bailiff exited the court to retrieve the new witness. Moments later, she was at the witness bench, accepting her oath. The conservatively dressed lady remained standing while the bailiff administered her oath and then settled herself into her seat.

Yvon rose from his table and approached the podium, with a folder tucked beneath his legal pad, ready to begin his questioning. "Ma'am, would you please state your name for the record?"

"My name is Patricia Thompson," the witness replied.

"And what is your occupation, Mrs. Thompson?"

"I've been an elementary school teacher for the DC public school system the past twelve years."

"Do you know why you were called to testify today?" Yvon asked.

"Not exactly. I just received a subpoena requesting me to appear." She shrugged her shoulders and shook her head. "All I know for sure is it has something to do with giving testimony about my background as an educator and my thoughts about the state of our educational system."

"That is correct. The full details of why your testimony was needed has purposely been withheld so we could ensure no potential bias would influence your testimony. We're looking for someone like you, an educator, to give us your opinion and views of the educational system in DC and/or the country if possible. Hope that helps."

"Yes, that does. And I'm glad someone is finally taking this issue seriously."

"We definitely are, Mrs. Thompson. Now, do you have any children?"

"Yes, I have a seven-year-old son."

"That's great!" Yvon responded with enthusiasm. "A second grader? What's his name?"

"Third grade, actually," she corrected. "Tyler, my son, he skipped a grade last year."

"You must be so proud of him," he said, prompting a beaming smile from Mrs. Thompson.

"I am. I know every parent says this about their child, but he really is smart. His current teacher is considering recommending he skip another grade, depending how he performs the rest of this year."

"Your son, Tyler, he's enrolled in public school or private?"

"Public school."

"He attends the school you teach at?"

"For the time being he does. His current teacher, the one suggesting he skip again, suggested I should consider enrolling him in a private schools in our district after this year is over."

"Are you still considering the transfer, or have you made up your mind about the private school?"

"Oh, I've decided. I submitted his application months ago, and he's already been accepted. He starts at the beginning of the next school year."

"Is there a specific reason why you want him to leave the

school he's currently enrolled in, one you're also a teacher at?"

"A private school will provide my son with opportunities he won't receive at a public school, even if I'm a teacher there. He'll get more specialized attention, more advanced-placement classes, additional access to technology, and special training to nourish his advanced appetite for learning. At least, that's my opinion."

"And your opinion isn't just one of a proud parent. These reasons also coincide with your professional opinion as an educator, correct?"

"Correct," Mrs. Thompson agreed.

"So your decision has nothing to do with the conditions of his current school? They have heat, books, enough teachers, and no issues with safety that concern you at his current school?"

"N-no. It's fine," she conceded.

"*Fine?* When I hear that word, it usually means there's opportunities for improvement."

"Every school has areas they can improve. No school is perfect, but my son's current school is typical for your standard public school. We have the usual range of good kids who are there to learn, and we have those disruptive few who present some challenges because of their behavior. But my son's teachers are good, and I don't doubt their or the school's ability to educate my son academically under normal circumstances."

The sound of one of the jurors sucking their teeth echoed throughout the courtroom.

"What do you mean by *normal circumstances?*" Yvon asked.

Mrs. Thompson paused, choosing her next words carefully.

"What I mean is that my son isn't your everyday average

kid, he's already skipped a grade, and we're considering skipping another. I'm sorry, I don't mean to come off as boastful, so if it did, I do sincerely apologize," Mrs. Thompson said, noticing some of the jurors had taken issue with her last answer. "For me, it just makes more sense to send him to a school where he'll be vigorously challenged in accordance with his cognitive level."

"And you don't think that will happen at his current school?"

"He may be fine for now, but as he starts progressing to the higher grades, I'd prefer a private or prep school environment for him. I think it would be better suited for him and his abilities."

"I understand." Yvon retrieved the thin folder from beneath his legal pad and held it in the air for Mrs. Thompson to see for herself. Sandy and the jury noticed her squinting her eyes, mouthing the words on the front. Then her eyes shot wide open. Yvon flipped open the folder, with the name of her son's school and crest on the front, to the first page.

"We also subpoenaed your son's academic records as well as the recommendations he's received from his previous teacher suggesting he skip a grade.

"Mrs. Thompson, at first glance it's clear your son is indeed very intelligent. He has the top scores and accolades from all his teachers starting from kindergarten until now." Yvon retrieved another folder. "My investigators were also able to find you've applied for some financial aid, federal loan forgiveness grants, and other educational scholarships. Can you tell us why you applied for financial assistance?"

"The prep school Tyler was accepted to has a pretty healthy tuition obligation," she responded. "I'm going to need help financially to pay for it starting next year."

"I see," Yvon said. "My investigators also discovered you were a finalist for Teacher of the Year in your district."

Mrs. Thompson blushed. "Yes, but I didn't win."

"But an award like that would look really good on your record. Help with promotions, etcetera?" Yvon asked.

"I guess it would have, had I won, but being acknowledged by my colleagues would have been sufficient to make me happy." Mrs. Thompson paused. "But my real motivation was the monetary prize that came along with the award. That money would have really helped with Tyler's tuition next year."

"It definitely would have." Yvon smiled while agreeing with Mrs. Thompson and flipping to the next page of his legal pad questions. "Mrs. Thompson, I must admit your story moves me. I would even speculate that your story of wanting better for your child even moves this court.

"Yesterday, before you even took the stand, our Honorable Judge Pisano agreed to allow me to call you to testify so you could share your story. I wanted His Honor and the court to hear about your experiences as an educator in our public school system and to recognize your hard work the past decade," Yvon continued.

Mrs. Thompson listened intently, seemingly unsure where his speech would lead.

"This court has a unique opportunity for you, Mrs. Thompson," Yvon said, raising the same manila folder he'd used with his first witness, the young police officer.

"Your Honor, may I approach the witness?" Yvon asked.

"You may." Just as he'd done with his first witness, Yvon spread the folder open, displaying the contract agreement and lump-sum check payment for ten million dollars made out to cash.

Mrs. Thompson, seeing the check, took a few deep breaths and fanned herself with an open hand. She looked back at Yvon and the judge for confirmation this was indeed not a joke.

"In the District of Columbia, a school teacher can retire at any age after thirty years of service. In front of you is a check for ten million dollars." Yvon retrieved a pen from his inside jacket pocket and extended it to Mrs. Thompson. "The contract in front of you, once signed, states you can retire today. Your payout will also be tax-free, so you will get all ten million of those dollars."

Mrs. Thompson shot back into the wood chair. "You mean, I don't have to pay Uncle Sam anything?" she asked.

"Not one dime," Yvon assured her.

"Oh my god, thank you! Thank you! Thank you!" she responded, making eye contact with everyone in the courtroom. She took Yvon's pen into her shaking hands and feverishly flipped through the three-page document without a pause. When she reached the last page, she scribbled her signature, looked back up at Yvon, beaming with excitement, and handed the pen and document back to him.

Yvon handed the check to her.

She snatched it from his hands, kissed the check, and let out a huge sigh. "Thank you, Jesus! You've just changed me and my son's life."

"Your Honor, I'd like to submit this legally binding document into evidence as defense exhibit D." The judge nodded in agreement. Yvon turned his attention to the bailiff guarding the back door and waved his hand at him.

"Bailiff, can you please bring Dr. Irving and the witness's son in from the hallway, please?" Yvon turned back around to face the witness again. "Mrs. Thompson, we just need to review the contract verbally so the court stenographer can document the agreement for the record." He retrieved the syringe and vial of black medication from his jacket pocket and placed them both on the ledge in front of her.

"Why are you bringing my son in?" Mrs. Thompson asked as the doctor and her son were escorted down the long middle aisle. Yvon waved the doctor forward to join him as the witness's son sat in the front aisle with the bailiff. Tyler saw his mother sitting in the witness chair and waved, excited to be in the huge room.

"Mrs. Thompson, this is Dr. Irving," Yvon said, directing her attention to the physician. "She will administer the medication in the vial in front of you per the agreement you just signed. After the injection you will be free to go." Yvon turned, locking eyes with young Tyler. "Along with your ten-million-dollar check."

Tyler's looked at his mother, displaying the largest of smiles. Several jurors also smiled seeing his innocent jubilation.

Yvon pounced. "There are only two stipulations to this contract. The first, you must maintain residence in the city you are currently living in."

Mrs. Thompson eyes volleyed back and forth between the syringe and the doctor while nodding her head suspiciously in agreement. "Okay, and the second?"

"The second stipulation is that you agree to the administering of this FDA-approved medication in front of you."

Mrs. Thompson's body language instantly changed.

"Don't worry, Mrs. Thompson. As the doctor who entered the courtroom with your son can attest, the medication is one hundred percent harmless."

"It has to do something, or it wouldn't be a stipulation. So tell me. What does it do?" she questioned.

"The medication increases the melanin levels in skin. The effects of the medication set in approximately twenty-four hours after it's administered. So, once we get your verbal approval for the court stenographer, the doctor will administer the medication and that's it. You and your son are set to ride off into the sunset millionaires."

"Melanin?" Mrs. Thompson questioned. "So it'll just make my skin darker? That's it?"

"That is correct. It makes the *recipient's* skin darker."

"There's no insane list of side effects you need to warn me about like I hear on the television commercials?" she asked, looking at the doctor.

"That is correct, ma'am," the doctor assured her. "There are no side effects. The medication will simply darken the recipient's skin tone. Nothing more, nothing less."

"So it'll be like a permanent tan?" Mrs. Thompson questioned once more.

"The *tan*, as you've described it, will be a bit darker than you may be accustomed to during a typical sunbathing session. If you're familiar with the actress Gabrielle Union, the dosage in the vial will darken the recipient's skin to levels equal to her shade of brown," the doctor advised.

Mrs. Thompson's gaze drifted toward the ceiling, and she pondered the doctor's explanation for a few short seconds.

"Fine, let's do it," she said, removing the blazer she was wearing, revealing bare arms from her sleeveless blouse.

The doctor pulled two new sterile gloves from her coat pocket and carefully slid them on.

"Excellent!" Yvon exclaimed, retrieving the syringe and vial and handing them to the doctor.

Mrs. Thompson released a large sigh, prepping herself for the injection.

Yvon turned toward Tyler again and smiled. "Mrs. Thompson, your son, Tyler, he isn't afraid of *needles*, is he?" Yvon watched as Tyler's eyes almost jumped out of his head at the sound of the word. Yvon turned back to face Mrs. Thompson. "We can have him sit on your lap if that'll make him more comfortable?"

"Tyler? I'm sorry, I'm confused. I thought *I* would be receiving the injection?"

"No, Mrs. Thompson. The agreement you signed states your son will receive the injection," Yvon said, flipping to the second page and pointing to it for her review. "See, there it is." He looked up at her, searching her face and body language as she repeatedly read her son's name on the contract she'd rushed to sign.

"Should we bring him over to you so you can comfort him for the injection, or can the doctor just do it over there where he—"

"No!" Mrs. Thompson shook her head adamantly. "I changed my mind. I can't agree to this."

"Is everything okay, Mrs. Thompson? You seemed okay with the procedure just a few seconds ago," Yvon asked.

"That was before I realized you wanted to inject my son. I'm an adult and he's a child. So I know how the world works. He doesn't. At least not yet. And I'm just not willing to roll the dice like that with my son's future," she responded.

Yvon motioned at the doctor once more, prepping her to be ready to speak on his behalf. "Oh, I see you may not have fully understood. There are no side effects, and this medication has been fully approved by the FDA. It will not affect him at all. Not physically or intellectually if that's what you're worried about."

"I'm not scared, Mommy. I'll keep my eyes closed just like at the doctor's office," Tyler said from the courtroom parlor.

One of the female jurors tilted her head at the brave young man and wiped away a tear.

"See, Tyler understands. No side effects, and like the doctor said, it will simply increase his—"

"I understand fully what it'll do!" Mrs. Thompson said sharply.

She looked over at her son and smiled as if trying to show him everything was okay. Like this was some big misunderstanding and Mommy would make it better once she explained it all. She turned to the judge and covered the microphone with her palm and whispered.

Judge Pisano nodded his head in agreement.

"Bailiff, please remove young Tyler from the courtroom. His presence is no longer needed." Upon hearing the judge's order, the bailiff took Tyler's hand and led him out of the courtroom. Tyler looked back at his mother and waved before disappearing behind the heavy, swinging double doors. "Now that the court-room is clear, let's continue."

"First, Mrs. Thompson, my apologies. I didn't mean to upset you. I just thought you needed some extra clarification. I clearly see now that you don't." Yvon looked at the jury. "However, could you please let the court know why you've changed your mind?"

"I was fine when I thought I would receive the injection. Mothers make sacrifices for their children. It comes with the job. But I'm not naive about the world we live in," she said. "I've had decades to learn how to navigate the unfairness of life. My son, Tyler, has not. He's innocent, so far, to the unfairness that lies in wait for him."

"I'm sorry, but I'm not sure I'm following you completely, Mrs. Thompson. A few minutes ago, you *and Tyler* were ecstatic about receiving the ten million dollars. You literally kissed the check." He paused, giving her an opportunity to respond before pouring on another layer of questioning. "Even after hearing the stipulations, you took a moment to consider but ultimately still agreed. Help us understand."

"For the past five years I've been a single mother living on a teacher's salary, so, yes, ten million dollars, *tax-free*, would change everything. I promised myself that if I were ever fortunate or lucky enough to win or earn that type of money, I'd buy a home in a better neighborhood and make sure Tyler had all the advantages in life. But I thought *I'd* receive the injection," Mrs. Thompson said with a tear falling down her cheek, visibly wrestling with her decision.

"But you're not comfortable with the stipulations now that

you realize it would be Tyler receiving the injection?"

"Correct," she whispered shamefully. "I'm not."

"Can you share with us, why?"

"You know damn well why," she shot back like a snake spitting venom ready to strike its prey.

"Mrs. Thompson, you will refrain from using that type of language in my courtroom," Judge Pisano directed.

"I'm sorry, Your Honor. It won't happen again," she said before turning her sights back to Yvon and pursing her lips at him.

"I'm going to be direct with you, Mrs. Thompson, and I'd appreciate you doing the same."

She sat in a defensive posture, arms folded across her chest, and nodded her head in agreement.

"Why don't you want to inject your son with this harmless medication you were so willing to receive yourself?" Yvon stared her in the eye, with both his hands placed firmly on the ledge of the witness bench, waiting for her response.

"You're really earning your fees today," she said wryly.

"I'll ask you again, Mrs. Thompson. Why have you changed your mind about receiving the money? You're under oath, and perjury is a prosecutable felony." Mrs. Thompson shook her head. "Why were you okay with the injection when you thought you were the recipient?"

"Like I said, I'm a single mother, and mothers make sacrifices for their children. I'm a teacher living in one of the most expensive cities in America. I know the obstacles waiting for me had I'd been the one injected and I also know how I would either avoid or overcome them. But Tyler, he's too young to understand or how to cope. Getting to skip a grade was a blessing, but it also made him a target. He stood out among the other kids. He's seven, and he's already being teased for just being too smart.

"That's one of the reasons I want him at the prep school next year. He won't stand out as much there because there, academic achievement is the expectation. It's a badge of honor not a Scarlett letter. He'll be just like everyone else, for the most part." She paused again, looking at the jury. Sandy could see the wheels in her head turning. "That injection will sabotage his anonymity at the new school. It'll make him stand out for a whole other reason. I've been an elementary teacher for over a decade. I know how cruel children can be. Even if a child was perfect in every way, other children will find something they're insecure about. When they find it, they'll poke and pick at it until they hit a nerve," she said.

"Even at a prestigious prep school, Mrs. Thompson? By the time he starts his first class next year, all anyone will know about you is that you're the new parent of the new kid. With his new uniform and his tuition paid, you and your son will be in the same socioeconomic status as his classmates. What's wrong with that?" Yvon prodded.

"You want me to say it, don't you?" Mrs. Thompson shot back.

"Say what, Mrs. Thompson?" Yvon questioned.

"Yes, he'll fit in academically and socioeconomically. But he'll stand out because of his color. And no amount of money will make people look past *that*." The courtroom went awkwardly silent until she broke the tension. "I can imagine what you're all thinking about me. But don't act like you didn't think it either. I mean, that's the reason why you chose me to come up here, isn't it? To watch me struggle with this decision and tell you why? You want to hear me admit that, yes, the public school my son attends is *okay* but it's not the best. The faculty, facilities, and extracurricular activities are not equal to what he'd have at the private school," she said.

"I want you to tell the truth so this court can hear it, despite how difficult it may be for us to hear," he assured.

"The truth? Okay, here's the truth. Yes, the money will make our lives much easier financially. Absolutely, one hundred percent! Did I consider what difficulties I would have to face twenty-four hours once I'd received the injection and my complexion changes? Yes, and I was willing to shoulder that burden for my son's sake. I'm forty-one years old and understand and have experienced people's inherent biases, even if I don't share those biases.

"But I will not purposely inflict those harmful experiences on my son. He's too young to even comprehend why people would treat him differently when they see his dark skin. I won't do that to him. Not for any amount of money."

"Thank you, Mrs. Thompson. Your Honor, I have no more questions," Yvon concluded.

"Prosecution, you may cross-examine the witness now," Judge Pisano instructed. The prosecuting attorney turned to the group of young attorneys huddled in the first row behind her table. One of them handed her a legal pad as she rose from her seat to approach the podium.

"Good afternoon, Mrs. Thompson. I'll make this as quick as possible. Are you racist?" Bertrand questioned.

"No! Of course not!" she responded. "My friends and family

would all be insulted by that question."

"How can you be so sure? The way the defense has painted your testimony, one would think the sole reason you don't want to accept the money offered to you is because you don't want your son to be mistaken for black. Is that a fair assessment?"

"No! It's not!" She sighed again before continuing. "Look, I get it now. It's his job to make me look that way, but that's preposterous. I'm not a racist, because Tyler is half-black." A few of the jurors perked up in their seats once they heard the mother's proclamation. "Yes, I'm white. I can trace my family's heritage back to Italy. I love my son, my family loves my son, and Tyler's father, who was black, loved his son and my family until we lost him a couple years ago to cancer. But accusing me of being a racist is laughable."

"Thank you, Mrs. Thompson. No more questions, Your Honor," the prosecution said.

"Your Honor? May I redirect?" Yvon requested.

"You may," Judge Pisano responded.

Yvon approached the podium, holding up the same folder containing her son's records. Then he raised another folder with a prep school name and crest on the front.

"I'm so sorry to hear about Tyler's father. Also, despite what you may believe, it's not my job to paint you as a racist. My job is merely to ask questions that pull the truth from your testimony. With that said, you just testified you're not a racist. As proof you offered Tyler's father's African American ethnicity. So I just have a few questions for you."

"Okay," she responded.

"When you filled out the forms for Tyler's enrollment application for his current school, where you're also a teacher, what box did you check in the section where it asks for your child's ethnicity?" Yvon questioned.

Mrs. Thompson paused for a moment, looking at the jury and then at the judge. "It was two years ago, so I don't member exactly, but I believe I selected mixed, biracial, or something to that effect."

"Your Honor, may I approach the witness?" Judge Pisano quickly approved. Yvon walked up to the witness stand and spread the folder before Mrs. Thompson. He placed his finger next to a color-coded arrow next to the "Ethnicity" section of Tyler's school admission form.

"Mrs. Thompson, do you recognize this document as the admissions form for your son's current elementary school?"

"Yes."

"The handwriting on the application. Do you recognize it as your own?"

"Yes."

"Could you read what box you checked in the section heading called 'Ethnicity'?"

Mrs. Thompson looked down at the application, the box, and back up at Yvon. Her face flushed red and her lip quivered.

"I checked 'Black or African American,'" she answered. Yvon nodded his head in agreement.

"Correct. You did indeed check 'Black or African American.'" Yvon then pulled a beige folder from beneath the open one. The beige folder had the name and crest of the prep school Tyler would be attending the next school year.

"Now, Mrs. Thompson, this folder contains the application

you submitted for Tyler's admission into the prep school he was accepted to attend next year." He opened the folder and placed it on top in front of her and positioned his finger next to another color-coded arrow. "Mrs. Thompson, do you recognize this application as your son's prep school admission application?"

"Y-Yes," she stuttered, visibly shaken.

"Is that your handwriting on the application?"

"Yes, yes, it is."

"Now, can you please tell the court what box you checked in Tyler's application for the prep school?"

Mrs. Thompson opened her mouth to respond. "Can I explain first—" Yvon raised his hand to halt her words.

"You'll have all the time you need to explain, but first I need you to read out loud what box you checked on Tyler's admissions application for his new prep school he'll attend next year."

Mrs. Thompson pondered her response nervously.

"Your Honor, will you please direct the witness to answer the—"

"I checked 'White'!" she exclaimed. "But I can explain."

Instantly, low murmurs erupted from the juror's box, interrupting her explanation.

"Order!" Judge Pisano banged his gavel lightly to silence the side conversations from the collection of diverse faces staring at the witness.

"Please continue, Mrs. Thompson," the judge advised.

"I know how this looks." She paused looking at the jury. "You think I'm ashamed of my son but that's just not true. I know checking the 'White' box was wrong for me to do, but I did it for him. I don't have to be black to see what's happening in this country. I'm a teacher in DC, for God's sake. I have students from all kinds of backgrounds. As many backgrounds as the jury box staring back at me. And you know what? I treat and love them all the same.

"Believe me, I'm not a racist or a bigot. But I'm no fool either," she said with the utmost seriousness. She scanned the jurors, looking each of them in the eye. "I'm raising a biracial child, and there have already been certain challenges he'll have to face other kids won't. As an infant and toddler, he was too young to notice the looks his father and I received from strangers when we were in public together. The store clerks pretending not to follow us when we shopped, the bad service we received at restaurants and bars, or the parents canceling play dates with Tyler if his father showed up to drop him off instead of me." Mrs. Thompson wiped away the tears falling from her eyes.

"I know marking 'White' was wrong, but I'd do it again. It's a harmless lie in comparison to the benefits my son will receive had I told the truth. I'm Italian, his father was extremely fair-skinned, and you've seen my son. He's extremely fair-skinned also. His hair is long and curly like mine. I saw your reactions when I revealed he was mixed. Be honest with yourself. Had I not said anything, would you have even noticed?"

Sandy looked at the jurors and saw their reaction. Some were shaking their heads no. "If checking a different ethnicity box fast-tracks all the advantages to my son that are reserved for people who look like me, then I'll make my peace with God when the time comes. Especially if it means sheltering Tyler from potential discrimination he'd receive had I told the truth on his application.

"So there's your answer, Mr. Yvon. I agreed to take the medication because I'm Tyler's mother. I can shoulder the burden of discrimination, harsh stares and words, maybe even violence, after my skin grows darker. Hmph, Gabrielle Union is gorgeous. Why wouldn't I want to look like her? But I draw a line when it comes to my son. And not because I'm a racist or ashamed of my son's ethnicity. Tyler is the mirror image of his father, and I loved that man dearly, even till this day. But I'll refuse *anything*, no matter how much money you offer me, that will compromise the only shroud protecting him from the true nature of his own country. I want my son treated like every other child and if that means I have to lie every once in a while to protect him then so be it."

"No more questions, Your Honor," Yvon said.

CHAPTER 25

Yvon Carlos's unorthodox strategy was on display for the select few privy to witness the court proceedings. He called witness after witness, all of them from different backgrounds and socioeconomic statuses. He presented each with their own unique scenarios where they had the option to become rich instantly if they traded in their whiteness. Despite the varying opportunities, all refused despite the money offered. It was a testament to the immeasurable price tag attached to their skin tone.

The jury stirred after every witness refused the large sum of money. Defensive witnesses declared themselves free of racism and bigotry and denied the existence of their privilege. Five witnesses and mountains of excuses later, the defense rose to call its final witness.

"Your Honor, I'd like to call Dr. Sandy Darboe to the stand." Yvon smirked at the stunned faces of the prosecution team. In line with his entire defense strategy, Yvon defied the most basic, conventional legal practice by introducing Sandy as a witness. Doing so meant she would have to hold her own against cross-examination. But it was the only way for Sandy to speak her truth to the prosecution, judge, jury, and hopefully her country.

"Place your right hand in the air and your left on the Bible, please," the bailiff directed, and Sandy complied.

"Do you swear to tell the truth, the whole truth, and nothing but the truth, so help you God?"

"I do," she responded.

"You may be seated," Judge Pisano said. Sandy's attorney approached the podium. He arrived empty-handed. The legal maestro, whom the courtroom had grown accustomed to hauling inches-thick manila folders, carefully clasped his hands, nodded at Sandy, and mouthed "ready?"

She responded with a smile and nod of her own.

"Good morning, Dr. Darboe."

"Good morning."

"Would you please state your name and residence for the record?"

"My name is Dr. Sandy Darboe, originally from Fort Worth, Texas, but now a resident of the District of Columbia."

"Dr. Darboe, I have one very simple question to ask you before I take my seat. Are you *responsible* for the deaths of Michael Drawoc and Shane Tumaini?"

"No, I am not."

"Your Honor, I have no further questions," Yvon said, handing his witness over to the prosecution.

The lead prosecutor, Kirsten Bertrand, slowly rose from her seat as if levitating. Sandy locked eyes with her adversary as Bertrand slowly walked toward the podium like a lioness stalking its prey.

Give me something to hit, bitch! Sandy thought, knowing her opponent would have more than one question she'd have to answer.

"Mrs. Darboe, did this court hear you correctly when you testified, under oath, that you were not the person responsible for the deaths of both Michael Drawoc and Shane Tumaini?"

"Yes, you heard me correctly," Sandy responded in a matter-of-fact tone.

"Mrs. Darboe," Bertrand scoffed, "we have multiple witnesses that put you at the locations where both victims were murdered. We have witnesses that identify you as the last person in contact with both victims before they were murdered. Is it your testimony today that these two different men, from different cities, in different states, were both murdered while you were in the vicinity by coincidence?"

"I'm not here to speculate what happened to them. I'm here to testify that I'm not *responsible* for their deaths."

"That doesn't answer my question, Mrs. Darboe, so I'll be more direct with you. Did you shoot Michael Drawoc and Shane Tumaini to death?" the prosecutor demanded.

"Yes! I shot them both, right in the face!" Sandy confessed without hesitation or remorse.

Tension filled every inch of the courtroom. The jury, the prosecutor's legal team, and Xavier rustled in their seats.

"W-what did you just say?" the prosecution questioned in disbelief.

"You heard correctly. I said yes. I shot them both," Sandy replied to the dumbfounded expression on the attorney's face.

The Prosecutor looked over at the judge and court stenographer, and they both acknowledged hearing the same response.

"So why perjure yourself when I first asked you?"

"I did no such thing. You just didn't ask the right question," Sandy said.

The jury looked at her with the same air of confusion as the rest of the court.

"Mrs. Darboe, in response to your own attorney's and my first question, you testified that you didn't kill them—"

"No! My attorney asked if I was *responsible*. You lazily piggybacked off his question, so my response remained the same. We can have the court stenographer read it back to you if you're having trouble remembering correctly, Ms. Bertrand." Sandy paused, stared the prosecutor in the eye, and silently mouthed "bitch" at her. "Now, would you like to know why I neutralized them?"

"The floor is yours, Mrs. Darboe," Bertrand responded with a smile.

"There are three reasons, backed by legal precedent, that answer to why those two predators are no longer breathing. Battered woman preemptive defense. Stand your ground. And US military strategy of preemptive strikes," Sandy said simply, forcing an awkward silence to set in. She stole a glance at the jurors as confusion swept over all twelve of them.

"Is that it, Mrs. Darboe? You present a riddle as your defense?"

"Ms. Bertrand, every human being is blessed with the *God*-given right to self-preservation. It's encoded in our DNA. The moment a man or woman takes their first breath after their birth, they have the right to *live*. As a surgeon, I know firsthand that the human body is a magnificent mechanism. If you hold your breath, against our own will our body will eventually force itself to take air.

"If our body temperature drops to far our body will begin to shiver in order to warm itself. If we overheat sweat will pour from our pores to cool it down. If in danger, our natural instinct of fight or flight will determine if we can successfully run away from the threat. And if retreat is not possible, adrenaline and fear will propel us to fight to the death. Even before we become self-aware of our own common sense and reason, our bodies will independently protect us from even ourselves and do everything within its power to adapt to its surroundings and ensure our survival. These are all abilities bestowed upon by our creator, by *God*.

"Then once humans evolved and developed civilized societies in the very country, our human right to live was reaffirmed, as stated verbatim, in our Declaration of Independence. The right to *life*, liberty, and the pursuit of happiness. I like to think the word *life* was listed by our founding founders *first*, purposely. They went to war with Great Britain over those very same principles and are celebrated as patriots.

"Well, I'm a patriot also. The only difference is I'm at war with America instead of the United Kingdom." Sandy looked around the courtroom for any indication that all eyes were not on her.

The prosecuting attorney didn't interrupt.

"Let's begin with the battered woman syndrome criminal defense. This defense cites a medically proven psychological disorder caused when women have found themselves held captive in *long-term* abusive relationships with abusive partners. Over time, this long-term abuse produces what doctors deem an irrational mental state of learned helplessness that limits free choice. This sense of helplessness places its victims into a spiral of conflict where they wrestle between the choice of enduring the abuse or fighting back against their abuser. The culmination of this back-and-forth conflict has occasionally resulted in a violent and fatal response to their abuser in order to escape further abuse.

"For example, in 2008, Barbara Sheehan of New York was such a victim. She was acquitted of second-degree murder after having shot her husband of twenty-four years, a retired *police sergeant by the way*," Sandy stressed to the jury. "Sheehan had suffered repeated abuse during their relationship until she refused to go on a trip to Florida with her abuser.

"Her refusal angered him, so he pointed a gun at her head and threatened to kill her. After he lowered his weapon, Barbara Sheehan grabbed one of his other guns and shot him before he could raise another gun at her. That day, she finally chose to live, not die.

"Now let's put this in perspective. The first kidnapped African slave was forced to come to Virginia four hundred years ago in 1619. After that, millions more were also kidnapped. This lasted for two hundred and forty-six years. During those years, slaves were watched and kept in line with violence, torture, and the threat of death. Then the Thirteenth Amendment made it illegal to own slaves in 1865. But a year later, the Vagrancy Act of 1866 made it illegal to be homeless or jobless, which most freed slaves were now. This purposely biased law was enforced obviously by police departments that were created twenty-seven years before slavery ended.

"If a battered woman of twenty-four years can legally be found within her rights to kill in order to preserve her life in the face of repeated battery and fear, then why can't an entire *nation* of kidnapped, brutalized, raped, tortured, and murdered women and men do the same? Why can't we choose collectively. . .to live? When I shot those men I decided, for *my nation,* not to be a victim anymore. I chose for us that we should live. And that's why Drawoc and Tumaini aren't here anymore."

Sandy took a drink of water and surveyed the courtroom. Every eye was locked on her. She carefully placed the glass down, took a deep breath, and continued.

"Now let's move to 'stand your ground,'" Sandy quickly transitioned. "The law states I have an established *right* by which I may defend myself or others against threats, real or *perceived,* even to the point of applying lethal force. Further, this right is bestowed upon me regardless of whether I can or cannot safely retreat from said situation.

"One of America's most gifted authors, James Baldwin, once wrote, 'To be a Negro in this country and to be relatively conscious is to be in a rage almost all the time.' And it's true," Sandy stressed. "Can you imagine living in a constant state of vulnerability? To navigate life's typical peaks and valleys and then deal with knowing the country you were born in, *built,* fought wars for, died in wars for, sacrificed for, does *not* love you back? Do you realize how helpless a person can feel knowing police aren't here to protect you but instead are charged with the task of controlling people who look like me?

"The police have been brutalizing and murdering people of color since their inception. So what are *we* supposed to do when the institutions put in place to protect citizens only protect a certain population of citizens? How do we manage surviving an institution who's trained and armed men and women who prey upon and murder us? Look, *we* know you don't care, but how long do you expect us to accept being brutalized and murdered by you?

"Finally, we have our US military who, at the beck and call of our government officials, have launched preemptive strikes to repel or defeat a perceived imminent offensive or invasion. Remember those 'weapons of mass destruction'?" Some of the jurors nodded their heads in acknowledgment. "Those four words launched our country's preemptive strike against the country of Iraq. Even though they never attacked or invaded this country, half a million Iraqis died because our government *perceived* them as a threat.

"What is the difference between what Barbara Sheehan and I did to neutralize imminent threats against us by standing our ground and what the US government did to neutralize a perceived Iraqi threat?"

Sandy went silent, forcing the jurors to pause and consider her question sincerely.

"A *perceived* threat was enough to bomb and invade another country, despite us finding zero weapons of mass destruction when it was all over. The threats I neutralized, Drawoc and Tumaini, had already proven themselves violent weapons of destruction when they both took innocent lives.

"So, in response, I removed Michael Drawoc and Shane Tumaini from this world. They were no earthly good anyway. Don't believe me? Let's examine Drawoc's life story. He stalked, chased, and murdered a teenager half his size and age. His wife divorced him after he'd threatened and pointed a gun at her.

After the divorce he was charged with felony assault of his new girlfriend months later. Then he was arrested on the suspicion of domestic violence towards that same new girlfriend. After that, he was removed from a restaurant after using racial slurs against patrons and the restaurant manager, trying to incite an altercation. Finally, he's charged and pleads guilty to *stalking* and *threatening* another citizen. These are all public record and indisputable facts.

"So, yes. I killed Drawoc. I found out where he lived and went to the apartment complex. I wanted to see for myself if news outlets had spun him into some bogeyman just to help them sell papers and advertising spots or if he was a cold-blooded killer. I parked my car awkwardly in front of his building, turned on my hazard lights, and waited.

"That's when Devonte Armstrong and I saw each other outside of the basketball court. Just like he testified, Devonte asked could he help, and I told him we were fine. As soon as the young man was out of earshot, Drawoc says, 'I had trouble with that gang of thugs when I first moved here. He and his friends always look like they're up to no good.'"

A few jurors sat back in their chairs, folded their arms across their chests, and shook their heads in disappointment.

"Drawoc didn't even need any coaxing from me. Bottom line, Drawoc was a predator biding his time until the next opportunity to kill someone, again. Whether it would be any of those young boys or his next ex-girlfriend, I preferred not to find out. Both Drawoc and Tumaini are no different than Jerry Sandusky and how he used the Second Mile organization to prey on and sexually abuse vulnerable boys. There would be countrywide outrage if *anyone* attempted to argue justifying Sandusky for his predatory behavior. Yet we constantly see people chopping at the bit, ready to argue down people of color left with no choice but to protect themselves from the serial, predatory behavior of racist and bigoted police officers."

Some of the jurors watched Sandy in shock over her candid declaration.

"Drawoc and Tumaini were cut from the same cloth. They were proven imminent threats against a humane society. They both murdered and this country's legal system failed to punish them appropriately." Sandy looked at the jury and exhaled in frustration. "Wake up, people!" she demanded emphatically. "We can't afford to deny this country's sickness one second longer. Drawoc, Tumaini, and anyone like them are viruses that warrant neutralization. And since this legal system has proven itself nothing more than a placebo, my placing a bullet in each of their heads finally served as a righteous cure.

"Believe me, I can only imagine the thoughts running through your heads right now. Perhaps you're wondering how an unassuming surgeon, who *seems* to have had everything going for her, is now sitting before you confessing these things? If I am correct, my reply is simple. *I AM...,*" she hesitated, "*I AM...* the warning shot across American's bigoted bow. *I AM...*the unsettling truth you all need to hear. *I AM...*a final forewarning to cowardice murderers who dare enter a place of worship to murder praying citizens simply because they are *not* white or Christian.

"I believe there is a God, and if he, she, or *it* hears can hear these words, I'm sure God empathizes with my feelings of hopelessness. I believe God understands that I'm just a person who *may* be wrong for enacting revenge, but what else would you have *us* do? What type of message does indefinitely turning the other cheek send to the predators infringing on our right to *live?* What other recourse does an entire community of people have when we know, after centuries of evidence, that we cannot rely on the scales of justice to tilt in our favor. Or, to protect and preserve our well-being in this country? *Any* victimized community's refusal to defend itself silently grants their perpetrators the consent to exterminate them with extreme prejudice.

"Another legendary American author, Zora Neale Hurston, once said, 'If you are silent about your pain, they will kill you and say you enjoyed it.' Well, we have *never* enjoyed it. The kidnapping. The forced servitude. The torture. The oppression. The rapes. The lynchings. The castrations. The racial profiling. The systematic harassment by racist law enforcement. The deliberate flooding of our communities with drugs. Or the murders." Sandy straightened her posture and scanned the jury with stern eyes.

"Continue to let my words fall upon your deaf ears. Continue to kill us with impunity," she warned, "and Dr. Sandy Darboe neutralizing a minuscule two predators will be the least of your worries."

CHAPTER 26

As anticipated, Sandy's testimony shook the courtroom and buried its listeners in an avalanche of truth. Her confession, carefully woven into the condemnation of predatory murderers like Drawoc and Tumaini, brought a dramatic close to the defense of her case. At the conclusion of her testimony, Sandy returned to her seat and exhaled. She sat there, content that she'd exorcised her truthful burden. She locked eyes with Judge Pisano as she settled into her seat. The two exchanged a moment of solace that Sandy would never be able to put into words.

She glanced over at the prosecution and saw the smiles they wore in between whispering in one another's ears. She watched as the prosecutor resigned to not ask any follow-up questions, confident Sandy's declaration had sealed her own fate and secured successful prosecution the moment she admitted to shooting both Drawoc and Tumaini.

Moments later the judge adjourned court for the day. The jury filed out of the courtroom, and soon after the bailiffs escorted Sandy through the chamber doors enroute to her holding cell in county jail. Tomorrow would mark the beginning of closing arguments, but Sandy's defense attorney wasn't done for the day.

Yvon needed everyone outside the courtroom to feel the weight of the pending decision. He needed the court of public opinion to weigh in on this groundbreaking case as well.

Before Xavier left the courtroom, Sandy's lawyer emailed a prepared statement along with an attachment that included Sandy's unedited transcript of her testimony. Yvon sculpted several paragraphs complete with quotable lines and sound bites the press could run repeatedly over the next news cycle. Judge Pisano's ban of media in his courtroom worked perfectly for an instance like this. It starved the press of any tantalizing headlines, so when Xavier emerged from the courthouse ready to reveal all that happened, the networks salivated.

Xavier's dish would be served just in time for the six o'clock news. WRC-TV broke the story first. They showed footage of Xavier in his police uniform reading the prepared statement before a cluster of microphones capturing every word.

"My name is Officer Xavier Darboe. My wife, Dr. Sandy Darboe, along with the approval of her attorney, have authorized me to release the following statement to the press and the American people." Xavier held up a stack of bound pages for all to see.

"Attached to the short declaration I am about to read is the full, unedited transcript of Sandy Darboe's testimony today. After reading my statement, I will provide copies of both the statement and transcript to you all. I will *not* answer any questions at the conclusion of the statement.

"Today, I took an oath before God to tell the truth. As such, I've confessed to the shooting of both Michael Drawoc and Shane Tumaini. Although I did squeeze the trigger that ended both their

lives, much like the black-hooded executioner of old, I bear no responsibility in carrying out the sentencing of these two murderous criminals.

"For centuries, the oppressed citizens of this country harmoniously sang tortured pleas for justice. Those sonnets have fallen upon deaf ears. Maybe with the execution of every predator like Drawoc and every bigoted cop like Tumaini, this country will finally realize its failed contrition in the presence of injustice.

"I charge all corrupt police officers with conduct unbecoming. I charge our justice system with gross negligence and incompetence for habitually failing to secure justice for its citizens against brutalizing police officers. Regardless of whether I'm found guilty or innocent, a new scale of justice tilts in the favor of the righteous black and brown people victimized for far too long. This day forward, I charge the oppressed people of this country to cease all peaceful protests.

"The oppressed masses must discontinue the practice of misplaced hope. The diseased mind of a racist or bigot cannot be altered through logical debate. Centuries of peaceful efforts have run their course and proven themselves a fruitless endeavor. Now is the time to strike down the opposition who taunts us and refuses to relinquish their power unless torn from their cold, dead hands. Since my enemies have proven themselves absent of any moral compass, I greet your subconscious death wish with my bullets. I pray more will mimic my efforts, as my enemies are your enemies, and our foes have proven themselves incapable of self-correction from their wicked trajectory."

●

Xavier sat in the middle of his empty sofa, processing the gravity of what he'd just done. He switched from one channel to the other while Sandy's mother was in Jason's nursery tending to his formula feeding. Xavier leaned forward, remote in his hand, absorbing the range of people's reactions to Sandy's statement. Within minutes of concluding the statement and providing the transcript of Sandy's testimony, breaking news announcements flashed across every television in America. He'd just threatened the establishment. Even worse, one he was a member of.

"This is Mary Anne Medley with WJLA, Washington, DC, and I'm here with Rodney Levy from Northwest, DC, to hear his take on the statement released by Sandy Darboe, the defendant charged with the murders of Michael Drawoc and Shane Tumaini," the reporter said into the camera in front of her. She stood next to a young, stocky DC resident patiently waiting for his turn to speak. "Mr. Levy, your thoughts on Mrs. Darboe's statement?"

"It's about time someone said it," Mr. Levy professed. "This country's been hiding its bigotry long enough. A lot of people thought racism would die with our parents' generation, but I knew better. There's a new generation of morons shouting at the top of their lungs, 'You will not replace us!' like anyone even cares to replace them. I'm telling you, ever since half this country voted a racist in for president, it's only gotten worse. Heaven forbid he wins a second term." Mr. Levy paused. "The country may never be the same again. The history books will mark these years as the beginning of the fall of America, much like the fall of the Roman Empire."

"So you think Sandy Darboe calling for violence and threating police officers is okay?"

"She didn't say *all* police officers. She said racist and bigoted police officers who have track records of brutality and murdering unarmed citizens. If you're a so-called 'good cop,' you have nothing to worry about, right?" Mr. Levy corrected.

"That's one way of looking at it," the reporter conceded. "She did say *just* the bad cops, but calling for even bad police officer to be met with bullets? Do you think she may have taken it too far?"

Mr. Levy looked the reporter in the eyes and scoffed. "Fuck them cops! I lost a cousin to a trigger-happy cop. He was unarmed and died because the cop claimed he 'didn't comply' before shooting him multiple times. The damn cop was so reckless two of his bullets hit his own partner. I wish a plague on ever racist cop's house."

"There you have it. One citizen's opinion about Sandy Darboe's ultimatum to *bad* cops everywhere. This is Mary Anne Medley with WJLA, Washington, DC. Back to you in the studio." Xavier changed to another station, where another field reporter was on the campus of Howard University, speaking with a young lady with a long, perfectly maintained lock hairstyle.

"I'm standing here with Rashida Bey, student body president of Howard University's student government association. Ms. Bey, can you share what the climate on Howard's campus is after news broke of Mrs. Darboe's confession of shooting Drawoc and Tumaini but laying the responsibility of their deaths at the doorstep of our country and its legal system?"

"I won't speak on the behalf of Howard University, its administration, or the student body as a whole. The opinions I'm about to express are mine and mine alone. With that said, the climate of Howard is what I would speculate the climate was like in October of 1995 when my parents watched the OJ trial while they were undergrads here at Howard. I obviously wasn't born yet, so I can't speak from personal experience of that time, but I wrote a term paper while in high school about the OJ trial.

"I remember interviewing my parents and others who lived through it. Based on what they described to me and from videos I found researching, those times were emotionally taxing. It's eerily similar to the emotions I'm experiencing following Dr. Darboe's trial. The clash of my generation's opinions along black and white color lines parallels what my parents described and the articles I read from 1995. It's literally like experiencing déjà vu."

"Did your parents tell you if they cheered when OJ was found not guilty? And did they say whether or not they thought OJ killed Nicole Brown and Ron Goldman?" the news reporter questioned.

"Yes, they cheered the not-guilty verdict," she confessed. "And, yes, they cheered even though they thought he was guilty from the beginning. But they didn't cheer because they thought he was innocent. They cheered because for once someone, who looked like us, beat the system that had been beating *on* us for the past four centuries," Ms. Bey said.

"Sandy Darboe has already admitted she killed both Drawoc and Tumaini. Will you, your classmates, or parents cheer for Sandy Darboe if she is found not guilty like OJ?" the reporter asked.

The young lady chuckled. "My friends and I actually debated this very question the other night."

"And?" the reporter asked as Ms. Bey folded her arms across her chest and looked up to the heavens as if asking for guidance for her next words.

"I will be *ecstatic* to see her go free and found not guilty," Ms. Bey confessed.

"But do you think that's right? Especially considering she confessed?"

Ms. Bey shrugged her shoulders. "At least she was honest when she confessed. When's the last time you heard a cop be honest and confess after taking an unarmed citizen's life?"

The large clock tower in the background began to chime. It was fifteen minutes before the hour.

"I must get to work soon but allow me to leave you with this thought." Ms. Bey turned to face the camera, speaking directly to millions of viewers. "When I arrive at work today, where I'm a teller at a bank, if I were to kill one of my customers who I *thought* had a gun, but it turned out they did not, I assure you I'd be arrested within minutes. I'd lose my job and serve time in the penitentiary. I would not be free, roaming the campus of Howard University, conversing with you.

"Then after serving my time, if I were ever released, I'd be placed on a list so I could never legally purchase or handle another firearm ever again. I would never be able to work for another bank ever again. My question to you is, why can't the same logical rules apply to police officers? Or are the police above the law like the moronic embarrassment currently residing in the White House?"

Xavier had heard enough and changed the channel once more and arrived at *Fox News*. The news anchor hosted a panel of two analysts discussing the legal ramifications of Sandy's testimony and prepared statement. At the bottom of the split screen the headline told Xavier everything he needed to know about the network's reporting. VIGILANTE ADMITS RESPONSIBILITY IN TESTIMONY in bold, centered letters gave viewers a half-truth introduction to the debate.

"Sandy 'The Vigilante' Darboe called for all-out war on police!" the anchor lied. Xavier could feel his temperament changing for the worse. He muted the television and changed the channel again. He watched the headlines in silence. One station after the other featured footage of his statement, with D.C.'s courthouse in the background. Followed by Sandy's mug shot despite Xavier and her lawyer providing news outlets with more suitable and flattering pictures of her.

Sandy "The Vigilante" Darboe. The unflattering moniker echoed in his head. His proud family name would now be synonymous with cold, calculated murder as Lewinsky was to Oval Office sex acts.

My family is going to be mortified. They'd always loved Sandy, so they wouldn't disown me or pressure me to leave her and start over. But they are a prideful and any besmirching of our family lineage would not be received well under any circumstances.

Xavier recalled the countless times his parents suggesting a "good African girl" for him to meet, court, and marry before he proposed to Sandy. He couldn't bear to hear his mother lecturing him, warning him—again—about "marrying an American girl."

Then there's my career. No matter the outcome, all my hard work in the academy and the sacrifices I made to advance my career will be swept away. Especially after Sandy desecrated the department's blue wall on social media like a graffiti artist tagging a subway train. The department will turn its back on me, and Kamara will be ostracized as well for befriending me.

The sound of his house phone ringing and the automated voice broke him away from his thoughts. "Incoming call from a blocked number." The quiet of Jason's nursery was replaced by crying. The unfamiliar noise stirred everyone in the apartment. Xavier rose from the sofa and grabbed the dusty phone he and Sandy had yet to use.

"Hello?" Xavier answered, mentally preparing himself to politely shut down the impending sales pitch of a telemarketer or an overzealous reporter fishing for a tantalizing quote for tomorrow's headlines.

"Xavier Darboe?" A voice unfamiliar to Xavier questioned.

"Yes, this is he."

"Oh, hello, sir," a chipper voice responded. "You're Officer Xavier Darboe?"

"I said yes. Who's calling?"

"Tell that bitch of a wife she's dead! You, her, and your piccaninnie son."

"Who the hell is this?" Xavier demanded, but as quickly as the words came out, he realized how foolish the question was. It wasn't as if the stranger would actually volunteer that information.

"I just finished the noose I'm going to hang your baboon baby from," the caller threatened. Xavier didn't respond, listening intently and hoping to hear something in the person's voice or in the background that would hint to their identity or location.

"Still there, porch monkey?"

Xavier finally broke his momentary silence. "Oh, I'm still here. So listen to this *porch monkey* very closely—5234 New York Avenue, Northwest, DC." Xavier said, slowly enough for the caller to catch. "You need more time for someone else to write it down for your illiterate ass?" Xavier said.

"Yeah, I got another noose for uppity coons just like you."

"Good, make sure you and whoever is stupid enough to come with you bring plenty of nooses. And I'll be sure to hang you all off my balcony like Christmas ornaments," Xavier threatened just before the caller hung up.

Coward!

CHAPTER 27

The news coverage of Sandy's statement sent the entire country into a whirlwind of debate. The anticipation of closing arguments and jury deliberations made Xavier anxious. Every time he'd tried to settle himself, a flurry of thoughts infiltrated his mind. Sleep would be impossible tonight. He rolled over in the king-size bed until he reached the remote lying on the night table. He rolled back over and propped up two pillows beneath his head, then flipped on the television.

The large screen woke from its slumber, still on the last station he'd watched before the revolving door of threatening phone calls began. They were all the same variety. A rotation of similar voices threating him, his wife, and their child with torture, lynching, rape, and death. Xavier responded to all the calls in the same fashion as the first call, countering with a threat of his own design.

He wanted them to know he was unafraid. He wanted them to know he loved and supported his vengeful wife and would protect his family, damning all consequences. He'd convinced himself it was all an overzealous dance of machismo between strangers and he would remain unflappable.

After the last caller refused to react to Xavier's threats and resigned to heavy breathing into the phone, Xavier finally turned the ringer off. Anyone important knew to call his or Sandy's mobile phone. He turned his attention back to the headlines on his television. He slowly increased the volume, not wanting to wake Jason and his mother-in-law. The headline increased Xavier's heart rate as the anchor recapped.

"This is an ABC News special report. Now reporting, Curtis Curry. And we are coming back on the air from commercial break to bring you the latest on the horrific shooting event in Dallas, Texas, earlier tonight. We have been able to confirm five police officers have been shot by what police believe to be a lone sniper. The shootings came at the end of what had been a peaceful protest against police corruption and its role in the killing of unarmed black men.

Again, five officers have been confirmed dead, and nine other officers have been injured. ABC has confirmed the shooter has been identified as Micah Johnson, a twenty-five-year-old army reservist up until last year.

"Preliminary reporting is still being gathered about the young man, especially his social media posts where he expressed anger towards police for their history of brutality and murdering unarmed citizens."

Xavier watched the mayhem unfolding on television. Video footage of the shooter firing, then moving to a new position, shooting again, and repeating the same maneuvers, were all too familiar to him.

"He's definitely military trained," Xavier mumbled to himself, watching the tactical precision the shooter used to wreak havoc in Dallas.

Xavier shook his head adamantly. *This isn't your or Sandy's fault. Don't beat yourself up, Xavier,* he preached to himself, but his conscience continued its torment. *As a unionized collective we police have claimed more casualties than a hundred Micah Johnsons ever could. But there is no denying the writing on the wall now. Sandy, Anonymous, and now Micah Johnson have had enough. They'd chosen armed rebellion.*

Xavier could feel his loyalties as a sworn officer being tested. The turmoil he felt inside was both confusing and liberating. Part of him reveled in the idea of bad cops finally being put on notice. *No more!* he exclaimed internally before his training corrected his recklessness. Micah and Anonymous, even his wife, were breaking the law. And no one was above the law.

No one is above the law . . . except for us cops, you mean. His conscience corrected him. More video flashed across his sixty-inch screen showing Micah Johnson exchanging gunfire with one brave police officer who dared to advance on the shooter's position for a close-range shoot-out.

They were both positioned behind large pillars of a downtown office building. The police officer peeked from behind his pillar, then fired several shots that grazed the pillar Micah Johnson took cover behind. As soon as the officer's firing stopped, Micah Johnson sprang into assault mode. In a stooping position and partially bent knees, he emerged from behind his cement pillar, releasing a succession of loud M4 semiautomatic rounds.

The rounds of his assault rifle broke off cement chips from the left side of the pillar. They fell to the ground at the police officer's feet. The officer instinctively rolled to the other side of the pillar away from Micah's gunfire. Micah looped wide right toward the officer's retreating direction. From his bed, Xavier watched as the officer turned directly into Micah's second flurry of bullets and died instantly.

Xavier couldn't help but wonder if the officer had a wife and children. He thought how the Dallas Police Department would place black stripes across their badges tomorrow, signifying the loss of not one but several of their own. He contemplated the grief the fallen officer's family would have to bear. Even if he wasn't married or didn't have children, everyone has a mother and father, possibly siblings, cousins, grandparents, who may still be alive.

Xavier knew whoever the officer's family was, if they'd seen the footage, the memory of seeing their loved one cut down would be forever etched into their memory. *He won't be taken alive. Dallas PD is going to fill him with enough bullets to kill him three times over.*

Xavier was ashamed for the thought that just ran through his head. Without even thinking, the muscle memory of his field training had within a few seconds tried, sentenced, and approved Micah Johnson's condemnation to death. No arrest, no opportunity to stand trial like Sandy, and no presumption of innocence. The cop in him knew Micah Johnson would die before he ever saw the inside of a squad car.

Sandy was right. There are too many of us power drunk after receiving our badges. And even worse there are too many of us who should have never been given the badge.

CHAPTER 28

The next morning, anxious reporters swarmed the curb of the courthouse like sharks amid a feeding frenzy. The endless flow of telephoned death threats generated from reading Sandy's statement made it easy for Xavier to decide to show up for closing arguments alone. Xavier called in a favor from his new friend and fellow officer, Kamara, asking him to stay with Sandy's mother and Jason. He didn't want to chance leaving them at the apartment alone just in case an overzealous crazy actually decided to show up at his home while he was at the courthouse.

When Xavier took his seat, he reached over the barrier and gently squeezed Sandy's shoulder.

She turned to face him with her usual large smile.

"Hey, baby."

"Hey, love."

"Just us."

"Just us."

They both could tell from the matching set of bags under both their eyes that neither slept well last night. He decided not to worry her about the calls coming to their home. Heaven forbid he confess his knee jerk reaction to taunt the callers in return. Xavier just locked eyes with her lawyer, and they exchanged nods, both knowing this would be Yvon's last chance to sway the jurors favor in Sandy's direction.

If Yvon failed to win the jury over, Sandy would have to watch Jason grow up through bulletproof plexiglass. Wish him happy birthdays and ask about his first days of school through germ-infested telephones. Her life wouldn't be her own anymore. She would need permission to sleep, eat, work, and even use the bathroom from correctional officers who were itching to make her suffer for the remainder of her life.

Sandy's body temperature rose, causing her to sweat, and her clothes to stick to her skin. Her heart pounded, and her anxiety pushed the limits of a panic attack as she watched the prosecution rise to address the jury.

"May it please the court, your honor, ladies and gentlemen of the jury. I want to first thank you for the time and attention you've put into this case."

Sandy internally scowled at every smile and overly gratuitous gesture her opponent made. *Brownnosing bitch!*

"It's not uncommon to begin a closing argument thanking the jury for their time," the prosecution continued. "However, I think we can all agree our experience serving on this case has been very unique. For the past two weeks all of you have had to live through an unprecedented courtroom hacking, the confession of an unremorseful murderer, and finally a brazen threat of continued violence against the men and women who keep us safe from harm. Yesterday's statement, read by the defendant's husband, with the approval of their attorney, is nothing short of a terrorist threat against law and order in this country.

"The same law and order you twelve citizens have sworn to uphold. Yes, ladies and gentlemen, it's an attack on you as well. I'll be honest with all of you. I won't ever be quite the same at the conclusion of this case. I take some solace in the fact that I am standing here, before my adversary, defiant in the face of her threats. And you know why? Because I am here for justice.

"The defendant, Mrs. Darboe, is charged with four separate crimes. She's charged with two offenses of capital murder. She's charged with premeditation to commit murder, and she's charged with using a firearm during the commission of a murder. First, we have the two capital murder offenses that she already confessed to committing during her testimony.

"She confessed," Bertrand repeated. "She said she did it, so I'm not going to waste your time trying to convince you she's a threat to society, because she's already made that crystal clear herself." The prosecutor paused for a moment and let her words resonate with the jury. "Then we have the charge of using a firearm during the commission of a murder." She turned her legal pad sideways and showed the jury in large block letters I SHOT THEM BOTH! RIGHT IN THE FACE! "Those were the defendant's words. But murdering those two men wasn't enough. No, she made a point to boast to us all about *how* she did it.

"Finally, we have the last charge of conspiracy to commit murder. Let me remind the jury that the deceased men were from two different cities, two different backgrounds and professions. Both shot 'in the face,' and the only commonality they shared was their murderer's malicious desire to carry out vigilante justice against these two people. These facts mean her killing them was not random.

"The facts support the prosecution's theory of how she researched these two men, found them, staged meeting them, and then killed them. In criminal law, a conspiracy is an agreement between two or more persons to commit a crime at some time in the future. And before you say, 'But she acted alone. Does that mean she's innocent?,' remember the courtroom hacking. Remember how eerily close the threats from Anonymous resembled the same threats from the defendant that were read by her husband yesterday. The defendant and Anonymous are in cahoots!" the prosecutor declared.

"These killings were willful, deliberate, and premeditated. We all see that. But the defendant didn't stop there. Even while on trial for the crimes I just described, she wants to intimidate us. She wants us all to believe this fanciful theory that the federal government and its judicial system are conspiring like a two-headed diabolical bogeyman. She is trying to influence the conduct of our government and its citizens, and that, by definition, is terrorism." The prosecutor scanned the jurors until she locked with each of their eyes.

"Yes, I said *terrorism*, because regardless of its form and its messenger, that's what her actions show us. She's evil, ladies and gentlemen of the jury. So I stand before you, asking that when you deliberate, remember her crimes and return with a verdict of *guilty*. *Guilty* of two offenses of capital murder, *guilty* of conspiracy, and *guilty* of use of a firearm in commission of a crime. A guilty verdict is the only right that will correct all the wrong she's done. Thank you again for your service and for your attention." The prosecutor turned from the jury, glanced at Sandy and her attorney, and took her seat.

"Defense," Judge Pisano said, "you may issue your closing remarks."

Sandy watched as her attorney stood up and walked to the podium, ready to address the jury. Another wave of heat flashed through her entire body. Fresh beads of sweat sprouted at the base of her neck. Her attorney grabbed the remote control to the courtroom audio system and pressed the power button. Within seconds all the courtroom monitors displayed a paused video with a African-American comedian holding a microphone on-stage.

"May it please the court, your honor, ladies and gentlemen of the jury. Before I begin my closing statement, I want to play you a video to lighten the mood after such a gloomy closing argument by the prosecution." Yvon smiled at the jury and aimed the remote at the large black glass case where the DVD player was sitting. The paused video began playing at the beginning of the joke.

"*I'm not saying fuck the police. I would never say that. You know why? Because I'm scared of those motherfuckers, that's why. <Crowd claps and laughs.> I'm not stupid, ha ha! Now, I know that's not a nice thing to say. I don't want to be scared of them. Shit, sometimes we want to call the police. Sometimes we have no choice to call them, right? Like this one time somebody broke into my house—that's the perfect time to dial 911. But I couldn't do it . . . mmm-mmm <Comedian shakes his head.> My house isn't like everybody's house. My house is what you call a mansion! <Crowd laughs.> Now, it ain't a Warren Buffett type of mansion, but it's nice enough that po-po wouldn't believe I lived in it. They'd be like—" <Comedian gasps and pretends to be the cop.> "'The robber is still here!'" <Comedian*

uses microphone to imitate a cop hitting the black homeowner with a baton.> "'Whew! That was a close one. Open-and-shut case, Miller. Hmm, weird. The same thing happened once before when I was a rookie. Apparently, this nigger broke in and hung wedding, vacation, and graduation pictures of his family all over this pristine white owner's residence. Welp, let's sprinkle some crack on him and get out of here.'"

Sandy's lawyer aimed at the DVD player again and pressed a button. The video paused, and he looked at the jury.

"That guy," Yvon said, chuckling, "he's one of my favorite comedians. I met him once after one of his shows. It was a brief but eye-opening conversation. I asked him what his favorite part was about being a comedian, and in true comedic fashion he said, 'Being able to smoke indoors and not get in trouble like you normal people.'" Some jurors laughed. "He's clever, right?" Yvon chuckled before continuing. "But then he answered my question seriously. And you know what he said? He said, 'I appreciate the simplicity of stand-up. Comedy is simply the purposeful exaggeration of reality. All a comedian does is take a normal, everyday occurrence, add extravagant embellishment, and—boom—you have a joke.' Sandy's attorney paused for a moment before continuing. "What the comedian said really made me think, because I never looked at comedy that way. As an extreme exaggeration of the *truth*. A truth, even if an unsettling truth, that also makes us laugh.

"Take the video I just played for you, for instance. Are we really to believe that, in real life, a cop or cops would respond to a 911 call and think the owner is the criminal? Then knock them over the head with a baton? *And* sprinkle crack on them just to get an arrest?" Yvon asked rhetorically. He scanned the jury, then hit the play button again. A still screenshot of a *New York Times* article displayed on the monitors. The article also displayed a color photograph of a middle-aged African American man with gray hair being led away from his home in handcuffs.

"What you are now seeing is the July 16, 2009, arrest of Harvard University professor Henry Louis Gates Jr. in his Cambridge, Massachusetts, home. Police were called to his residence because a neighbor suspected Professor Gates of breaking into his *own* home. Professor Gates came home and found the front door to his home jammed shut and, with the help of his driver, tried to force it open. The responding Cambridge police sergeant eventually arrested Professor Gates and charged him with a crime."

Sandy watched the faces of the jury change from indifferent to serious. Some jurors sat back in their chairs, shaking their heads in disappointment. Some nodded, once they recalled the story that ended with Professor Gates, the arresting officer, and then President Barrack Obama sharing beers at the White House, discussing race relations.

"Well, at least they didn't sprinkle crack on Professor Gates before they arrested him," Yvon said sarcastically before pressing play again. The screenshot disappeared, and another video began to play. This time it was another African-American comedian performing his stand-up routine.

"White folk love them some excitement. Not us though, not black folk. Being black is excitement enough. <Crowd claps and cheers.> We get our adrenaline rush from everyday shit. <More claps, cheers, and laughter.> My white coworkers ask me all the

time, 'Getting into anything fun and exciting this weekend?' 'Well, I'ma drive home, and when I pass that speed trap, I'ma hope I just get a ticket and not my ass whupped. Then I'ma slooowly pull out my wallet to show the police my license, registration, proof of insurance, voter registration card, and birth certificate to prove I'm an American citizen, and I'ma do all this hoping and praying I don't get shot forty-one times. What about you, Peter?' <The audience erupts in cheers and laughter.> I'm serious! And heaven forbid you ever drop your wallet in front of the police. <The audience groans, and the comedian shakes his head.> Don't you do it! Don't you bend over and pick that wallet up. You hear me? <Audience claps in agreement.> If I ever . . . ever, ever, ever dropped my wallet in front of the police, I will NOT pick that motherfucker up. I'll kick that shit all the way home with my hands in the air! 'Mmm-mmm, nice try but you won't get me today, Officer!'"

Yvon paused the DVD player again and returned his attention to the jury. Sandy could see they were growing more uncomfortable. This time only the minority jurors chuckled at the joke.

"My apologies for the comedian's language, but I didn't want to doctor the video, so you could hear the jokes unedited. Despite his use of profanity, he's a funny guy. He's another favorite of mine. He said he would kick his wallet home instead of picking it up in front of police." Yvon chuckled again. "Which brings us back to what the first comedian said about exaggerations. None of us can really expect anyone to be that fearful of picking up their wallet in front of police, right?" Yvon hit play, and another screenshot displayed.

"The screenshot you're now seeing is another *New York Times* article. It's a reporting on the facts behind the shooting of Mr. Amadou Diallo. February 4, 1999, Mr. Diallo, a twenty-three-year-old immigrant from Guinea, was unarmed and shot to death by four New York City plainclothes officers after they mistook him for a rape suspect from one year earlier. The officers fired a combined total of *forty-one* shots. That's where the second comedian got being shot forty-one times from. But only nineteen bullets struck Mr. Diallo outside his home in the Bronx.

"Despite the four officers' terrible judgement and total disregard for life, all four were acquitted of second-degree murder." Yvon looked at the sullen faces of the jury. "See? Comedy is exaggeration. The second comedian doesn't really fear being shot forty-one times while trying to pick up his wallet. In reality he's really only afraid of being shot nineteen times. Chances are the other twenty-two bullets will miss him," Yvon said sarcastically before hitting the play button again. The video displayed the second comedian again as a guest on a cable talk show, promoting his new book *How Not to Get Shot Forty-One Times*.

Talk show host: "How old were you when you had your first encounter with the police?"

Comedian: "I was seven years old."

Talk show host: "Seven? Really? That young for your first encounter?"

Comedian: "Yeah, I was seven. I grew up on One Hundred and Fifteenth street in Harlem not that far from Central Park. One day I'm coming home from my school and the police pull up on me and my friend. Now, mind you, this was the day after that lady jogger was raped in Central Park."

Talk show host: "You mean the same time of the Central Park Five?"

273

Comedian: "Exactly! The police rolled up on us and questioned us about some guy in my neighborhood. They was like, 'Where is he?' And we said, 'We don't know.' Then the cop detained us and told us to put our hands on his police car. And I said, 'Sir, your police car is hot. It's burning my hands.' And he said, 'You little nigger! You take your hands off that car I'll put a bullet through each of your hands.'"

Yvon paused the video. Some of the juror's mouths hung open in shock. Yvon pounced. "Oh, come on. Police wouldn't bully a seven-year-old, and they definitely wouldn't shoot a child. This is just more comedy. More *over* exaggeration just to get a laugh, right?"

Yvon pressed play. Another screenshot of a news article showed a picture of ten-year-old Michael Thomas Jr. of Chicago leaning against the front fender of a police cruiser with his hands cuffed behind his back. The child was visibly distraught, crying, and so afraid that the front of his light-blue sweatpants were now a dark navy blue because the Chicago youth had urinated himself.

"The screenshot you're seeing now is from an article published by a local Chicago newspaper. Ten-year-old Michael Thomas Jr. was walking down the street when police pulled up to him, detained him, and placed him in handcuffs outside of his grandmother's home. Chicago police said they stopped Michael Thomas Jr. because he 'matched the description'"—Yvon made air quotes with his fingers—"of a teenager with a gun that they were looking for. The innocent young man was eventually let go without charges after his grandmother showed the police officers her ten-year-old grandson did *not* have a weapon by pulling up his T-shirt, displaying he wasn't armed."

Yvon pressed play again. The video showed a snow-covered park where a child was playing near a large gazebo. Moments later a police cruiser sped into the frame and stopped ten feet in front of the child. Only two to three seconds passed before the video showed one of the police officers fire two bullets into the child. The child falls to the ground, motionless.

Gasps rang out from the jury box. Faces tightened and jaws clenched.

Sandy watched multiple trails of tears fall down the cheeks of both male and female jurors.

"For those of you who are not familiar with the gruesome video I just played, that's how Tamir Rice was murdered while playing, like all children do, in a park. Let me say that again. He was playing in the park. Just like I've done. Just like all of you at some point in your lives. Tamir was a twelve-year-old living in Cleveland, Ohio. Two police officers were dispatched when someone called police about Tamir playing with a toy gun. At the beginning of the call and again in the middle, the caller says the gun is probably fake and stated the child is probably a juvenile. But those warning of innocent child's play didn't stop the officer in the passenger side of the police cruiser from shooting Tamir Rice twice in the torso. Young Tamir died because of the wounds he sustained the following day.

"What did the second comedian say? Comedy is simple life overexaggerated. Right?" Yvon exclaimed, shrugging his shoulders, continuing his sarcasm. "The little boy who urinated on himself, Michael Thomas Jr., the police eventually let him go, and you can wash out urine, right? And Tamir Rice didn't have bullets shot through each of his hands, like the cop that threatened the comedian. Tamir Rice was shot in the chest instead." Yvon pressed play once more. "And finally, the last video I wanted to show you is by a different comedian."

The video showed the comedian dressed in a dark all-purple outfit accentuated by shiny pants and matching jacket, pacing back and forth across the stage of a theater in New York. He's laughing, and the crowd is cheering the tail end of his last joke.

"People all over the country are mad! I blame social media. Social media gave people the perfect platform to vent about all their stupid shit! And who's the maddest? White people! <He points to white audience members throughout the sold-out theatre.> Okay, not all of y'all are mad— some of y'all all right. <Crowd erupts with laughter.> Once you overpay to come see one of my shows, we Kool & the Gang. Like Meek Mill and Drake, the beef is over. But seriously, you ever watch 60 Minutes? *Or worse,* Fox News? *<The crowd groans.> Yeah, I heard that. You've definitely watched* Fox News. *What did you see, huh? A bunch of pissed off white people. They're 'Making America Great Again.' <The crowd groans even louder.> And why? Because they think they're losing the country. You watch* Fox News *and they're like, 'We're losing! We're fucking losing everything! Fucking Muslims! Illegal aliens! We're fucking losing the country.' <Comedian pauses.> Losing? Shut the fuck up! Y'all ain't losing shit. If y'all losing, who's winning? <Crowd laughs.> Not us! <Crowd erupts into louder laughter.> Try drinking the water in Flint, Michigan. Try being a brown immigrant seeking asylum at the Mexican border. Talking about losing? Shit, there isn't a white person in this room that would trade places with me. None of you, none of you would trade places with me. AND I'M RICH! I bet you there's a dishwasher that saved their money for months just to buy a*

ticket to my show that's thinking, 'Hmmmm? Naaah! I'm going to see this white thing all the way through and see where it takes me.'"

Yvon hit the stop button. The monitors returned to blank black screens. He slowly walked from the podium toward the jury box. One juror offered another some Kleenex as some wiped away their remaining tears with their fingers and bare hands. Yvon stared them all down, forcing the uncomfortable silence to linger.

Sandy watched it all play out. Her shackles clanked against each other as she raised her hands up from beneath the table to wipe her own eyes.

Her attorney leaned on the front railing of the jury box. "I'm going to pose a rhetorical question because obviously I don't expect you to answer me directly. Not out loud, anyways. But don't be afraid to answer it silently, to yourself. And be honest with yourself when answering. No one will ever know what you're thinking, and we can't force you to reveal what your answer is. So, right here, right now, in the recesses of your own mind you've have a safe place free of judgement and the pressure of being politically correct.

"You all saw me call four different witnesses to testify, none of them associated directly with this case. They had nothing to lose *but* everything to gain. Four different people, with different backgrounds, different levels of education, and socioeconomic levels." He stood back from the witness stand, folded his arms across his chest, and looked each juror who was not a minority in the eye. He bounced from white juror to white juror until all seven of them met his gaze.

"So my question is, Is this comedian right?" He reached into his inside jacket pocket to retrieve the syringe and vial containing the same medication he'd placed in front of the witnesses he'd called days earlier. He placed both the syringe and vial on the ledge of the jury box. He removed his tailor-made suit jacket, unfastened his gold cuff links, and rolled up the sleeves of his bespoke white shirt embroidered with his initials.

Sandy watched as the jurors in the front row of the jury box sat back into their seats, seeing the vial and needle. Yvon picked up the needle and pressed it into the vile containing the medication. After drawing enough until the syringe was one-quarter full, he pulled the needle out and tapped it a few times with his finger before carefully pressing the plunger until a small amount of the medication shot out of the needle's head.

"Counselor! What are you doing?" Judge Pisano demanded.

Sandy's lawyer turned toward the judge and stuck the needle into his shoulder and slowly injected himself.

Sandy watched as all the eyes in the jury box lit up. Their jaws dropped, and some covered their open mouths with the palms of their hands.

"Whew! I was never a fan of needles," Yvon declared as the judge's fury grew. He looked at the jury. "My question still remains. Had any of you not been selected for jury duty and I called any of *you* to the witness stand, would you have taken the injection, or is being white more valuable to you than winning the lottery?"

The sound of the judge's gavel startled everyone. "Today we're having an early lunch. Counselor! My chambers! Now!"

CHAPTER 29

Following Judge Pisano's impromptu lunch break, Sandy watched her lawyer emerge from the judge's chamber as if punch-drunk. The opposing attorney wore an evil smirk on her face while Yvon's brow glistened with fresh sweat. He pulled out the chair next to Sandy, let out a large sigh, and plopped down into his seat.

Sandy leaned forward in her chair, anticipating bad news. A young lawyer with red hair flowing down to the middle of her back was seated next to Xavier, scrolling intently through her smartphone until Sandy broke the silence.

"That bad, huh? Just how screwed am I?"

Sandy's lawyer dabbed his brow, poured himself half a glass of water, and swallowed a mouthful. He turned toward Sandy and winked. "Periodic slaps on the wrist come with the territory. Nothing to be alarmed about," Yvon responded.

Suddenly, the young attorney slid forward and shoved her phone in Yvon's face. Her full lips spread, revealing a large and bright, perfect smile, which distracted Sandy enough to question if she wore porcelain veneers. Yvon read his assistant's phone screen and nodded his head in approval.

"Oyez, oyez, oyez!" the courtroom deputy bellowed, bringing everyone to their feet. "All persons having business before the Honorable, the District Court of Washington, DC, are admonished to draw near and give their attention, for the court is now in session. God save the United States and this Honorable Court. The Honorable Myer Pisano presiding."

"Bailiff, please bring the jury in," Judge Pisano instructed.

Moments later the jurors filed back into the courtroom and took their places. They all at some point looked at Sandy's lawyer. It was evident to Sandy some were still wrestling with Yvon's last words before plunging the syringe into himself. Several locked in on him, staring and squinting as if they were watching a horror film, anticipating the changing of his skin tone before their eyes. Like a werewolf morphs from a man to a beast everyone feared.

"Defense Counsel, you may continue your closing remarks," the judge said.

"Thank you, Your Honor."

"Counsel?" Judge Pisano stressed. "Tread very carefully."

"Yes, Your Honor," Yvon conceded before continuing what remained of his closing remarks. He patted Sandy's hand beneath the table and leaned over toward her, whispering in her ear. "Closing time."

He rose from his chair and approached the jury box again. "May it please the court, ladies and gentlemen of the jury. I hope I didn't leave the impression that what you witnessed before our lunch break was a stunt. If you do think that, I assure you it was not. We live in a complicated world, and part of the deal we all accept being in this world is enduring its hardships. The videos I showed you were indeed harsh. A politically correct person would apologize to you for displaying content that evoked so much emotion, but I will not apologize."

He paused and turned to face Sandy. "Dr. Sandy Darboe especially cannot afford for such indifference, when addressing the turmoil our country is in. Political correctness has no place here. Not today. So I'm going to be as direct and honest as I can be with you because that's what this trial demands in order for you all to make a sound and fair decision. The preservation of our humanity demands it and demands it now." Yvon paused and nodded at the young lawyer assisting him.

She hit a few keys on his laptop and then picked up the remote control for the courtroom video displays. When they turned back on, all the screens mirrored Yvon's laptop screen. It showed the Google home page. The young lawyer typed "Trending news" in the search text box and hit enter. The top five search results referenced the same breaking news.

"I want to bring to your attention the time stamp of the results," Yvon directed. "This *murder* happened only ten to fifteen minutes ago." Yvon pointed at one of the members of the jury. "While you dried your tears"—he pointed at another—"while you were probably having small-talk conversations with other jurors, and while you all were enjoying the lunch this Honorable Court provided, this country lost another precious life." Yvon nodded at his young attorney. The first link referenced a video. She clicked on the link and pressed the play button.

The monitor displayed police body-cam footage of a police officer shooting fifteen-year-old Jordan Edwards in the back of the

I AM . . .

head while he was riding in the front passenger seat of a vehicle. Young Mr. Edwards was simply a passenger in a car of friends who were leaving another friend's house and heading home.

"While I and the prosecuting attorney were in the judge's chambers. While you were contemplating the details of this case, living and breathing, another young black man was killed by police." Yvon paused and nodded again at the attorney. She pressed more keys and clicked the mouse attached to the laptop. Seconds later a slideshow appeared, listing the most recent and high-profile cases where police had shot and killed unarmed citizens.

"What more proof do you *need*?" he questioned sincerely. "I know you see it because you've all at some point averted your eyes. I know you *feel* it by the empty box of Kleenex you've discarded onto the floor," he said, singling out jurors who were crying. "Edmund Burke, an Irish political philosopher, once said, 'All that is necessary for the triumph of evil is that good men *or women* do *nothing*.' This country, despite its storied ascension to a world power, has fallen into a shameful state of paralysis." The slideshow of slain black and brown faces continued while Yvon continued.

"It's time for the citizens of this country to have the uncomfortable conversation we've avoided for far too long. It's going to be painful but embrace it! That pain is necessary to exorcise our demons. Ladies and gentlemen of the jury, we must acknowledge our country's deep-rooted racism and xenophobia."

He paused, scanning the jury box. "I know, it's not an easy thing to say. It's even more difficult to acknowledge. And, yes, sometimes it feels impossible to admit. But that's the only way we'll quash it. Running from this truth has not and will never save us.

"We've tried running from American's greatest original sin, the decimation of the Native American. And look where it's gotten us. Before Christopher Columbus, before colonization, this country was the home to over one hundred and forty-five *million* Native Americans. Only two hundred years after Columbus arrived, one hundred and thirty million Native Americans *perished* from European disease, murder, and fighting to resist European colonization. One *hundred* and *thirty million* people," he repeated. "That's ninety percent of an indigenous population wiped out over the course of three to four generations.

"Just imagine, those of you who have grandchildren, imagine your *great*-grandchildren being born into a land where no one speaks their language or even looks like them anymore." Yvon paused and eyed a male juror who refused his gaze. "Running from the truth will not save you." The slideshow continued, displaying fresh faces of men, women, and children who had been lost to bigotry at the hands of police over the last few years.

"Then there's America's second-greatest sin. The kidnapping and enslavement of twelve million African people." Yvon looked at the four African Americans on the jury. They returned an unwavering gaze. "After stealing an entire country from the Native American, someone had to build up all this new land, right? So America trafficked—yes, you heard me correctly. America human-trafficked twelve million people from their homes along the west coast of Africa and forced them into slave labor. But that number, twelve million, is only a fraction of the overall number. Lest we forget not all Africans who were kidnapped arrived in the Americas safely.

"Approximately six million died as captives, in the over-crowded bowels of the ships transporting them across the Atlantic. For over two hundred years kidnapped Africans endured mutilation, torture, starvation, rape, and murder while America rode their whipped backs to wealth and prosperity. America would *not* have risen to world prominence had the African not been forced to build it for free." Yvon paused again. "Running from this truth will not save us," he repeated. The slideshow continued with more fresh faces of slain men and women.

"Then there's America's third-greatest sin." Yvon scanned the jury box and locked eyes with all the women on the jury. "Lie to yourself if that helps you sleep at night but know this—America does *not* love you either," he said firmly. "Ladies, this country only *tolerates* you. It tolerates you because it wants you to cook its food, serve its meals, lie on your backs, birth its children, and work the same occupation as a man for less money."

Yvon's testimony was met with trembling lips fighting back a mix of anger and a flood of more tears.

"Ladies, let me remind you, during the same time Africans were forced to endure slavery, you also were a second class citizen. Remember during this time you had *no* right to vote. It wasn't until 1920 when the Nineteenth Amendment gave women a voice in the political process. As of today's date you haven't had the right to vote for a century yet. Now, let's put that date into a better perspective.

"In 1920, African slaves had already been *freed* for fifty-five years. That's fifty-five years this country still didn't think its very own white women deserved to vote. *Your* white fathers, uncles, husbands, brothers, nephews, and the adult sons *you* birthed into existence allowed fifty-five years after the freeing of African slaves to pass before deeming their own women worthy to cast a ballot."

Yvon stared at each of the five women in the jury box. "The only thing America hates more than brown people . . . are *women*. Just ask Hillary Rodham Clinton." Yvon went silent and let Hillary's name sink in. "Over a decade ago America elected its first African American president. Yet, here we are terrified of the idea of electing a female president or even vice president. Every election cycle we're overcome with acute paralysis as our pens hover over check boxes adjacent to female candidates from a political field overflowing with more than qualified candidates."

Sandy watched imaginary light bulbs go off for the female jurors. Painted lips that once were trembling with sorrow had now stiffened with anger. Eyes with full lashes and once-stained faces from streaking mascara were now dry as a desert. They returned the same resolute gaze their African American jurors had worn moments before.

"Running from the truth will not save us," he repeated while the slideshow of the murdered continued.

"At the beginning of this trial my client, Dr. Sandy Darboe, pled not guilty. In my opening statement I proclaimed this country as the true culprit, responsible for the deaths of Drawoc and Tumaini. After all the evidence presented, I ask you, where is the lie? I firmly believe we all love this country. But our love for this country should never justify blind loyalty in the face of the evils it has committed. We must hold America accountable to the dream it promises. It is our right, but more importantly it is our duty!

"In closing, I'm going to pose another question for you to ponder privately in your own minds. If you would allow me to direct you, I'd like you to close your eyes. I'd like you all to think about your favorite family member. I'm talking about that one person that you love dearly. That one person you'd give your last dollar to. Now, I want you to imagine one day you and that one favorite family member are at the beach. You're having a great time wading waist deep in ocean waves.

"Then suddenly, without warning, that favorite family member knocks you off your feet into the waves and holds your head underwater."

All the juror's eyes shot open in shock.

"I know, it's unexpected and jarring, but that's what's happening. They are holding your head beneath the water. Your eyes are burning from the salt. You're holding your breath. You're pushing with all your adrenaline-inspired might against the sandy floor, trying to raise your head out of the waves. But your family member is in a more advantageous position. They've caught you by surprise so no matter how strong you are, you can't overpower them.

"You're thinking to yourself why is this happening? You may even be praying for it to end. Your heart is racing now because your body is oxygen starved. If you don't find a way to get your head above water, you *will* drown. Then suddenly, in the sand, your hand finds a sharp seashell. It's big and jagged. Jagged enough it can be used as a weapon. Now, what do you do? Do you take that jagged and sharp seashell and begin cutting and slicing away at your favorite family member before you drown, even if it means you may have to kill them to survive? Or do you love them so much you'd rather drown before hurting one hair on their head?"

Yvon looked at the jury as they all looked at one another and Judge Pisano, pondering the bizarre question. A question no one should ever have to answer out loud.

"I'm sure some of you are asking yourselves what does that have to do with this case? Well let me explain. For centuries this country has held people of color's *and* white women's heads underwater. Despite the unwarranted assault, they've continued to love this country, endure its unfair hardships, and pray for these hardships to end. They've exhausted all their sinew to stop America from drowning them.

"They've hoped and prayed this sadistic game would come to an end, but America stubbornly maintains its death grip. Now, we've reached the point in our history where America's victims can't breathe, and they don't want to die. And Dr. Sandy Darboe has appeared to them, in the sand, a jagged and sharp instrument here to save them. Dr. Darboe, Micah Johnson, and Anonymous, they're the jagged seashells for the countless Americans waiting in the balance, oxygen starved. We haven't reached a precipice where we much choose to use the only weapon at our disposal to fight . . . but . . . I ask again. How long can we expect them to wait?

"You've seen the videos. You've seen the slideshow of murdered men, women, and children that has yet to repeat a single face the entire time I've been speaking to you," Yvon said, pointing to the monitors showing a never-ending procession of lives that ended prematurely at the hands of bigoted police officers. "Self-preservation is a human being's most natural instinct. It is

God-given. Which means it supersedes any flawed law defined by man.

"The US government has demonstrated over the span of centuries it is either unwilling or incapable of protecting *all* its citizens. So these citizens' God-given right to *live* must be acknowledged and upheld. Even if that means they must now, since under duress, *proactively* and *preemptively* preserve their lives against those wishing to do them harm. My client, Dr. Sandy Darboe, just wants to live in peace. She wants to see her husband and newborn child live in peace. She wants nothing but *every* citizen in this great country to live out the rest of their lives in *peace.*

"You heard the testimony of people who knew Drawoc and Tumaini. They proved themselves to be the worst of us. They forced her to correct the wrongs that America had failed at correcting for centuries. I have faith this jury won't fail, though. I truly believe, before you render judgement and determine my client's fate, you will remember how you felt watching the videos I showed you. Remember the scenario I posed that forced you to walk in her shoes for just a few moments. And ask yourself. Did *you* allow yourself to drown? Or did you fight back with that jagged seashell to save yourself like my client?"

CHAPTER 30

For a third consecutive day since the end of closing arguments, Xavier and his mother-in-law took refuge in the courtroom's canteen for lunch. Xavier cradled Jason while he napped. He eyed every lawyer, court clerk, and civilian that shuffled into the modest eatery. He searched the face of every person, before being disappointed when none of them were Sandy's lawyer. The waiting game associated with the rendering of verdicts was beyond stressful.

Xavier and his mother-in-law volleyed their theories behind the meaning of the delay. Did it indicate that the jury would be sympathetic to Sandy? Or was it simply the jury needed three days to sift through the evidence and decide what punishment would be most appropriate considering the four charges against her? Even when Xavier pressed Sandy's lawyer for his expert opinion, Yvon only provided canned, inconclusive responses designed not to get his hopes up.

His mother-in-law sat quietly, methodically stabbing with her fork the assortment of green and red vegetables that her garden salad was comprised of. Xavier took slow bites of the dry prepackaged turkey–and–cheese sandwich he'd chosen until Jason began to stir. Xavier readjusted his posture to cradle the infant better when he realized the front of his son's diaper was slowly expanding.

Xavier couldn't help but smile. His mother-in-law looked up at him and returned the same smile.

"What is it?" she asked.

"The little guy just makes me happy," he responded. The small nuances of being a father were still pleasant surprises for him. Never did he think something as simple as changing a diaper would bring him such joy. The fresh memory of Sandy's first lesson on how to properly change their son's diaper momentarily distracted him from their monotonous wait.

You're a lucky little man to have such an amazing mother. Your daddy is pretty lucky too. Xavier hoped as the months multiplied into years Jason would see that for himself. Although he was not a very religious man, he prayed every morning and evening that his son would grow up knowing his mother as a free woman and not a convict. Xavier looked down at the multicolored diaper bag with decorative teddy bears dancing across each side and thumbed through the contents.

Diapers, wipes, baby powder—

"Xavier!" his mother-in-law said, taking a firm grip of his forearm. He looked over at her, and her pale face stared past him toward the entrance of the eatery. He traced her stare toward the doorway. Sandy's lawyer was power walking toward them. Anxious, Yvon bent over their table and spoke in a low tone.

"The judge has ordered the court back in session."

●

Back in the courtroom, Judge Pisano took his seat and

signaled for the bailiff to usher in the jurors. They marched in single file before breaking off to take their respective seats in the jury box. Once seated, the judge swiveled his large chair toward them.

"The court has received your note that after three days of deliberation, you have thus far been unable to reach a unanimous verdict on any of the four charges," Judge Pisano declared. A slender middle-aged woman with glasses rose from her seat.

"Yes, that is correct, Your Honor," the jury forewoman confirmed. "We've sincerely tried, but I'm sorry, Your Honor, we are deadlocked." Judge Pisano nodded in acknowledgment.

"You may take your seat," the judge instructed. "While I appreciate your most sincere efforts, I must implore you all to return to deliberations and press forward with the intentions of rendering a verdict. Along with those instructions, I caution you not to change your position merely to render a unanimous verdict and end this exercise prematurely. You must consider the evidence, weigh it against your conscience, and make an honest and true decision. If after continued deliberation you are not able to come to a consensus, *only* then will I consider other alternatives, such as a majority decision, or ultimately a hung—"

Suddenly, the familiar, distinct, and unbroken sound of a siren filled the courtroom's audio system. The prism of vertical colored bars with the words EMERGENCY BROADCAST in the center reappeared on the court video displays like it had during the courtroom hacking. The piercing sound startled Jason awake, and he began to cry. Xavier jumped up from his seat and exited the courtroom. Sandy watched as he disappeared through the double doors, escorted by a bailiff.

The heavy doors shut behind them, and the siren finally stopped. The colored bars displayed on the monitors, as they did weeks ago, slowly broke into a synchronized wave.

Judge Pisano signaled to another bailiff, who ran out of the courtroom, yelling into a walkie-talkie. The same 3-D animation of the pointed-chin Anonymous white mask displayed on all the courtroom screens. The jurors stirred in their seats. The animated Anonymous mask slowly scanned from left to right. Judge Pisano grabbed his gavel with nervous hands and raised it. An even louder siren filled the courtroom.

"Judge Pisano, do not bang that gavel!" a computer-generated voice ordered angrily. The bailiff with the walkie-talkie burst back through the doors. This time he was accompanied by two men cradling laptops and banging away at their keyboards. Judge Pisano complied with the Anonymous order, carefully placing his gavel down, and retrieved two foam ear buds to shove in his ears. He shot a helpless gaze at the bailiff and the cybersecurity team the court had hired after the first hacking attack.

"This is Anonymous. Despite your amateur-hour firewall installations and meager security countermeasures you've put into place, we've continued to monitor these proceedings."

Judge Pisano looked at the two cybersecurity professionals for some indication they had the situation under control. The bailiff looked up at the judge from the back of the courtroom and shook his head in disappointment.

All the video displays but the few in front of the jury box changed to a digital clock displaying twenty-four hours. The eyes of the Anonymous masks on the three monitor displays mounted in front of the jury box filled in red. The front row of jurors jumped from their seats, retreating to the back of the jury box.

"Ladies and gentlemen of the jury, please do not be afraid," Anonymous reassured. "Please take your seats, as your service thus far has been exemplary." The retreating jurors looked among one another and reluctantly returned to the front row and settled back into their seats.

"Thank you," Anonymous acknowledged.

Judge Pisano looked to his technology team again, and the bailiff returned the same disheartening news.

"As Judge Pisano instructed the jury just moments ago, Anonymous also must implore you to come to a decision. However, unlike the judge's sentiments, a majority decision or hung jury will not be acceptable. It is not Anonymous's objective today to sway your decision in either direction of guilt or innocence. Our purpose is to ensure your decision is free of ambiguity. This is a volatile moment in our country's history. Your ruling in this case will set legal precedent that will determine the future course of our country's justice and law enforcement systems.

"A unanimous decision *must* be made, and you have twenty-four hours to do so. If a unanimous decision of guilt or innocence is not made by the time the digital clock reaches zero, Anonymous will deploy a technological shut down of the US government and allow anarchy to prevail. Your twenty-four-hour countdown begins now." The white mask disappeared from the monitors, replaced by the countdown clock.

CHAPTER 31

I t was the first weekend following the second courtroom hacking. Two days after the jury rendered their unanimous verdict, and Xavier needed to get out of their apartment. After the turmoil of the past few weeks, a pleasant change of scenery was in order. After he and Sandy had relocated to DC, Jason was soon born and their child instantly had become the priority. This meant they hadn't had much time to explore the city. Xavier decided that would change today.

After a fifteen-minute drive Xavier parked his SUV on Fifteenth Street NW. He unpacked and unfolded Jason's Chicco Shuttle stroller from the trunk, then placed Jason inside and situated the diaper bag in the bottom compartment. Blocks away, across the street to the left, was the entrance to Meridian Hill Park. He'd heard from friends it was the perfect scenic destination with its large cascading fountain.

The short drive from the apartment had lulled Jason to sleep. Grateful for this moment of solace, Xavier took a moment to appreciate the serenity of his surroundings before pushing the stroller down the street of the Northwest, DC, neighborhood. It was a beautiful day, complete with voluptuous white clouds slowly gliding across a sky-blue backdrop. Several homeowners busied themselves attending to their lawns while others took in the beautiful day on their front porches, enjoying afternoon drinks with their significant others.

Xavier and Jason were two blocks away from where he'd planned to cross the street and enter the park. Out of his peripheral vision, he noticed a Metro DC police squad car slowly trailing behind him. Xavier looked back and not recognizing the driver, shot the officer a friendly wave and continued down the street. When he came to the intersection of that street, the police cruiser sped up, made a sharp right turn, and impeded Xavier from crossing. He jerked Jason's stroller back out of the intersection and back onto the sidewalk. Jason was jolted awake. He instantly began crying, and Xavier fumed.

"Are you fucking nuts?" Xavier yelled at the officer emerging from the patrol car. The officer shot one more glance at Xavier while speaking into the shoulder-mounted walkie-talkie. The circling blue lights periodically flashing in Xavier's eyes. The homeowners he'd passed moments ago craned their necks with curiosity from their porches. Blinds and curtains slowly were parted by those who wished to remain anonymous from what was developing in front of their homes.

"Can you tell me what you're doing here?" the officer questioned. Xavier returned a peculiar facial expression.

"I'm taking a walk with my son."

"Where are you headed?" the cop questioned. Xavier's head tilted and his face scowled.

"I'm on the job," he responded, hoping the coded term would temper the officer's aggression. The cop took a step closer and placed three vertical fingers down the width of his utility belt.

"I know *exactly* who you are," the cop said. A chill climbed Xavier's spine. "I said, 'Where are you headed?'" the officer repeated. "And let me see some ID." Xavier looked down at his son, now screaming at the top of his lungs. Xavier reached for the pacifier hanging around Jason's neck. The officer yanked his weapon from its holster.

"Show me your hands!" the officer shouted from the cover of his squad car. His service weapon aimed directly at Xavier. Xavier's heart leaped, his eyes widened, and a hot flash spread throughout his body.

How could you be so stupid? Xavier scolded himself, realizing his reaching inside Jason's covered stroller had just given the officer all the excuse he needed to shoot Xavier.

De-escalate the situation.

"Hey. Take it easy," Xavier said between quivering lips and a forced smile. "My son is crying, and I just wanted to give him his pacifier. I'm not armed, and like I told you before, I'm a cop," Xavier said. The cop curved his top lip into a snarl.

"Step away from the carriage with your hands up and walk towards me," the cop ordered over the noise of the passing traffic and Jason's wailing. Xavier surveyed the sloping sidewalk resting under Jason's stroller.

"Officer, as you can see, I have my child with me. The sidewalk is on a decline. If I raise my hands, the stroller will roll forward into the street. I'm happy to comply with your commands, but first I need to lock the wheels on my son's carriage before I can let go of the handlebars," Xavier implored while the officer behind the squad car, ready to shoot.

"I'm giving you a lawful order!" the officer yelled. "Step away from the carriage with your hands up! Walk towards me slowly or I will fucking shoot you!" The cop's left eye squinted taking aim. Xavier looked over at the row of houses and its onlooking owners, helpless. More residents gathered outside to witness the exchange. Xavier flashed back to the videos Sandy's lawyer played during his closing arguments. Sweat trickled down his back. His legs trembled. He had a death grip on Jason's carriage.

This can't be happening.

He appealed to the officer again.

"Officer, my name is Xavier Darboe. I'm a sergeant with the DC Metro Police in the third district. My commanding officer's name is—"

"I'm giving you a lawful order!" the police officer repeated. "Comply or I will shoot you—"

"Not while we're here, you won't!" an old raspy voice interrupted from the front lawn of the corner home to the right of Xavier. Xavier watched a couple his parents' age slowly walk down the length of their lawn. The officer's gun remained aimed at Xavier. The wife had her phone out, recording.

"Sir! Ma'am! Stay where you are! This is a police matter—"

"I'm live on Facebook, Officer. I've been live since the moment you stopped this young man. *Everyone* is seeing this," the older lady advised. When the couple reached the pavement, they both glanced into the stroller at Xavier's screaming child. Then they positioned themselves, shoulder to shoulder, between the carriage and the officer's aim.

"Sir! Ma'am! Step aside or I'll arrest you for interfering with police business," the cop ordered, but the couple remained, defying the officer's order.

"This young man has done nothing wrong. He hasn't broken any laws and has his child with him. Your aiming your weapon at him is placing both him and his child's life in danger," the husband said while other residents from the neighborhood gathered closer, brandishing more smartphones to record the exchange.

"This is your boy Mack, and I'm out Northwest where this punk-ass cop is about to shoot some dude for no reason! It's getting crazy out here, Joe!" a witness said twenty-five feet from behind the officer's position.

The cop maintained his aim on Xavier with one hand and squeezed the mic on his shoulder-mounted walkie-talkie with the other.

"This is Officer Lucentio. I need backup at Fifteenth Street Northwest now!" he said with trembling hands. Xavier looked down at the plastic wheel locks and slowly moved his foot to press them both down, securing Jason's stroller so it wouldn't roll once he released the handlebars. Xavier gently let go of the carriage and softly nudged it to make sure the locks were engaged.

"Officer," Xavier exclaimed slowly raising his hands in the air, "my hands are up and I'm heading over towards—"

"No you're not, bro!" another voice shouted from the street left of Xavier. A large man with a protruding belly walked next to the older couple in front of Jason's carriage and took a position to the left of the older man. "We've all been watching, and you didn't do anything wrong. This cop is an asshole and better lower his weapon before shit gets out of hand," the bulky man threatened, crossing his thick, tattooed arms across his chest and resting them on his belly.

"You tell 'em, baby!" a young tattooed lady said, also with

her phone out recording. Xavier finally noticed the crowd had exploded into a mix of young millennials and middle-aged adults, reflective of the diverse melting pot synonymous with DC culture. Xavier, with his hands still up, slowly stepped out from around the three-person barrier. Officer Lucentio adjusted his aim to follow Xavier.

"It's okay, everyone. No need for anyone to get hurt over a misunderstanding—"

"Nah, bruh! Ain't no misunderstanding. This bitch-ass cop and every other cop like him needs to learn their place. Our taxes pay their salaries," a tall, slender, young man with locks in his hair said. "We hired you to protect and serve, not prey and murder. Now put your gun down. We're sick and tired of this shit!"

Suddenly a chorus of police sirens from three additional squad cars roared around the corner and accelerated toward the scene. They came to a screeching halt once reaching the perimeter of the crowd. Six additional officers exited their vehicles and ran over toward their colleague.

Xavier watched as the husband standing in front of Jason's stroller leaned over to his wife, whispering a few words. A look of concern appeared on her face before her husband gently motioned for her to head back to the house.

"We're still live on Facebook where the police are harassing a man who was walking down the street with his child. The cop has his gun drawn, pointed at us, ready to shoot, even though we've done nothing wrong," the older man's wife narrated to the growing number of viewers on the social media app. The husband signaled to a few more men he knew from the neighborhood. They all broke from the crowd, forming a multicultural line of seven men, shoulder to shoulder, in front of Xavier and the stroller.

The new set of officers shouted people back, attempting to create a perimeter, but the crowd disregarded their orders, refusing to back down, growing bigger, stronger, and more defiant with every passing second. The older husband standing at the center of the seven-man line yelled out to one of the newly arrived officers.

"Sergeant! Your officer illegally detained the man behind me for walking down the street with his son. He then pointed his weapon at him and threated to shoot him. This young man has not broken any laws. And as you can see from the growing crowd, we have several devices that have captured this cop violating this young man's civil rights.

"Now I must warn you, all seven of the men protecting this young man from being gunned down by your fellow officer, as well as several other of our neighbors in the growing crowd surrounding you, are lawfully licensed concealed-carry weapon holders. So this can go one of two ways. You can arrest that poor excuse of a cop, take our witness statements, and we'll gladly provide you the video evidence of that cop's harassment and violation of this father's civil rights. Or"—the older gentleman looked at the collection of neighborhood men to his left and to his right—"you can ignore my sensible and rational suggestion and force all of us to stand our ground." The older gentleman then shrugged his shoulders. "Choice is yours, Sergeant . . . and whatever happens, happens."

CHAPTER 32

The weather in Southlake, Texas, was perfect. A month of being ushered back and forth between the county jail and Judge Pisano's courtroom gave Sandy a new appreciation for the freedom she'd taken for granted. When Sandy and Xavier left Texas for DC, Sandy and her best friend, Camila, promised each other the distance would not affect their friendship, and today was a testament to that promise. The first weekend after the jury returned a verdict of not guilty, Sandy booked a flight, kissed Xavier and her young prince goodbye, and headed back to the south for the weekend.

Fifteen minutes after picking up her rental car at the Dallas/ Fort Worth International Airport, she pulled her rolling luggage up the driveway of Camila and Hector's walkway. She rang the doorbell, and within moments she could hear Camila's heels knocking against the wood floors. Her friend opened the door, and they both shrieked at each other and embraced in a hug that lasted forever. Once they finally separated, Camila looked Sandy up and down.

"Look at you. Already lost the baby weight and jail buff with those thick thighs and Michelle Obama arms."

"Girl, it's called the Solitary Confinement Diet. Between the disgusting prison food and countless air squats in my cell to pass the time, I had no choice but to come out snatched."

Camila laughed, grabbed Sandy's bag, and rolled it to the guest room on the first floor.

"Where's Hector?" Sandy asked.

"Oh, he's in the basement," she said. "It's his turn to host the guy's monthly poker game, so they're all down there smoking cigars, drinking too much, and losing money to one another."

"I should go down and say hello before we go."

"Girl, we don't have time for that. I've been ready to go since you landed. You can say hello when we get back later tonight," Camila said, positioning Sandy's luggage in the corner. "I'm going to go get my purse from upstairs, and we're out of here." She gave Sandy another strong hug before the two let each other go. "Girl, I've missed you so much. We all have."

"Me too." Sandy replied.

Camila headed out the guest room toward the main stairwell while Sandy checked her new hairstyle and fixed her clothes in the large mirror attached to the wood dresser. After all the attention her case garnered, she thought it wise to chop off her curly, thick mane. Now she sported a shorter, blond, and straight hairstyle. Sandy walked out of the guest room into the living room. Everything was as she remembered it when she and Xavier last visited their home before leaving Texas.

Pictures of Emmanuel, ranging from the day he was born until his last birthday, lined the wall around the stone fireplace. Tears welled up in her eyes.

Don't you dare cry! You're here for Camila!

"I'm coming now," Camila shouted from upstairs, followed

by the hurried sound of her shoes trotting down the hallway. She had a large, black Kate Spade bag resting in the fold of her elbow and the biggest smile Sandy had seen since she lost Emmanuel.

"Okay, let's go!" Camila said, rushing them both out the door.

Three hours later they were seated at their third local bar of the night, snacking on bar food and people watching behind their matching sunglasses.

"I like the new look, girl. You make me want to try something different with my hair," Camila teased.

"Whatever! You know Hector would have a coronary if you cut off all your hair. I *had* to change my appearance, though. Everywhere I went I got looks from people who recognized me from newspaper articles or television news footage of the trial. People even recognized Xavier, but you know my man's just too big and bald. It's nothing he can do to hide that, ha ha. I'll admit this shorter style is much more manageable though."

"Yeah, I can't go anywhere without some group of people arguing about the verdict."

"I know. I had to delete all my social media accounts because of trolls flooding my pages with so many comments and threats. Alerts would sound all day and night."

"Same here," Camila said before pausing. "After Emmanuel, I just couldn't take it anymore. All the negativity, the back-and-forth about who was to blame. It was slowly driving me mad. I finally took a leave of absence from the hospital. Hector deleted all his social media too. With his tech career requiring he have security clearance, the last thing we need is him losing his position for saying something in the heat of the moment to some troll."

"Hey," Sandy said, consoling her friend. "You don't have to talk about it. You don't have to do *anything* you don't want to do tonight."

"I'm *fine*. Don't worry about me," Camila said in return, taking a large sip of beer, "I couldn't wait for you to get here."

"Okay, take it easy. Last thing we need tonight is 'Crazy Camila' making an appearance," Sandy said scanning the bar. "Okay, it's time to go." Camila swallowed the remaining half pint of her beer.

"This one's on *me!*" Camila said, throwing thirty dollars on the bar before they both headed for the door.

"I'll drive," Sandy said.

Camila climbed into the passenger side of Sandy's black rental car. Ten minutes into their drive, Sandy pulled into a gas station and got out of the car. Camila waited in the car, fumbling through her handbag while Sandy put her shades back on and went into the convenience store. When she pushed through the door, a bell chimed. The person working the cash register looked up; seeing Sandy's petite frame, he returned his attention to ringing up his customer's items on the cash register.

The same couldn't be said for another customer coming down the aisle toward the front of the store with a twelve-pack of beer he'd just pulled from the refrigerators. Sandy walked by him and through the invisible yet pungent cloud of beer trailing the already drunk customer. He tried to force eye contact but Sandy refused.

Fail, you loser.

She could feel his eyes undressing her as they followed her back down the aisle. She threw her hips extra hard with her last two strides before stopping in front of the section where engine oil and other car supplies were kept. She dipped her hip hard and studied the car products.

That's right, get a real good look, creep. If Xavier were here, he'd whoop your ass and you'd wake up in the ICU.

Then she saw what needed and squatted so deep her backside almost touched the linoleum floors. Her toned figure was on full display in her skinny jeans and thigh-high stiletto boots. Out her periphery she saw the drunk turn away from the register and head back down the aisle toward her.

So predictable.

"Excuse me, little lady. May I be of some assistance?" the drunk slurred. Sandy refused to make eye contact.

"My oil light came on," she responded.

"Do you know which one you need?"

"Aren't they all the same?" she questioned, prompting him to chuckle.

"No, ma'am. You put the wrong brand in and you can ruin your engine."

Sandy shrugged. "It's not my car. It's a rental, so as long as the engine doesn't quit on me the next twenty-four hours before I return it, I really don't care."

"Only here for the night, huh?"

"That's right," Sandy responded.

"Well, where's your car? I can check and pick the right brand for you. That way you don't have to worry about the rental place blaming you for ruining their car."

Sandy stood up. "It's just outside. But I don't want to inconvenience you."

"No inconvenience at all for a pretty lady like you. It'll only take me ten minutes, tops, to see what you need, and I'll even fill you up if you want," he said with a sly tone. "We wouldn't want to get oil on those nice clothes of yours."

"Well, since you put it that way. Sure, follow me," Sandy agreed, flashing a bright smile before leading him outside. Again, she could feel his eyes locked onto her ass as they headed toward the car. When they both arrived, the car was empty.

"Do you know how to pop the hood?" he asked.

Sandy handed him the keys. "Would you mind?"

"Not at all," he replied smiling. He unlocked the car, then found and pressed the button near the bottom left of the steering wheel that popped the hood. He walked around the front of the car, slid his hand beneath the partially open hood, released its safety latch before pushing the hood open, and over his head. He pulled his keys out of his pocket and turned on a mini flashlight connected to his key chain.

"Isn't that a nifty little gadget?" Sandy said.

"Yeah, it really comes in handy on these little countryside roads where you can't always find street lighting." He searched the darkness under the hood with the flashlight until he found the oil cap. He unscrewed it and shined the light on the underside of the cap where it specified the type of oil.

"A lot of cars put the oil type on the cap so you don't have to memorize it."

Aww, look at you. Such a proud man-splaining moment for you isn't it?

"Now all we need is a funnel."

"Don't rental agencies keep those in the trunk along with the jack?" Sandy suggested.

"We could check, but if not, they have some in the convenience store. I'll check the trunk." He pressed the button on the car keys to automatically open the trunk. Seeing it slowly rise open, he walked toward it, past Sandy, and smiled again. She returned the smile.

"I can't wait to thank you for everything you've done, Officer Danny Shore," Sandy said, catching the drunken off duty police officer off guard. An extra second passed before he'd finally realized she knew his name without him telling her. But it was already too late. Now, Officer Shore was staring down into the spacious trunk, lined with thick, clear plastic, and Camila's tiny fame curled up inside.

Camila clutched a semiautomatic handgun equipped with a silencer she'd purchased on the dark web per Sandy's instructions before she and Xavier left Texas a year ago. Sandy stole a quick glance of their surroundings ensuring there were no witnesses. To Sandy, time seemed to move in slow motion as she observed Camila's firm grip on the weapon was steady in her small manicured hands. Sandy caught one final glimpse of the friendship bracelet with the Puerto Rican flag around Camila's wrist before countless muzzle flashes lit the corner of the dark parking lot. Officer Shore collapsed backward onto the gravel parking lot, lifeless. Multiple small red circles formed through his white T-shirt and expanded by the second. Sandy rushed past the cop's corpse to help Camila climb out the trunk of the car. They positioned themselves on each end of him.

"One, two, three!" Sandy directed from a deep, squatted position; her arms wrapped under his shoulders. Camila matched Sandy's posture, grabbing his legs so they could lift his lifeless body into the trunk of the rental car. The car's suspension dipped adjusting to the deadweight. They looked down at the officer who'd stolen Emmanuel's life so haphazardly and frivolously.

"I got you, *puto!*" Camila rejoiced, slamming the trunk closed.

CHAPTER 33

S andy was jolted awake as the tires of her returning flight to the DMV met the tarmac. She slid the shade of her window up and squinted as her eyes adjusted to the sunlight beaming through the modest window.

"Ladies and gentlemen, I'd like to welcome you to Reagan National Airport. The time is now twelve thirty-two, with a temperature of seventy-two degrees. We'd like to thank you for choosing to fly with us today, and we look forward to being able to serve your traveling needs again in the future," the plane's captain said over the intercom.

Sandy pulled the hood of her sweatshirt over her head and slid on her new favorite pair of sunglasses in preparation to depart the plane. She kept her head low, looking only at the ground. She was both eager to discretely deplane and rush home to shower both Xavier and Jason with hugs and kisses when she finally arrived home.

●

Thirty minutes later Sandy stepped down from the airport shuttle steps with her single carry-on luggage trailing behind her. She navigated her way through the aisles of the Economy

311

parking lot, her car keys raised above her head, pressing the panic button until her car alarm sounded. After loading her luggage into the trunk, she jumped behind the steering wheel, paid the attendant in cash, and exited the parking lot.

Ten minutes later she breached the DC city limits and reached into the glove compartment. From there she retrieved her smartphone and pressed the power button. The instant it was on, a chorus of text messages, missed calls, and voice mail alerts lit up the locked screen. At the top were several messages from Xavier imploring she call him right away. She punched in the code, secured her phone in its dashboard mount, and called him. The phone only rang once before he answered.

"Are you okay?" he questioned.

"Yes. Is everything okay at home?"

"Yes. Jason and I are fine."

"Thank God!" she said, finally having a reason for her heart rate to lower. "I saw all the messages and didn't know what to think."

"You don't have to worry about us, love. How did everything in—"

"Xavier!" she interrupted. "Let's talk more after I get home."

"You're right."

"It's okay, love." An awkward silence lingered until Xavier finally broke it, prefaced by a deep sigh.

"Something happened while you—" Xavier stopped himself this time. "Something happened yesterday, when I took Jason to the park."

"Is Jason okay? What happened?"

"Yes, baby, we're fine. But I had a run-in with police while he was with me. A cop recognized me, pulled his car in front of us, and almost hit the carriage."

"Xavier? Are you sure you and Jason are okay?"

"Yes, Sandy. I promise we're fine, now. But that damn cop, he was being an asshole, harassing me, trying to instigate a reaction. Even *after* I told him I was a cop. He threatened to shoot me. The look in his eyes, San. He wanted to shoot me. Luckily for us there were a lot of witnesses with smartphones, so the captured everything. But I can stop thinking about what would have happened if those people weren't there. There was even a standoff between me, the neighborhood residence and the cops."

"What?" Sandy questioned in disbelief.

"Yea San, the people from the neighborhood, they literally stood between us and the cop who drew his weapon on us."

"He pulled his weapon on you and Jason?"

"Yeah," he responded. "I've never seen anything like that before. The entire neighborhood surrounded cops and said they wouldn't stand by and watch them hurt us. Some of them were even armed."

Sandy listened petrified, her knuckles turning white as she clenched the steering wheel, unsure what was coming next.

"Then one of the cops he called for backup, a sergeant, arrested the cop who threatened us. But had that sergeant not shown up, Sandy . . ." Xavier paused again. He contemplated how the event brought him face-to-face with his and possibly Jason's mortality. The shock of it returned, forcing him to ramble on recounting the standoff. "That fucking cop had his weapon aimed at us. Threatening to shoot me, even worse," he paused again. "His eyes, San. The look in his eyes. He wanted to shoot me. He didn't care Jason was in the line of fire."

Sandy couldn't respond. An overload of horrific scenarios flooded her imagination. She'd lost all track of how long she'd been sitting at the green light only a few blocks away from their home. Cars stuck in the lane behind her leaned on their horns, urging her to proceed through the intersection before the light changed to red again. Sandy disregarded it all as she snatched her phone from its mount. She swiped the screen once, entered her password, and tapped the icon labeled "To Do List" as more cars added to the line trapped behind her. A security window prompted Sandy for a secondary password as drivers yelled obscenities at her motionless car. After she entered the second password another request prompted her for her thumbprint.

"Sandy? You there?" Xavier questioned.

"Yes, love. I'm here," she responded coldly while an app similar to a notepad opened.

On the notepad a list of names displayed one after the other, each name occupying its own line. Some name were highlighted in red while others remained in black lettering.

"Xav?"

"Yes, San?"

"What's the name of the cop? The one who aimed his gun at you and my child."

THE END